Ethel Lina White and

Ethel Lina White (1876–1944)

Ethel Lina White was born in Abergavenny in Monmouthshire, Wales. White started writing as a child, contributing essays and poems to children's papers. Later she began to write short stories, but it was some years before she embarked on books. Her first three, published between 1927 and 1930, were mainstream novels. Her first crime novel, published in 1931, was *Put Out the Light*, and she went on to be one of the best-known crime writers of the 1930s and 1940s in Britain and the US. Her novel *The Wheel Spins* (1936) was made into the acclaimed film, *The Lady Vanishes*, by Alfred Hitchcock in 1938. Ethel Lina White died in London.

By Ethel Lina White

The Wish-Bone (1927)
Twill Soon be Dark (1929)
The Eternal Journey (1930)
Put Out the Light (1931)
Fear Stalks the Village (1932)
Some Must Watch (1933)
Wax (1935)
The First Time He Died (1935)
The Wheel Spins (1936)
The Third Eye (1937)
The Elephant Never Forgets (1937)
Step in the Dark (1938)
While She Sleeps (1940)
She Faded into Air (1941)
Midnight House (1942)
The Man Who Loved Lions (1943)
They See in Darkness (1944)

Put Out the Light

Ethel Lina White

An Orion book

Copyright © The Estate of Ethel Lina White 1931

The right of Ethel Lina White to be identified as the author of this work has been
asserted in accordance with the Copyright, Designs and Patents Act 1988.

This edition published by
The Orion Publishing Group Ltd
Orion House
5 Upper St Martin's Lane
London WC2H 9EA

An Hachette UK company
A CIP catalogue record for this book is available from the British Library

ISBN 978 1 4719 1701 1

www.orionbooks.co.uk

CHAPTER I

The Shadow

WHEN MISS VINE WENT TO BED SHE WAS ACCOMPANIED BY her shadow thrown on the white marble wall.

At first, it was a blurred, servile shape, that slunk behind her, dogging her heel. Then it attained her own stature and grew clearer, keeping pace with her as a friendly silhouette.

But, at the bend of the staircase, it changed and became terrible. A monstrous distortion, it shot up—taller and taller —until it leaped over her head and rushed before her, to her own room.

At that moment, Miss Anthea Vine always felt afraid. In the turgid depths of her heart she knew that it was stealing on to search for that other darker shadow, which, one night, would be waiting for her. . . .

By day, Oldtown was a homely huddle of roofs, clustering in a tree-lined valley; but, by night, it was a black bowl filled to the brim with shadows.

Timid, fluttering shadows; squat, swollen shadows; mean, sneaking shadows; starved, elongated shadows; poisonous, malignant shadows, they foamed up in the brew and overflowed the rim, into the streets—hiding in corners, stealing into windows, following people home.

Fighting the shadows, were the lights of Oldtown, which swarmed over the black bowl, like golden bees. It was easy to trace the chain of lamps in the High Street and the glowing dial of the Town Hall clock amid the chaotic straggle of the widely spaced illuminations.

One other light was distinct in character and received definite recognition. Every evening, at eleven o'clock, it glowed from out the left wing of the great pile of Jamaica Court. The porters at the hillside station always watched for it, as it was more punctual than their scheduled trains. In addition, it was informative, for it broadcast a parochial news bulletin.

Miss Anthea Vine was going to bed.

At twelve o'clock, to the stroke, the light went out.

CHAPTER II

The Victim

"THAT'S A WOMAN WHO'S GOING TO BE MURDERED." MISS
Pye spoke with calm authority, as she poured out the breakfast coffee, in the small dining room of the Cherry Orchard.
She was fair, fat and she liked to be taken for forty. A
pleasant woman, of strong character and sound common
sense, she was fixed of purpose as the Pole Star, although
she clouded her issue behind a Milky Way of words.

At the word "murder," her brother, Superintendent Pye,
pricked up his ears. He was bull-necked and massive in build,
with great cheeks like ripe plums, and choleric blue eyes. His
reputation was that of a good mixer and a competent football referee.

For generations his people had lived in Oldtown, where
they had been, originally, landowners, and Pye, himself, was
essentially of the soil. His present job was one of Fate's mis-
deals. While he was in general request as judge, at every
local dog show, the prevalent opinion was that, from long
cold storage in Oldtown, his brain had mildewed.

Only his sister, Florence, believed in him; for she worshiped her Maker, in public, every Sunday, but she worshiped
her brother, in private, every day of her life.

Oblivious of criticism, Pye's ambition was static. He
yearned to handle a subtle murder-mystery. And all Provi-
dence sent him was dog fights and drunks.

3

At his sister's words he glanced across his garden, where the friable dark soil was spiked with the green tips of bulbs. On the tarred road stood two young men and a girl, engaged in noisy conversation. The youths presented a contrast in figure, as one was short, and thickset and the other, tall and slender. Both were well-dressed in conventional country style, and betrayed more than the usual correct slouch of boredom.

Only the back of their companion was visible to Pye, but her slim form, in its short tweed suit, held the allure and grace of girlhood. Her grass-green beret revealed short golden curls which glittered in the pale spring sunlight. As she poised on one toe she looked like the Spirit of Youth Triumphant—hovering for one golden moment of laughter, before she winged on her eternal flight.

Youth—never lingering—always passing on.

Superintendent Pye pointed to the girl's back, with his pipe.

"D'you mean Miss Vine, Flo?"

"I do," replied his sister. "She's just asking for it. Carrying on with those boys, just like Queen Elizabeth."

"No. Queen Elizabeth had quite a good brain—for a woman."

As Pye spoke Miss Vine suddenly spun round on a slender stem of silken leg, revealing the painted, triangular face of an elderly woman.

He swallowed a gulp of repulsion.

"Murdered?" he grunted. "Well, she'd be the better for it. It might cure her complaint. Silly, vain old maid, pink and hollow as an Easter egg."

His sister took no offense at his Gilbertian contempt for spinsterhood.

"You can't call Miss Vine a fool," she objected. "Think of the fortune she's made."

"Not she. *Men* have made her fortune for her. She's lucky with her managers."

"Well, doesn't it show brains to get men to make money for her?"

"I call it a canker. She squeezes them dry and then sacks them. A very different kind of business woman to our Doris."

Pye's face beamed with pride as he mentioned his favorite younger sister—the proprietress of the Timberdale Arms. She had not only been a pretty girl, but, as the widow of Major Law, she had, at one time of her life, been honored by association with a man.

Miss Pye began to collect the china and stack it together on the tray. At a sudden gust of loud laughter from the road, she stood with a teacup in her hand.

"I wonder what she's telling those boys," she remarked.

"Some ripe, old-fashioned story, you bet," grinned Pye. "They say that little lady can go one beyond the limit. Not that I've ever heard her. Not in her class."

Miss Pye's mild eyes gleamed fiercely behind her glasses.

"Does she patronize *you?*" she gasped.

The next second she had regained her calm.

"It doesn't matter," she said. "She's going to be murdered."

Her brother tapped his pipe over the grate and then stood, spread-eagled, before the fire.

"And who told you that?" he asked derisively.

"The cards tell me, Adam. Every time I lay them out I see the murder of an old woman, by night."

At the Superintendent's laughter, Miss Pye crossed over to the window. On the opposite slope arose a vast erection of gray stone. It had no claim to artistic architecture, but it was solid, imposing, and kept up on a scale that advertised wealth.

The glass roofs of its conservatories, billiard room, and covered entrance flashed back scores of miniature suns.

It was Jamaica Court—the residence of Miss Anthea Vine —owner of a chain of "Dahlia" lingerie shops and of terracotta Munster hotels.

"Is that a happy house?" demanded Miss Pye. "There are three young people cooped up there with that horrible old woman. All of them in her power, hating her like poison. Can you deny that things are ripe for murder?"

Pye scratched his nose. Everyone was familiar with the situation at the Court. Years ago Miss Vine had adopted three children from poverty-stricken homes. Two of these, Charles and Francis Ford, were her third cousins, while the girl—Iris Pomeroy—was an orphan, acquired through an adoption society.

She had surrounded them with luxury and spared no expense over their education. The boys went to public schools, and, later, qualified for professions. But when Charles' name was on the rolls, and Francis had completed his articles with an architect, Miss Vine, apparently, considered her obligation at an end. The boys were forced to put up their plates in Oldtown, the soil of which was already soured with professional men of long standing. As they did not make enough income to pay their office rent, she kept them chained to her side, as her cavaliers and slaves.

When Iris returned from her finishing school on the Continent, she found herself in a hotbed of rebellion and discontent. All three were gifted with strong wills, good looks and plenty of brains. They wanted to spread their wings and lead their own lives; but, whenever they fluttered towards freedom they found themselves hobbled by economic pressure.

"They must be a precious spineless lot to put up with it," observed Pye.

Again Miss Pye dissented.

"They're none of them that. Charles is a regular dare-devil, with his ugly face and wicked grin, and Francis is too quiet and polite. Still waters run deep, remember."

"Well, take it from me, Flo, and I ought to know, the last thing either of them will do is murder the old bird."

"Why?"

"To begin with, they'll never unite against her. She's got them split with jealousy. People take Charles and Francis for brothers, because they've got the same name, but they're only cousins. They say blood's thicker than water, but, in the long run, it always makes bad blood."

"You forget the girl," hinted Miss Pye darkly. "Look at her eyes. She's one of your moderns, who'd think nothing of banging Miss Vine over the head with a chopper, and then calling it a complex."

The Superintendent's shrug advertised his private opinion that he argued with a fool. But he could not resist the temptation of airing his views on his favorite subject.

"Listen to me, Flo. Before you can have murder, you've got to have two other things. Motive and opportunity. Now, I'll grant you those three have opportunity, as they're on the spot. But, where is their motive?"

"Her money, of course," replied his sister.

"And how do they know they're going to get any of it? She's the sort that never makes a will. If she dies intestate, her money will go to her brother in Australia."

Miss Pye hung on to her point.

"Well, the girl's got a motive. She and Miss Vine are in love with the same man."

"Who?"

"The new young doctor—Dr. Lawrence."

"And how d'you know they're in love? Did you read it in the *Herald?*"

7

Pye's sarcasm was wasted on his sister.

"I count on juxtaposition," she replied. "Every day, he pays a visit to the Court, where he sees Iris Pomeroy. He must be sick of that mouthing old mummy. And think of the opportunities he has of poisoning her."

"And is it likely that a fellow with no practice would kill off his one good patient?" asked Pye impatiently.

Miss Pye did not continue the argument. Having cleared the table, she took up a pack of patience cards and began to lay them out in the shape of a horseshoe.

"I wonder she dares go to bed, at night," she murmured, "never knowing if she will wake up again."

She saw Miss Vine's wealth as cheese—bait to tempt the rats from their holes in her own larder, or the sewers of the underworld. But her brother only laughed.

"You've only got two ideas in your head, Flo. Servants and sentiment. Leave crime to them that understand it. Stick to your Betsy."

"Perhaps it takes some brains to have a Betsy, at all, these days when every girl calls herself 'Betty'," said Miss Pye quietly.

As she counted her cards, she watched the group on the road. Charles Ford had untidy hair, with a cowlick stirring in the wind; but, although he was ugly, there was definite charm in his expression.

His eyes were not in complete alliance with his impudent grin. They called his bluff. One had but to divide his face to read the history of his frustration in two chapters; the upper-half, which supplied the capital, and the lower-half, which denied the labor.

Francis was better looking than his cousin, with regular features and satin-smooth hair, but his nose was too long and his mouth too small. His expression betrayed complete boredom as he stood, silent, while Miss Vine and Charles capped each other's story.

Presently he betrayed his first sign of animation at the sight of a tall man in gray plus-fours, who was swinging down the road, his hat in his hand.

Dr. Glyn Lawrence was handsome and possessed a Southern poise and grace; it was easy to imagine him dancing a tango or fighting a duel. Yet there was a hint of the Orient in his slanting eyes, drooping lids and thick chiseled lips.

"Here's your friend Lawrence," remarked Francis.

He scarcely opened his lips, yet his diction was so perfect that his words were clear-cut and cold as icicles, dropping into the rapid current of Charles's slurred speech.

Miss Vine's eye lit up, for her court was never large enough to satisfy her. As she pouted and gesticulated, she always carried with her an invisible companion—her imaginary self. She saw a rose-flushed face, piquant with mischief, soft with the bloom of youth.

"You've a smut on your nose, Anthea," remarked Francis.

Instantly, she pulled out her pocket mirror. In the tiny circle of glass she saw no smut, but two little old eyes, like shriveled nuts, peering through a feathery foliage of artificial lashes.

"You are supercritical, Francis," she said quietly. "But thank you for your interest. And here's my faithful Lawrence. Don't you envy a doctor his opportunities, Francis? He can cure, kill, or kiss."

"No," was the prim reply. "I'd rather be a parson. It must be so nice to tell people not to do the things one does oneself."

"He'd make a dashed good parson, too," grinned Charles. "We've shocked this pure young lad with our smutty tales, Anthea."

"Oh, darling." Anthea spun round to Francis. "Sorry I was coarse."

9

"Don't apologize," remarked Francis in his cool, precise voice. "I'm always interested in the revelation of character."

Miss Vine's eyes gleamed between narrowed lids. While Charles charmed her, Francis held her interest. He was never boorish like his cousin, but, under his invariable politeness, she sensed his hostility.

Her smile grew possessive as Dr. Lawrence joined the group.

"You're the man I want," she said. "Come up to the Court, Wednesday afternoon, and reassure me about my heart."

Dr. Lawrence's smile was too suave, as he shook his head.

"It would be my personal delight to reassure you, my dear lady," he said, "just as it is my duty to preserve the health of such a valuable member of the community."

"He means your butcher's bill, Anthea," cut in Charles. "I've always got to translate this bloke."

"But," went on the doctor, taking no notice of the interruption, "I have to operate on Mrs. Learoyd, Wednesday afternoon. Adenoids."

"Oh—the grocer's wife?"

"Exactly. May I suggest coming up to the Court in the morning?"

Miss Vine's eyes gleamed. These were the moments for which she lived, when she directed destinies from her own altitude.

"And may I suggest that another doctor is capable of performing a minor operation?" she said.

"I agree. Williams is probably more capable than myself. Unfortunately, he is also capable of pocketing the fee."

"In that case," declared Anthea, "you can charge me double your miserable adenoid charge. But you must come to the Court, in the afternoon. I have two board meetings for the morning."

"How dare a wretched grocer's wife stop the way of a guinea pig?" asked Charles. "I used to know Mrs. Learoyd when she was barmaid at the Crown. Pretty woman, eh, Lawrence?"

"I know her only as a patient," replied Dr. Lawrence stiffly.

"And patients don't count as women. What have you got to say to that, Anthea?" flashed Charles.

Her face radiant with triumph, Anthea enjoyed the scene. She loved to incite her menagerie to fight, for it stimulated her with a sense of power. If, sometimes, they turned on her, she could always crack her whip.

As she looked at them, in turn, she wondered which was most dangerous. Charles was good-tempered, but inclined to snap. You could put your head into the lion's mouth once too often. One day, he might, by pure accident, snap too hard. . . . Francis was the intractable tiger, who slunk from her and watched her with unfriendly eyes. Yet, at a pinch, he might prove the most reliant of the three. And what of Lawrence —the graceful, beautiful beast, who never growled, or showed his teeth? He was the unknown quantity.

Inside the dining room of the Cherry Orchard, Miss Pye continued to lay out the cards.

"There it is again," she murmured. "Plain as plain. Queen of spades, which means an elderly woman. Of course, it should be diamonds, but who can tell what her real color is? Surrounded with treachery—all the knaves in the pack. Ace and nine of spades, both reversed. It only means one thing. *Murder.*"

Miss Pye stared across at the great stone mansion which topped the rise. The humble Cherry Orchard was over-shadowed by it, like an impudent white dog that dares to stand up to the gray bulk of a crouching beast of prey.

Its chimneys seemed to bristle and its smoke curl upwards with defiance—as though to suggest a plucky little animal that would fly at the throat of its adversary, and hang on until death.

The Pyes—brother and sister—always hung on.

CHAPTER III

And So to Bed

AT ELEVEN O'CLOCK, THAT NIGHT, THE LIGHT GLOWED, like a beacon, from the dark pile of Jamaica Court. The bored porter at the high-level station, shouted to his mate.

"Eleven, Jim."

Jim glanced at his watch.

"Gosh, I'm five slow. Not Wednesday, is it?"

On Wednesday night they had learned to expect irregularity in the appearance of the light, although it never failed to go out at the stroke of twelve.

As he moved the hands of his watch on to eleven, he heard the faint chimes of the Town Hall clock, which were only audible when the wind was in the rainy quarter.

For the past twenty minutes, Eames—Miss Vine's maid— had been busy behind the drawn curtains of the spectacular blue-and-silver bedroom. Although she was never allowed to assist at the rites of the evening toilet, she had to make the preparations and foresee every possible need.

Face cream here. Skin food by the side. Astringent behind, but where it could be seen at a glance. Ice on the plate-glass slab. Strips of plaster, cut into assorted sizes. Powder. Perfume.

The maid took the temperature of the bath, making allowance for slight cooling, and added the correct proportion of aromatic salts. Then she glanced at her watch—for there was no clock in the bedroom—and crossed to the window.

The gesture with which she drew aside the curtains was almost dramatic, as though she were in league with the darkness and were giving a signal to the shadows lurking in the black bowl of the valley.

Although, viewed from the station, the Court rose up as a bleak rock, behind the blinds, it was a stronghold of youth, blazing with lights and vibrant with noise. A group of young people were gathered round the roulette table in the drawing room, shouting against the blare of the loud-speaker. With the exception of a girl, they were greedy youths, drawn to the Court by the bait of unlimited free drinks and tobacco.

A few had an eye to bigger profits—a Stock Exchange tip, or even a furtive fiver, given and accepted, as a boon. Not even the boldest attempted to pluck his hostess at cards, for she played poker too well. Her monetary favors were bestowed on those endowed with the silver tongues of diplomatists, or else the jargon of the gutter. She was only responsive to contrasts. She could assimilate large doses of flattery, and also of abuse; the first was a tribute to her charm, the second a challenge to her power.

According to her custom, at this hour, Anthea was alone in the dimness of the Moorish library. Almost lost in its carven magnificence, she sat at her desk, under one green-shaded light.

In front of her was a sheaf of papers, containing the figures for the board meetings which had taken precedence of Mrs. Learoyd's adenoids. From time to time she jotted a note on the margin; but for several minutes she had ceased to write.

Her golden head was sunken on her breast, when Charles put his head round the corner of the door.

"Eleven, Anthea," he said, consulting his watch.

A feature of the Court was its absence of clocks, except in the servants' quarters. Anthea disliked any reminder of the passage of time, so that it was her secretary's duty to see that she was punctual for her appointments.

As she made no reply, Charles clapped his hands together, in a pretense to slaughter a moth.

Miss Vine started upright and stared at him blankly. Her blurred eyes made her appear defenseless, and almost pitiful.

"Bedtime, Anthea," announced Charles.

"So soon? How quickly the time passes when one is working."

"Quicker still when one's asleep." Charles perched on the arm of her chair and threw one hand carelessly on her bare shoulder. From this point of vantage his eyes roved over the papers on the table.

"Been dreaming of your lovers, past and present?" he asked.

She slapped his hand playfully, but her eyes grew shrewd.

"No," she replied, "it's for them to dream of me. I've been deep in finance. Ah, Charles, this little head. All I have to help me. And so much to do."

"You need a man," suggested Charles. "Why not let me in on the ground floor of your next scheme?"

"No, Charles. I trust no man."

"Not even me?"

"You, least of all." She tilted his chin with her finger. "You see, I'm rather fond of you. That's fatal. A woman should always be on guard against her heart."

"What do you trust? Your corns?"

"Don't be vulgar. I trust my *head*."

She scooped together her papers.

"I'm making more money for you, Charles. Look at all these figures. No, that's enough. I did not say 'read them.' "

As she spoke, she locked the documents in a drawer.

Charles watched her, while the smile faded from his lips. In that gesture she had put him definitely in his place.

A minute before she had been his puppet, posturing and smiling as he pulled the strings of flattery. His arm was around her shoulders, in careless possession. But her manner of turning a key reminded him, not only that the wealth which surrounded them had been created by her own vision and enterprise, but, also, of his own position.

Tonight she might be the conquest of his curly hair and insolent smiles; but tomorrow he must go to her, cap in hand, to beg for a new pair of flannel bags.

At that moment he hated her with all the force of his young manhood. As he withdrew his arm roughly she smiled up at him.

"What's the matter, sonny-boy?"

He blurted out his request, like a sulky schoolboy.

"I'm short on my allowance, Anthea. And decency demands trousers."

Miss Vine pulled his hair.

"Slip them in on my own bill, Charles," she advised. "Tell Phibbs the old woman will never notice."

"You, an old woman, Anthea? I like that. Now—how old are you? I mean—how young?"

She probed the mockery of his eyes.

"Young enough to retain my faculties," she told him. "I'm neither deaf nor blind."

Then she passed her hand over her brow.

"But—I'm tired."

The scorn faded from the young man's smile.

"You slog too hard," he said. "Why the hell don't you retire? You've all the money you want. What's the good of it if you croak, and leave it to others, who've never made a penny of it?"

Miss Vine's smile was inscrutable, as she stared at her cousin.

"Are those your true views, my noble boy?" she asked.

"They are."

"Then you want me to leave you out of my will?"

Charles laughed.

"Now, you're being funny," he said. "You bet, little Charles wants his share of pie, with the rest. . . . Only, that's a long way off. And, honestly, Anthea, it's a bit raw to be slacking while you are slaving, day and night."

"And where would *you* be without my money, Charles?"

He reddened to his eyes.

"In the gutter—where I belong—judging by the company I keep," he muttered.

His insolence seemed but to amuse her. She loved a clash of wills, because she could always force her opponent to his knees.

"It's sweet of you to offer me your grandfatherly advice," she said, "but my health is Dr. Lawrence's affair. I don't keep a dog and do my own barking. Ring the bell for Morgan."

Charles hesitated with his finger on the electric button inserted in the desk.

"You're not going to keep that girl up late again, are you?" he protested.

"That is my own business." There was a rasp in Miss Vine's voice. "I don't pay a secretary and do my own typing."

Miss Sally Morgan entered the library with such promptitude that she might have been waiting for the summons, outside the door. She was a pretty girl, dressed in black satin, but her youth and attraction were sunken in her own imitation of the perfect secretary.

Her Spanish heels were too high, her lips too red, the line of her permanent wave too correct. In her endeavor to be

17

efficient, tactful, and resourceful, she spoke only to answer, and always gave the impression of thinking in shorthand.

As Miss Vine took no notice of her, she stood silent, in her employer's line of vision. Charles knew that this demonstration of indifference was punishment for his interference, and he came to the rescue.

"My aunt—I mean, my cousin—isn't really asleep, Miss Morgan," he said. "She's deep in finance."

Instantly, Miss Vine picked up a sheaf of papers, which she handed to the girl.

"I want these typed tonight," she said curtly.

"Certainly, Miss Vine," Sally assured her.

"You can use this room. Tell Bates not to sit up. You can put out the light."

"The ideal employer. Always thinking of her servants," remarked Charles. "Looks like an all-night sitting for you, Miss Morgan. But there—*you're* young."

Miss Vine rose and put her arm through his, in a possessive manner. She rubbed her finger over his sleeve and spoke in a gentle voice.

"You're positively shiny, darling. You'd better slip in a new evening suit on my bill, as well as the bags. . . . And now to bed."

Charles escorted his lady, with his eyes fixed on the carpet; but, at the door, he looked back at Sally. She was already seated before her machine, but she was not typing.

There was a sudden landslip of her pretensions, as youth cried to youth. At the girl's sympathetic expression Charles lost his crestfallen air, and spoke with his usual impudence.

"Oh, Anthea, shall I give Bates orders to bring Miss Morgan some nourishment, if she's going to be late? Bread and water is what she really likes, but if you've got such a thing as an old bone, she would adore it."

"Thank you, Charles, for anticipating my wishes," replied Anthea. "Give Bates his instructions."

Her smile was acid as she turned to Sally Morgan.

"My cousin is always so generous," she said. "I believe he'd give away my last penny."

Charles pretended not to hear the insult as he opened the door of the library with exaggerated courtesy.

Miss Vine's court awaited her, under the domed roof of the pillared marble hall. The visitors were waiting to bid their hostess "Good night," for it was the rule of the house that her retirement was the signal for their departure.

Tonight it was plain that she was in her most majestic mood, and had receded beyond the reach of flattery or familiarity. Under the thin arch of her brow—like a strand of copper—her eyes looked blankly into distance.

"Good night," she said, staring at the roof. "Charles. Ring."

When the visitors had hurriedly slipped away, she turned to the girl. She was a lovely creature, exotic and overpainted, like a delicate pink azalea.

"Where's Francis?" she asked.

Iris shook back her long mane of leaf-brown hair.

"How should I know?" she murmured.

"Haven't seen him since dinner," volunteered Charles.

"Ah, you never give each other away, do you?" sneered Miss Vine. "Always reminds me of the loyalty of the underworld."

Dr. Lawrence—who never joined in the general exodus, smiled slightly, in recognition of the hit.

"Here's your strayed lamb," he said, as Francis lounged into the hall.

Anthea's peaked face suddenly sparkled with new life.

"You've kept me waiting," she reproached him.

"I'm frightfully sorry to be guilty of discourtesy," Francis assured her. "But, I thought you would probably be late. You see, I saw Charles go to the library, and drew my own conclusions."

The distrustful glance he shot at his cousin was not lost on Miss Vine. She fluttered her lashes, to indicate her consciousness that two young men were jealous of her favors, as she turned to Charles.

"Take off my necklace," she appealed.

Charles obeyed stolidly. He might have been a robot, wound up for a special duty. Coiling up the string of pearls, he thrust it in his trouser pocket.

The doctor's eyes narrowed at the sight of the jewels.

"I wonder you trust them out of your keeping," he said.

"Why?" asked Anthea. "Do you think they might tempt someone to wring my bonny neck?"

"Well—it might be a risk."

"But Charles always puts them in the safe at night. And I can trust Charles. He's my heir."

"But, darling," laughed Iris, slipping her arm around Miss Vine, "I thought *I* was."

"So you were, angel. Francis's turn tomorrow."

Miss Vine shook herself free of the girl's embrace and turned to Dr. Lawrence.

"You see, doctor. I can sleep in safety, because I know I have the protection of three strong young people. If I were to die tonight my money would go to my brother. I haven't made my will."

"Very naughty of you, dear lady," ventured Dr. Lawrence.

"Oh, but I'm going to. Today—tomorrow—soon. Besides, death is still a long way off."

A long way? Even as she spoke, in the lamp-lit parlor of the Cherry Orchard, Miss Pye laid out the cards.

Charles broke the strained silence.

"So now you're wise to the position, doctor. Anthea, you'll lose your beauty sleep."

With the condescension of a maiden queen, Miss Vine extended her cheek to her three dependents and stretched out her hand for Dr. Lawrence's kiss. They stood, in homage, watching her stately white satin figure slowly ascend the great staircase.

Half way up the first flight she turned and held up her finger at a burst of dance music, from the radio.

"Shall I come down and dance with you?" she called.

"Yes, do," they urged in chorus. "We'll scramble for you."

"Then—I won't."

Shaking her golden curls, she ran up the stairs, like a girl. Her heart was pounding with exertion, but it also beat with triumph.

Young men clustered round her, like moths round a candle flame. She reminded herself that Cleopatra had reached her zenith at the age of forty, which would be an Eastern equivalent of her own years.

The young people stood in silence and watched her slim white figure disappear round the bend of the staircase. Then Francis called after her in his sweetest voice,

"Slip on the top stair, girlie, and break your bonny neck."

CHAPTER IV

The Cruel Looking Glass

WHEN MISS ANTHEA VINE REACHED THE BEND OF THE staircase her shadow began to grow. It blotched the white marble walls, and then took its flying leap over her head. Like a monstrous bat, it flitted down the corridor, leading the way to Miss Vine's bedroom, as though expectant of grim company.

Tonight? It reached the door, flickered, and then sank into the floor, crushed under the heel of Miss Vine's silver slipper.

It could wait. It began to rise again, to herald the approach of the mistress of the house. A smile was on her lips at a memory of a flushed girlish face, radiant with triumph, as it mocked the desire of youth.

She felt swollen with power. Four suppliants were at her feet, eating out of her hand. They had strength, talents, good looks—but no future. That was hers—because she had what they lacked—her wealth.

They could not afford to let her die. Until she made her will, she was the jewel in their crown.

Her room was in the left wing, beside that of Iris, who occupied what was, in reality, her dressing room. Charles and Francis slept in the same block. This was the intimate family sleeping suite. The picture gallery, the billiard room and the guest chambers were in the central building, while the servants' quarters were situated in the right wing.

As Miss Vine entered her apartment her maid met her in the doorway. She appeared a pale neutral creature, without a positive characteristic. Glancing apprehensively at her mistress, she flattened herself, to let the great lady pass.

Miss Vine inclined her chin slightly, and the maid took the nod as an invitation to speak.

"Good night, madam."

Flattered by the servility of the tone, Miss Vine was gracious in her response.

"Good night, Eames."

The woman closed the door noiselessly and then slunk along broad carpeted corridors, past the blazing well of the great staircase until she reached the right wing. As she opened the small door, which led to the servants' bedrooms, she heard a buzz of voices and an undercurrent of laughter.

In response to the atmosphere of warm humanity and fellowship, Eames changed miraculously, from a robot, to a vital young woman. Bursting open the first door, she plumped herself down in the middle of a bed, interrupting a game of nap.

"Believe it, or believe it not," she declared, "but the Queen wished me 'Good-night.' "

"Go *on*," said a housemaid incredulously. "Something must have pleased the old girl. Did you find a man under her bed?"

Their burst of ribald laughter was not heard in the cloistered left wing, where Miss Vine slowly advanced to the long triple mirror. She saw her reflection, slim and white, with the reedlike grace of a young girl. With the instinctive urge to play to some unseen gallery, she extended her arms in a dramatic gesture.

"Maiden's bower," she cried. "Chaste and chilly. Oh, Heaven, send me a man."

As she drew nearer to the glass she flinched suddenly, and then stood still, like a dreamer awakened to an ugly reality.

Almost immediately she regained her self-control, as she spoke in tones of biting scorn.

"Fool. *Old* fool."

She peeled her satin gown over her head and threw it on the carpet. Lighting a cigarette, she began to undress, spilling her ash, and dropping each article where she removed it. Filmy garments lay strewn everywhere, like shredded butterflies' wings; rings and bracelets were scattered, like pebbles, on chair and floor.

Since tidiness was second-nature to Miss Vine, her actions were deliberate. While she had her toilet secrets to preserve, she bitterly grudged her maid her nightly hour of leisure, and wished to make extra work for her in consequence.

Presently, she flung on an orchid wrapper, frothing with ostrich-tips, and went to the bathroom of green-and-rose glass, with concealed flood-lighting, to give the effect of sunshine.

A cloud of steam, perfumed with the scent of roses, hung on the air. But while she steeped herself in the hot, aromatic water, her mind foamed with the figures for Wednesday's board meetings.

"Having passed a nine per cent preferred ordinary dividend, there remains £43,227 to be carried forward.... Net profit of £104,750 compared with £106,667 for the preceding twelve months."

From her bitten lips and desperate eyes, Miss Vine might have been facing beggary. She reviewed expedients—reconstruction, increased advertisement, paring of overhead.

Best of all—the ax.

Wearily she climbed out of her bath, poorer than when she had stepped into it. Before her stretched the terrible ordeal of her exercises. Sway, swim, rotate, frog. Stooping to pick imaginary daisies—reaching for the moon. No pause —lest she slackened in her efforts—no respite to regain her breath.

She stopped and pressed her hand, for a moment, over her heart. A slim and supple figure was ensured for another twenty-four hours, at a cost of heart-breaking drudgery. Tomorrow and tomorrow stretched out ahead indefinitely, with their threat of more drastic treatment as time gained yet another point in the losing battle.

But she wasted no vital energy in self-pity. With resolute courage, she crossed to the toilet table and faced the relentless mirror. Before her, on the plate-glass slab, reposed a small fortune, converted into lotions and creams.

She was up against yet another stage in the terrible work of reconstruction. As she rubbed an unguent into her relaxed skin, preliminary to a course of facial exercises, she looked around her with appreciative eyes. Possessed of the mind of a jackdaw, she had copied her scheme of decoration from the ladies' salon in the *Kurhaus* of a German Spa.

The effect was theatrical, for the walls were of dull silver, and the ceiling blue as an Italian sky, and studded with stars. The silver bed, and silver suite, together with the Persian handmade carpet had been on view, as an advertisement, in the window of an important London furniture store.

Although it was destined for an Oriental monarch, Miss Vine entered into negotiations for a copy. Followed by the attentive manager, she walked into the shopwindow, as though she were making an entrance upon a stage. Always covetous of attention, she was thrilled to notice that people in the street lingered to watch her, in her rôle of potential customer.

She felt herself indicated as a lady of wealth, so she played up to her audience, trying every chair, looking at herself in the mirror, and posing on the bed.

But even as she arched her brows in criticism, or smiled her approval, she became aware that the faces pressed against the glass were laughing at her postures and her pantomimic conversation. Instantly her pleasure turned to gall. At her furious gesture, the manager had the blinds pulled down.

The first night she occupied her new bedroom she was puffed up with peacock pride of circumstance. It was good then to recall that long-ago day of late summer, when she had first seen the original apartment in the *Kurhaus*.

She had been on a conducted tour—a youthful outsider in a party of sightseers. She hated those women, because they were different from herself. While she was flat and pale, they had piled puffs of hair and curved figures. Some were married, while others were accompanied by men. She was sure that they derided her solitary state and were holding her up to ridicule. All the time her eyes kept flickering to the faces of the unconscious strangers, to detect the covert smile and glance.

She thought of them again as she gloated over her glittering splendor. Where were they now—those victorious women of yesterday? Probably hemmed in by cheap bedroom suites of pitch pine or fumed oak, paid for by instalments. Handles that came off—drawers that stuck. The ultimate triumph was hers—expressed in her blue-and-silver magnificence.

Suddenly her pleasure was dulled by a familiar sense of uneasiness. She felt that someone was laughing at her. She glanced nervously at the drawn blue satin curtains, for she could not rid herself of the impression that faces were pressed outside the glass. In spite of her common sense, which reminded her that her window was on the first floor, she was obsessed by the conviction that the crowd was still outside, jeering at her.

Miss Vine did not try to overcome her weakness, because an unnecessary effort only drained her of vitality. Since her room could not be overlooked from the grounds, she merely drew the curtains apart.

Her serenity was instantly restored; and, after that night, a blazing star in one window of Jamaica Court shone out during the hour that Miss Vine prepared for bed.

As she frowned, grinned, and grimaced in futile endeavor to keep wrinkles at bay she thought of a new enterprise, little more than an embryo, but ready to fructify in her brain.

This was a new terra-cotta Munster Hotel for Timberdale.

At present the little seaside place was only a secluded bay, unvisited by trippers or char-à-bancs; but, with her uncanny intuition for anticipating the morrow, Miss Vine was always a leap ahead of her competitors. She had heard the stir, which was the forerunner of the whisper, of building development in Timberdale.

She opened and shut her jaws for the last time, and applied fresh cream. The end of facial exercise was but the beginning of massage.

No pause yet—no rest. She stroked her cheeks and pinched her throat, while her lids were dropping for lack of sleep. Rub, pat, knead, flick. Always upwards. Across the lines. Butterfly touches around the eyes. As it was yesterday—as it would be tomorrow.

Miss Vine's mind worked in sympathy with her aching wrists. She had taken lunch at the Timberdale Arms, a few days previously, in order to spy out the land.

"That old pub is no opposition," she gloated, "Run by a

woman, too. I can smash her inside of three months. Only
one bathroom, no central heating, telephone in bar, and cold
meats for lunch. Custom running to waste. I counted twenty
cars passing inside of ten minutes. They'll stop when I open
my Munster. But the place does a good counter trade. Men
like these moldy old pubs, dating back to the Flood, where
they can swill home-brewed and crack jokes with the landlady. She's a fat fool, but a draw with customers. Might
be a sound plan to buy her out, and build on, so that they
could still come to the old place. She wouldn't stick up the
price, once she's scared of competition. I'll put Casey on
the job. He'll take her down the garden."

She stopped to apply the welcome ice pack. The end of
her drudgery was near. There only remained the strips of
plaster for the elimination of lines.

As she stuck them to her face, her thoughts winged on
another flight.

"Those young ones. They hate each other. Good. Always
aim to split. Coalition is dangerous. And now my secretary
is helping on the good work. Charles is jealous of Lawrence,
and Iris hates the girl. Who does little Morgan hate? No
matter. I keep her too busy to hate. She's my machine. And
I'm above them all. They all feel me. Tonight, they only
looked at *me*."

Her toilet was finished. It was a terrible indictment on
human vanity—so much time, money and effort expended
for such inadequate result. Yet, it was illuminative of the
qualities which had created a woman of wealth out of a
penniless nonentity.

Miss Vine had worked according to timetable, although
she had neither clock nor watch to consult. Each operation
occupied so many minutes and she never allowed the stages
to overlap, in proof of a perfectly planned routine. More
significant still was the fact that she never slackened in her

movements, or yielded to the rebellion of her aching muscles. Directing her least action was the power of her will.

Dressed in pale petal-pink satin pajamas, Miss Vine lay in the great silver bed. Her hand was raised to the electric switch. Before her stretched the hours of darkness, when the rats crept out to gnaw the cheese.

A whistle shrieked in the valley and the eleven-fifty-seven puffed into the hillside station. Among the straggle of passengers who passed through the wicket, were two season-ticket holders, who always returned to Oldtown on this train. One was a musician in a cinema orchestra, and the other kept a restaurant.

As they stumbled down the steep stony lane leading to the town, the saxophone player grumbled to his companion:

"Never knew the blinking train so slow. We must be late."

"No," dissented the restaurantkeeper. "It's not gone twelve. Miss Vine's light's still on."

He pointed to the star blazing somewhere in the left wing of the dark pile of the Court. As though to confirm his words, while they watched, the Town Hall clock struck twelve.

At the same minute, the light went out.

CHAPTER V

Lions

MISS VINE LAY RIGID IN THE GREAT SILVER BED, SMOTHERED by lace and bows of ribbon, which festooned her silken pillows. But, in spite of the pads over her eyelids, she could not sleep. Her mind was a brimming cistern, overflowing with the stored emotions of the day.

Presently, she made a conscious effort.

"I *must* sleep," she thought, "or I'll have no bloom tomorrow. Seven men, tonight—all young. They come for Iris, but they stay for me.... Beautiful? That girl? She's nothing but a scrag—all lashes and lipstick.... Yes, but she has youth. I hate her because she's young. And I hate the boys, because they're like those other boys, who always passed me by and asked other women to dance.... But I have my revenge, every day, every hour. Three of them, all thwarted, stunted, clipped. In my power.... And they cannot rebel. No, I've guarded against that. I've made them distrust and hate each other. Those boys have just enough common blood to know each other's blind spots. And you despise your own faults, in another.... But I mustn't think. I *must* sleep."

A delicious lassitude crept over her and she began to doze. She made her mind a blank, forcing out stray memories with the driving power of her will. Presently her stiff limbs relaxed in the gentle heat from her hot water bags.

The air-cell blankets, satin-bound and palest azure, like a summer dawn, were light as a snowflake, but warm as the sun.

She gave a slight start and her brain was a dissolving mist. This was the critical moment, which swept past her, like a wave, rushing out to sea. If she could catch it, and ride it far enough, it shook her off into a bottomless pit of sleep, where she slumbered, like a log, until Eames' tap upon her door.

She felt herself swept forward. Almost immediately, she began to dream. She had a vivid vision of a lion's cage, where a trainer stood, surrounded by his beasts. He had no need to crack his whip, or force them to submission. One lion had a noble, majestic face—another washed its paws like an amiable domestic cat. A third was playful as a kitten, while a fourth purred and rubbed his head affectionately against his trainer's knee.

Suddenly the trainer's foot slipped, and he fell. In a flash the lions were on top of him. Anthea saw a red splatter arising from tooth and claw, and she awoke with a faint scream.

Her heart was pounding and the palms of her hands were clammy. Worse than her fright, she realized that she had lost her moment. She was now doomed to wakefulness—face to face with the threats of the darkness.

Three young people in her power—driven by the passions of their thwarted youth. Did they hate her? She seemed to feel the air curdle with the poison which she, herself, had generated in the dark jungle of her own brain.

"They're not asleep," she thought. "They're only pretending. They're awake, thinking of me. Plotting. I can feel their hatred."

Was there one she could trust? She sweated and picked

at her satin sheets as she remembered that the lion which had fawned upon its master had been first to spring.

Miss Vine was right, in one respect. As though infected by her own unrest, the light was still burning in more than one room in the left wing.

On the other side of the partition wall, Iris sat before her toilet table, smoking a cigarette. Her narrow slip of a room had none of the spectacular splendor of Miss Vine's suite, who dramatized herself as Royalty. But, in common with the other bedrooms, it had its handsome furniture, its soft thick carpet and its distinctive color, until the shade-card gave out, to the glory of Miss Vine.

As Iris stared into the glass, she saw the brilliance of her eyes and her mane of hair, like a drift of autumnal leaves, falling over the collar of her apple-green pajama jacket.

She scowled at it, in a mutiny of passions.

"I hate myself," she thought. "I haven't the spirit of a dead fish. This awful humiliation. I'm lumber. Waste. I'm kept. And yet I put up with it. I feel utterly, utterly ashamed. I ought to go away. . . . Where? What can I do? . . . Nothing. I can only wear beautiful clothes. Besides, I should hate a life of drudgery."

She threw a glance at the leaping fire and the soft depths of a rose padded chair. Exchange this for a mean, narrow room in some boardinghouse, and a gas fire, with a slot meter.

She shook her head.

"No. I'm a luxury product. Anthea made me so. It's all her fault. She's got us tied by the leg, with our wings clipped. We may sulk, but we all open our beaks, at feeding-time. Utterly degrading. There's no hope of escape for me, unless I marry. And nobody comes to this house but a pack of sponging boys—and Lawrence. Lawrence can't marry me. He depends on Anthea to live. Yet he's losing any chance of building up a practice, as long as he comes here every day. People are talking about them. They smell out a scandal. That hurts horribly. . . . She throws us practically in each other's arms. It's not fair. It's cruel. And yet I couldn't live if I didn't see him every day. . . . I seem to be lost in a maze, and every path only leads back to myself. I know I'm my own enemy. If I were strong, or brave, I could hack my own way out. But, it's all hopeless. I'll never be free, until Anthea dies. *Until—she—dies.*"

At that moment Charles was also looking in the glass. He stopped pacing his room, struck by his own reflection. He was collarless, for he had begun to undress, and his hair was ruffled to an untidy shock.

At the sight he burst into a laugh.

"My gosh. Portrait of English gentleman, in evening rig. Living in marble halls. Eating and drinking like a lord. And not a bean to call my own. Hell. . . . There's that girl, all alone, downstairs, hammering away at her infernal typewriter. Wonder what she thinks of us all. We must seem a precious school of young pikes. Wonder what she thinks of *me*. Rotten of Anthea to keep her up so late. Wonder if old Anthea's cracking. I had the deuce of a job to wake her tactfully, tonight. No use trying to sound Lawrence. He's a tight-wad, on purpose, just to rub in the beauty of our special position. I don't like the way he strings poor old Anthea along—laughing at her up his sleeve. I may do it, myself, but—hang it all—she's family. Besides, in a queer sort of way, I don't dislike the old bird. There's a curious fascination and flavor about her, like putrid game. One day, I'll probably brain her with the poker, all for the general good. Gosh, it's late. Wonder if she's finished her typing yet."

And while Charles dreamed of a girl, Francis lay, at his ease, smoking, and thinking of a house.

"If the Court were mine I'd turn it into a hotel. Anthea's precious hall would be ideal as a lounge. Ridiculous place, with its marble floor, and marble pillars and marble statues, like a museum. It only wants a sign—ADMITTANCE FREE. Anthea's bedroom, with Iris' room thrown in, would be the Royal Suite. I could divide most of the bedrooms. I should have to put in lifts, but the central-heating could stand, and there are enough bathrooms for an English hotel. Might add a swimming pool—and what price a hangar? Ought to be ready for air development. JAMAICA COURT HOTEL. It ought to pay. On the London Road, and close to the coast. . . . Come to think of it, it's nothing but an hotel, at present, only Anthea boards us free. What's more, she pays us to stop with her. . . . Wonder what Charles touched her for in the library, tonight. I'll have a dig at her, myself, tomorrow. After all, she's only here to be bled. Poor old Anthea."

Unaware of actuality, and still strapped in the prison of her own terrified mind, Anthea sweated in the great silver bed. The time was at hand when she always heard sounds. Some were the fictions of a nightmare imagination—low chuckles in the corners of the room, and rustlings behind the curtains of her bed.

But others were real. Often, at night, when she was semi-torpid, she heard doors open stealthily and footsteps creep down the corridor. They were always muffled, and hinted of furtive purpose. Presently she would catch the murmur of voices.

She knew what it meant. Conspiracy. Jets of ice-cold water spurted down her spine as she listened. Because she was in bed, trussed, plastered, blinded and defenseless, she was afraid of the three. Iris was no longer a badgered love-sick girl, wearing her Paris frock, only by favor of her own; the boys were no longer her economic slaves.

Because they were united against her—they were youth. They were vengeance.

As she strained her ears, the footsteps began to steal along the corridor. She lay rigid, scarcely daring to breathe. The sounds drew level with her door, where they stopped. ... They passed on again.

And after the footsteps, there came whispers, which were followed by a burst of smothered laughter. In its turn, the laughter was succeeded by a burst of jubilant song.

Unable to solve the riddle of the midnight drama, Anthea shook in a palsy, waiting for the combined attack. But to-night, like the other nights, nothing happened. Their plans were not matured. A murder must leave no trace.

Worn out with emotion, Anthea suddenly slipped from her waking nightmare into deep sleep. In the morning, she would awaken, her usual autocratic, vigilant self—ruthless and unafraid. Her lions would be only her menagerie, caged and tamed.

Meanwhile, a little comedy had been played in the corridor. A door was pushed cautiously open, and Iris, in her pajamas, came out of her bedroom. She stopped to listen, and then crept down the corridor, creeping with the long strides of a young tigress. At the sounds of the padding of bare soles over the carpet, behind her, she began to run.

But, in spite of her efforts, Charles leaped past her, thrust her aside, and placed himself, triumphantly, on guard, before a small door.

"Beaten you to it," he exulted.

"Charles, you beast," panted Iris. "I was first."

"No, you don't. Hang it, play fair. You've miles of start."

There was a large superlatively fitted bathroom in the corridor, a temple of hygiene, expressed in silver and marble, and radiant with concealed flood-lighting. But, by the perversity of youth, this splendid apartment was usually neglected, while there was strong competition for a little ordinary tiled bathroom.

As Charles turned the handle there were the sounds of the splashing of water and Francis's voice, as he sang, with intense religious conviction—"I know that my Redeemer liveth."

"*Well*," gasped Iris. "As if he really meant it. I call that the limit in blasphemy."

"That pure snooping young lad ought to be scragged," said Charles.

They held their sides as they rocked in laughter.

Miss Anthea was fast asleep, safely delivered from her terrors of the night, when Sally Morgan put the cover on her typewriter.

As a matter of fact, she had rather enjoyed the adventure of being alone in the vast obscurity of the ground-floor area, for she had little imagination, and no nerves.

Charles saw her as the youthful victim of Miss Vine's tyranny, condemned to work while the household slept. But had her employer ordered Sally early to bed, so that she might finish her typing before breakfast, the lady would have considered herself ill-used. Like most young people, she liked late hours, and was a heavy sleeper, in the morning.

It was queer and fascinating in the dim magnificence of the Moorish library, surrounded with screens of fretted wood, and hangings of dark stamped leather, which might conceal the dried gouts of blood, from old assassinations. Her typewriter clicked like a ghostly clock.

She was also well-sustained, for Bates, himself, had brought in her tray of sandwiches and coffee, in order to register his personal sympathy.

"Is there anything else you might require, miss?" he asked, conscious of a lavish provision.

Sally, whose excellent appetite made her appreciative of

the good fare at the Court, was on the point of telling him that everything was gorgeous. She remembered the dignity of her position before she disgraced herself in his eyes.

"Nothing, thank you, Bates," she replied. "You need not sit up. I will see to the lights."

"Very good, miss. Thank you, miss."

At the door, he turned and spoke with renewed respect.

"Would you fancy a small bottle of champagne, miss?"

Those upper-servants knew how to be generous with Miss Vine's money. But, as the perfect secretary, Sally could not encourage extravagance.

"No, thank you, Bates."

Bates withdrew, full of compassion for the pretty young lady.

Sally clicked away briskly, entirely engrossed by the figures she typed. Sheet after sheet was unrolled from the machine; carbons withdrawn and copies numbered.

Presently her job was finished. Sally relaxed for a minute, as she brushed back a wave of hair which had fallen over her eyes. Her thoughts drifted to Charles, and she saw him again, as he had sat on the table, a few hours ago, swinging his legs while he teased Miss Vine.

Sally had a great respect and loyalty for Miss Vine. She stood as a working model of a successful business woman, to be copied—as well as an employer, to be propitiated.

Suddenly she saw her in another guise, as a vampire of youth. At a memory of the expression in Charles' eyes, when Anthea had taunted him with generosity, Sally's calm face flexed with anger, and she hit the table with her clenched fist.

"I hate her." Her voice choked with passion. "I *hate* her."

CHAPTER VI

Nocturnal

EVEN AS MISS VINE SLEPT, IMMUNE TO FEAR, THE shadows were stirring in the valley. They crept along the roads, rode the walls of houses, and climbed into windows.

Had Miss Vine seen them she would have been afraid. But it was a long chain of events which led out from the safety of four silver walls, and up to a dying gurgle in the dark. It twisted and serpentined, while it looped itself around the small obstacles of chance incidents.

Thus it came to pass, that, on this night, a small mongrel pup was, for a second, overlord of the Masters of Fate. It was an ironic gesture on the part of the mocking gods, for Miss Vine kept no dog, even for defense. She hated all animals, and the canine tribe in particular.

But Miss Vine's fate was already sealed in a long-distance call to Death—because, aeons ago, the star decreed that a spinster should be murdered by night.

The puppy, whose name of Wendy was a double-fault— both as regarded his sex, and also his instincts, which were destructive rather than protective—lived at the Moat House. It was a low, white residence, set amid extensive water-fed grounds, and two miles, as the crow flies, from Jamaica Court.

Nominally, the puppy was the property of Mrs. Antrobus —the widow of a judge, and the official owner of the Moat

House. She was a lady of strong character, and had ruled her late husband with an iron hand. In the puppy she met her master. She allowed the small creature to impose his will on hers, and to rule the house.

In one direction only was his ambition frustrate. She decreed that all respectable and law-abiding little dogs should stay at home, after dark. Every night, at nine o'clock, the housemaid carried him into the kitchen and put him to bed, in his basket. He made no protest, beyond looking like a martyr, but lay, curled up in feigned slumber, while he listened to every word of the servants' gossip.

When their supper was finished and the creaking of the back stairs told him that they were safely on their way up to bed, he leaped from bed, butted open the kitchen door, and padded back to the deserted drawing room.

A little lord of creation, he was now free to choose his own sleeping berth—the best chair or the forbidden brocade settee. But, first, he always crossed over to the French windows, where he stood, wistfully gazing out into the darkness of the garden.

His instinct told him that he was missing the best things of life—scufflings and rustlings in the undergrowth, strange strong scents, and a whole world of adventures and perils which lay hidden outside in the gloom.

On this especial night he had made his usual survey, and was blissfully snoring on the plum-brocade settee, when something drifted from the belt of wood which walled one side of the lane, at the bottom of the garden.

It was a shadow.

It clung to the darkness, as though it were a detached scrap of the night. Almost invisible against the trunk of an oak, it stared up at the Moat House.

The low, white building lay in total eclipse. No crack of light outlined any of the long dark windows. Apparently, every fire was drawn, every door locked, every inmate asleep.

The shadow crossed the lane and opened the front gate, slowly and cautiously. At the sound of a betraying creak—which was magnified by the stillness to a rusty scream—it flitted back to its shelter, and melted again into the bark of a tree.

The minutes ticked away—and each tick was the beat of a heart. The silence of the night was unchallenged. Creeping out again, the shadow slipped through the open gate, and into the tenebrous shadows of the drive.

Slowly, as though feeling every inch of its way, it pressed on. In the shade of the trees it looked blind and formless—without limbs or features, as though some elemental passion had achieved experimental materialization.

But when it came out into the open it was revealed as an indefinite figure, muffled in a cape, and with its face blacked out by the mask of a dark handkerchief.

The shadow paused. On the other side of the moat which gleamed ahead, like a black, sluggish canal, seeded with stars, was a wide expanse of lawn, where the Judge's widow gave garden parties, in summer.

When it had slunk over the drawbridge, the shadow knew that its Rubicon was passed. Although the house looked dark and silent, even now some wakeful person might be standing behind the window curtains, looking up at the stars.

A drove of wild horses thundered through the shadow's head—and each hoof-beat was the galloping of its own heart. Conscious of its peril, it crossed the grass, and reached the French windows of the drawing room. Without a pause wherein to weaken, it drew out a bit of bent wire and began to pick the lock of the door.

Careless through long immunity, no one in Oldtown took elaborate precautions against burglary. But, although the mechanism was simple and the shadow worked with dexterity, it was nervously conscious of a race with time. Two separate chimes sounded from the clock-tower of a village church before the door yielded to pressure and swung open.

The shadow tried, in vain, to pierce the gloom of the interior. It knew itself to be a black silhouette in the doorway, while the room kept its secret.

Had it been seen? Then, someone was waiting for it, in the darkness. It was walking into an ambush. An undergraduate nephew of Mrs. Antrobus was staying at the house; he was a footballer of repute, who would welcome the chance of a tackle.

The shadow could not afford to linger. Risking all, it drew out its electric torch and flashed the light over the floor and walls.

The room was empty, although it showed the recent tenancy of its mistress by the comfortable disorder of dented cushions and open library book. It was a large, pleasant apartment, rather too ornate in its decoration, and over-crowded with furniture and ornaments. The walls were almost covered with water-colors, in gilt frames, depicting Italian landscapes with pansy-blue skies and groves of olives.

The dancing circle from the torch flickered like a will-o'-the-wisp, over many a valuable ornament in carved ivory or finely wrought silver, which were souvenirs of the Judge's years of office in the East. Then it rested on the marble mantelpiece, where a Dresden china shepherd and shepherdess smiled at each other, over the barrier of the gilt French clock.

The shadow took its bearings, and then snapped off the torch. Working its way between the furniture, it stole noiselessly to the fireplace, and snatched the nearest Dresden figure—the flaxen-haired shepherd in sky-blue breeches.

It was on its way back to the open French window, when

the sound of footsteps outside the house caused it to hug the wall, as a bat hooks itself under the eaves.

Mrs. Antrobus' nephew, who, by all the rules of the game, should have been snoring dreamlessly upstairs, was cutting diagonally across the lawn, on his way to the front door. Although he had nearly drunk in the dawn at a stag-party, he was still sober, and aggressively fresh after his long walk home.

The shadow had no real fear of detection. The nephew stood in wholesome awe of his aunt, and was obviously intent on getting into the house quietly, in view of the late hour. The shadow could see his broad back and muscular shoulders in the shelter of the porch, and it strained its ears for the creak of the front door, which would be its signal to slip out into the garden.

But, even as it listened, it heard a snore from the settee. With eyes grown accustomed to the gloom, it saw a fat white puppy, just stirring out of its sleep.

The small creature yawned, blinked—and suddenly spotted the shadow. Instantly, it was erect, every hair bristling.

The shadow knew that the game was up. At the first yap, the nephew would turn his head and see the open French window. The intruder would be bottled up if it stayed in the room, and overtaken if it tried to escape.

Quicker than light, two instincts flashed together in warfare within the puppy's mind. It knew its business, which was to arouse the household. But, even as its jaws opened, its wicked eye espied the French window.

It stood ajar. The barrier which guarded Paradise had mysteriously fallen during the night.

The stronger instinct won. Wagging its tail feebly, basely pretending to be invisible, accepting the stranger as an inmate of the household, the puppy sneaked across the carpet, and shot out into the garden.

Its flight across the grass was noiseless as a flash of lightning. The crisis was over. As the nephew entered the house, the shadow, in its turn, slipped out of it, cautiously closing the French window.

When it reached the drawbridge, it stopped to drop the Dresden china figure into the moat, where it sank from sight, down in the opaque olive-green water.

CHAPTER VII

Dresden China

THE LOSS OF THE DRESDEN CHINA FIGURE WAS DISCOVERED, the next morning, by the housemaid at the Moat House. Although, at different times, she was entered in the books of the local registry office as "Gloria," "Greta" and "Norma," she was always known as "Fletcher"; for true to national type, she had quite overlooked the opportunity of her own name which was the same as that assumed by the Queen of Hollywood—Mary.

Fletcher was a local beauty, with a complexion of strawberries-and-cream and enormous, rather stupid, gray-green eyes; she had vague ambitions of a film career, and took every chance to look at herself in the glass.

Consequently, the mantelpieces at the Moat House were the best dusted in the neighborhood. And, since her first job was to obtain the requisite light, she began operations by pulling up the blinds.

She saw Wendy nosing soberly about on the lawn, but merely concluded that he had been let out by the cook, who was an earlier riser than herself. The fact that he was not indulging in his usual idiotic capers, with which he expressed his joy of life, escaped her notice. When he saw her, he walked across the lawn, with a serious expression on his face, and scraped at the French window.

She opened it with some slight difficulty, let him in, and

then began to dust the mantelpiece, looking arch, proud, amorous and terrified, in turn. Presently, however, it began to dawn upon her that something was amiss; her hand kept groping for an accustomed article, in vain.

Reluctantly she looked away from the mirror, and rolled her big eyes over the shelf. As she stared, first at a china shepherdess, with flaxen hair and rose-garlanded skirt, and then at an empty space, on the other side of the clock, without any effort she registered utter surprise.

Presently, she spoke aloud.

"It's the boy."

Having settled the point, she finished dusting in her usual perfunctory manner, looked at herself again in the glass, and then strolled into the hall, to collect the morning papers.

After she had made a leisurely examination of these, in a vain quest of a photograph of Norma Shearer, she went into the kitchen, where the other maids were at their breakfast.

"Which of you've took the boy?" she asked.

"Boy?" echoed the cook.

"One of them china figures on the drawing room mantelpiece is gone," explained Fletcher.

The cook fixed her with an accusing eye.

"Where have you put the bits?" she asked directly. "The dustbin isn't safe."

Fletcher tossed her head.

"*I* haven't broken it," she declared. "It's gone, of itself, in the night."

"Then you'd better arrange that it comes back, of itself, in the morning," advised the cook darkly. "You know how nosey-parker she is over her bits."

As Fletcher only rolled her eyes helplessly, the cook got up and went to the drawing room. The first thing that caught her eye was the half-open French window.

45

"Why is that left open?" she asked.

"It's stuck," explained the housemaid.

"Was it stuck when you shut it, last night?"

"No."

"Well, why does it stick now?"

"I don't know."

The cook began to examine the door, and discovered the scratches around the lock. Immediately excitement ran high, and Fletcher's innocence was vindicated. Hopes soared, as the maids rushed to examine the silver chest and plate basket.

Although nothing appeared to be missing, Cook took advantage of the situation to make a dramatic announcement to her mistress, when she entered the drawing room.

"Please, mum, the burglars have been."

Mrs. Antrobus was a handsome, elderly woman, who made no attempt to disguise her age. Her thick wavy hair was iron-gray, and there were numerous fine lines around her wonderful violet-blue eyes. It was her custom to walk about the house, smoking a cigarette and wearing black satin breeches, while she issued her morning orders.

The fact that she was without her skirt did not detract from her dignity as she listened to Fletcher's story with a magisterial air.

"I'll test this for myself," she said.

The servants stood and watched with interest, as their mistress made a minute examination of the room, after the fashion of a stage detective. Presently, she rose from her knees, lit another cigarette, and spoke to the housemaid.

"What have you done with the pieces, Fletcher?"

Although the cook had asked precisely the same question, without the aid of any elaborate preliminaries, the servants were impressed.

Fletcher began to protest her innocence passionately.

"I didn't. May my Heavenly——"

"Can it be mended?"

"It's not me. It's burglars."

"Do you expect me to believe that childish story?"

"But, madam, look at the door."

"I have. And I've seen marks, made by a chisel, which anyone could make. They are not conclusive."

Fletcher began to experience the mental paralysis of a victim of circumstantial evidence, as Mrs. Antrobus proceeded.

"There are white hairs, from the puppy's coat, on this settee, Fletcher. They were not here, last night. He slept here."

"Oh, no, mum," interposed the cook. "Wendy always retires in the kitchen."

"You mean, he ought to, but it is evident you forgot to shut the door. It is also evident that no strange person could have entered this room, last night, without him barking the house down."

The puppy, who was listening to the conversation, at once, gave a demonstration of his talents, with an air of conscious virtue.

"There, good little dog," said Mrs. Antrobus. "But that's enough. Mistress knows her little man can bark. *He* understands his duty, if no one else does."

Goaded by desperation, Fletcher made rather a brilliant effort.

"He might have left them hairs *after* I done the room," she said.

On her mettle, as a detective, Mrs. Antrobus rubbed the brocade with a delicate withered finger.

"In that case," she said, "there would be marks of mud or damp, as the puppy's been in the garden. I'll hear no

47

more. Bring me those pieces, and nothing further will be said. Breakfast in ten minutes, Cook."

At the door, Mrs. Antrobus stopped to give another order.

"In future, the puppy's basket is to be taken to *my* room, at night."

When she was out of earshot, the cook spoke to her mistress.

"What you've always wanted, my lady, only you was afraid we'd think you soppy."

After the truce of breakfast, Mrs. Antrobus took the puppy for his morning walk. In spite of the signs of the spring visible in the green tips of the hawthorn hedges, it was a cold morning, with lacy cloudlets frozen against a pale-blue sky. At the first milestone from Oldtown, she met Superintendent Pye and stopped for a chat.

They had a mutual liking for each other; he admired her as a sensible, good-looking woman, who had collected a husband, while she liked him as a doggy man, although she thought nothing of his acumen in the profession he had mysteriously chosen.

"And how's the big hound?" asked Pye. "I suppose your mistress always wipes out your eyes with boracic, after your walk? I know she does. *You're* in good hands, my lad."

Mrs. Antrobus smiled flintily to acknowledge his compliment. Then her violet eyes grew soft and wistful.

"Mr. Pye," she said, "of course we both know he's a mongrel. But—does he *look* one?"

"He looks like an English sportsman. I can give him no higher praise than that."

Clearing his throat, Pye delivered a short lecture on canine welfare, under the impression that he was giving her delicately wrapped-up hints, while Mrs. Antrobus asked questions, and congratulated herself that she was picking his brains, without his knowledge.

Presently, there was a roar, and, almost simultaneously, a great car shot by them, giving them a momentary glimpse of an imitation of a fair-haired girl, who was clutching the wheel.

Mrs. Antrobus snatched up the puppy, just in time to save him from a sinner's just fate, and spoke wrathfully to a vanishing snarl.

"Road-hog. Why did you get in the road, you little fool? That appalling Vine woman. She tried to kill Wendy."

"You were in the wrong," observed the Superintendent. "He shouldn't have been off the lead."

Having done his duty, he relaxed in gossip.

"Would you say that looked like a mighty sick woman?" he asked.

"How can you tell with a permanent schoolgirl complexion?" snapped Mrs. Antrobus.

"Well, she's so ill, she can't wait even a few hours for medical aid. I've just been talking to Learoyd. Dr. Lawrence was due to operate on his missus for adenoids, but he cried off, to attend to Miss Vine instead."

Mrs. Antrobus pursed her lips.

"The man's a fool," she declared. "Who's going to call him in, if he can't be depended on to come?"

"Just what I say. Learoyd told me his missus will throw a nice scene, when she knows about it. They're going to spring it on her, just before the operation, for fear she'll refuse to have it done. Like all the women, she's mad about Lawrence."

"I wonder if that is wise policy," said Mrs. Antrobus thoughtfully. "Well, good-bye. It's so nice to meet someone of the same likes—and dislikes."

When Mrs. Antrobus returned for lunch, she inquired if Fletcher had produced the broken bits of the china ornament.

"No—and never will," was the determined reply.

Notice—on either side—was in the air. Then Mrs. Antrobus remembered the extra work entailed by her nephew's visit, and, being a strategist, decided to let the matter slide, for the present.

But she disliked the look of her drawing room mantelpiece. It not only gave the impression of being lop-sided, but also of sorrow.

The shepherdess seemed to mope for her swain. Her roses appeared to wilt and her blue china eyes were always staring sadly at the vacant place, where her sweetheart had played his pipes, for her delight.

"The poor little shepherdess is missing her shepherd," Mrs. Antrobus told her nephew, who grunted at her inexplicable descent into sentiment.

But that same night the shadow came again to the Moat House. This time, although it was prepared for emergencies, there was no risk of alarm, for the puppy was sleeping upstairs, in his mistress' bed.

A few minutes later there was a flash of white, a splash of olive-green water, and under the mud and the lily-roots, two china lovers were reunited.

CHAPTER VIII

The Joker

THE FOLLOWING MORNING, AS THE PYES WERE AT breakfast in the shabby comfort of the dining room, they were disturbed by the loud shrilling of a bell.

"Telephone," said Miss Pye, who always explained the obvious.

The next minute Betsy entered, her mouth pursed with importance.

"Official, please," she announced.

With astonishing speed for his build, Pye lumbered out into the hall. He was always expectant whenever he answered the telephone, even though he knew that he was doomed to disappointment.

"Some woman's set her chimney on fire on her neighbor's washing-day," he thought acidly, as he took up the receiver.

When he returned to the dining room his blue eyes looked fierce, which was a sign of suppressed pleasure and excitement.

"Burglary at the Moat House," he announced. "Look sharp with the car, Flo."

His sister lost no time in getting the secondhand Morris from the garage and bringing it round to the front gate. She helped her brother into his coat, without an unnecessary question.

51

At last a chance had come to Adam. Although her powerful voice contained only three notes, full of holes, she sang loudly as she picked a buttonhole of early snowdrops, to decorate the hero, on his return.

Pye's hopes were high when he reached the Moat House. The housemaid who opened the door was in such a state of palpitation, that she might have been the heroine in a drama. He concluded that her excitement was symptomatic of a wholesale loss of silver. When he was shown into the drawing room Mrs. Antrobus also fostered the illusion, for she welcomed him with the enthusiasm of a girl.

"Thank goodness you've come at last, Superintendent," she cried.

"Glad to be of use," he said, waving aside the cigarette she offered him. "Now, don't talk, please. It will save time, if you answer my questions. I understand that your house has been burgled. What was taken?"

"A pair of Dresden china ornaments," replied Mrs. Antrobus.

"Thanks, I will, after all, if I may change my mind," remarked Pye, striking a match in an heroic attempt to hide his disappointment.

"I know it sounds unimportant," said Mrs. Antrobus, vaguely aware of a flop. "But there are unusual features in the case, which will interest you. In fact, they constitute a real mystery."

Pye stared at a brown rose on the carpet, in a creditable effort to register concentration, as he listened to the story of the initial theft, embellished with Mrs. Antrobus' own deductions. It seemed to bear a family resemblance to one of his sister's stories about Betsy.

"And I took her for an intelligent woman," he thought. "They're all alike. Scrambled eggs for brains."

Then he became aware that Mrs. Antrobus was waiting for his comment.

"You were right," he said. "Just a servant's trick. You should do what my sister does. Lay a trap for her."

"No," declared Mrs. Antrobus crisply. "I was wrong. Last night we had a second burglary, which proves I misjudged Fletcher. After the first incident, I gave orders for the French windows of the drawing room to be shuttered at night. We'd grown careless in the matter, as we never have burglars here."

"I'm glad we're of some use, after all," Pye reminded her. "And what way did your gentleman come, last night?"

"Through the conservatory. Come and see for yourself."

Pye followed her across the room and into the small greenhouse, which was built out of it. Here, one of the lights was smashed, and a pot of cyclamen overturned.

"I've not touched anything," declared Mrs. Antrobus virtuously.

She was vexed that the Superintendent fell short of her own standard of investigation. He merely blew out a cloud of smoke, looked around him with interest and then pounced down on a drooping plant.

"Not yours, I hope?" he asked.

"No. I'm housing it for a neighbor, who's gone abroad."

"Run it out, at once, unless you want your vines infected. It's got mealy-bug. That's all here. I'll just have a look at the lock that was forced."

After a cursory glance at the French window, he plumped down again on his chair.

"And what did you say was taken last night?" he asked.

"The remaining Dresden figure," said Mrs. Antrobus reproachfully. "Surely I told you that? The shepherdess."

"Were the ornaments genuine?"

"They were on *my* drawing-room mantelpiece."

"Sorry. But we have to ask these questions in the force. I can see for myself you have a very tasty room. Now, you're sure no other valuable is missing? Been through everything?"

"With a fine comb."

Mrs. Antrobus' opinion of Pye was rapidly sinking.

"The man's a fool," she thought.

"Well, Superintendent," she said, "what steps do you propose to take?"

"I propose to do nothing," replied the Superintendent.

As she remained silent through sheer indignation, he proceeded to explain.

"To begin with, these burglaries are the work of a rank amateur. Your pup would make a better job of breaking in a house than he's done. It's plain he was all on the jump, no nerve and no head. His first visit, he must have heard some sound which startled him so that he hopped it, with only one figure; and the second time, he's clumsy as a steam-roller. No, madam, wash him out. He's not a serious proposition. You probably know him as well as you know me."

"What do you mean by that?" demanded Mrs. Antrobus frigidly.

"Well, your burglar is either a bright young joker and done it for a rag, or else he's a rival collector, who coveted your figures."

Mrs. Antrobus' violet eyes grew thoughtful.

"There might be something in your last deduction," she said, "if only the first figure had been taken, it might have been wanted to make up a pair. But, together, they're not of outstanding value."

"Then we must leave it as someone's little joke," observed Pye, heaving out of his chair, as a sign that the interview was over.

Mrs. Antrobus could restrain her annoyance no longer.

"Do you mean," she asked, "that I'm to sit down under this outrage and make no attempt to punish the offender? Look at those lovely rose cyclamens. And the broken light. Who's going to pay the glazier's bill? Why, it's positively monstrous."

Pye glanced at the clock, and edged nearer to the door.

"That's my advice," he said.

Mrs. Antrobus mechanically followed his eye.

"Oh, I *wish* the Judge were here," she cried petulantly, as though the deceased magistrate were five minutes late for an appointment.

Pye had a fellow-feeling for her disappointment.

"It's because of the respect I had for the Judge," he said, "and also, because of my respect for you, that I don't want you to advertise your loss. You'll only have a pack of brainless idiots laughing in their sleeves at you. I want to preserve your dignity."

Mrs. Antrobus' face softened as she held out her hand.

"That's nice of you," she said. "I'll be guided by you."

Pye paused in the doorway, in an attempt to atone.

"If you find you've got the mealy-bug," he said, "lose no time. Send for me."

"Yes," remarked Mrs. Antrobus bitterly, when the door had closed behind him. "That's about your mark. Mealy-bug and dog-biscuit. And you stand for the law. Oh, if only the Judge were here. He'd know what to do."

For the first time, she seemed to be finding the flaws in her complacent widowship.

In his turn, Pye arrived home in a bleak mood. His grim red face slightly brightened, however, as he saw a smart blue Baby Austin blocking the road for him, before the Cherry Orchard.

Miss Pye—big and fair—met him, at the gate; and another woman—bigger still, and fairer—stood at the open door.

"Doris is here," announced Miss Pye.

"You don't say so," murmured Pye, as he smiled and nodded to the proprietress of the Timberdale Arms.

Miss Pye took no notice of his sarcasm, as she caught his arm.

"Well, Adam, what was it?" she asked.

"Oh, she'd lost a pocket-handkerchief in the wash," was the acid reply. "Hullo, Doris, old girl."

In his eyes, his favorite sister was still the slim, golden-haired girl who had rushed Major Law's defenses during his sole leave, although nothing was left of the war idyll but the golden hair and the Major's pension.

"Go on. She never called you in about a hanky?" asked Miss Pye.

"Well, perhaps, it was a nightie."

"Nothing we don't know, in our business, about lost nighties and the funny places they turn up in," said Mrs. Law, whose humor tended to be Rabelaisian in brand.

"Naughty girl," remarked Pye, playfully slapping her. "What's for dinner, Flo?"

"Steak-and-kidney pudding," replied Miss Pye.

The sun shone again as Pye addressed the Universe.

"Now, who wants women to have brains when they can make a crust like you, Flo? That's women's business, bless them. Stopping for dinner, Doris?"

Mrs. Law shook her golden head.

"No, Adam. I only just dropped in to ask Flo to cut the cards for me."

"Why? Nothing's wrong?" asked Miss Pye.

"No. Everything's fine."

"Worried, then?"

56

"Golly no. But I just wanted to know what's going to happen."

Mrs. Law was a heavy smoker and her ash fell continuously on the cards, as she leaned over the table. In spite of her frequent bursts of loud laughter and her broad comments, it was plain that her mind was not at rest. She fed Miss Pye with questions, as though trying to force a favorable fortune.

"Can't you see a letter for me, with good news? Can't you see a pleasant surprise? Those hearts are good, aren't they? You can't see treachery threatening me, can you?"

Miss Pye, who took her soothsaying seriously, did her best to give the beloved younger sister a promise of good luck. But the cards were not too propitious, and even Doris cried out at certain ominous combinations.

"No good stringing me along, Flo, old girl," she said. "I know a bad card as well as I know a bad florin. Well, well, such is life, and may the best woman win. I'll have to rush back to relieve the bar."

She brushed the ash off her smart black-and-white suit, dusted her red face with powder, lit another cigarette, and hurried out to her car. As she grasped the wheel, while her brother and sister watched her in admiration, she gave them a clue to her uneasiness.

"You never knew anything like the rumors we get in the trade. I bet the war was started in a pub. Guess the latest. Some smart aleck was saying there's going to be a Munster Hotel in Timberdale. All hot air, I say. The place would never cover two hotels."

Adam's eyes grew anxious.

"Would it injure you?" he asked.

Mrs. Law shook her head with an explosive laugh.

"Don't worry, old son. I'm too well dug in. My place is historic and I've got a following. A real first-class connection. I can hold my own against any opposition. I'm much more bothered about what's going to win the Lincoln and National double."

After Mrs. Law had driven off, puffing at her cigarette in gay defiance, Pye and his sister remained staring into each other's eyes.

"That dam' painted scarecrow," thundered the Superintendent, glaring up at Jamaica Court.

"Don't excite yourself before eating," urged Miss Pye, "or the meat will poison you."

But directly after the cloth was removed Miss Pye again took out her pack of cards and laid them out, in the form of a horseshoe. As she counted and sucked in the corners of her mouth, she seemed to find grim consolation in her pastime.

For there it was again. Murder of a spinster by night.

CHAPTER IX

Aftermath

As DR. LAWRENCE WALKED INTO ANTHEA'S BLUE-AND-silver bedroom, the following afternoon, he thought of his other patient—little Mrs. Learoyd. She always reminded him of a French doll, for she was small, with short black hair and a bright color. Unfortunately, however, she had not the placid disposition which accompanied sawdust stuffing, for she was a mass of sensitized emotions and romantic inhibitions, which she fed, thrice weekly, at the pictures.

Lawrence had great difficulty in persuading her to consent to the little operation. It was in vain that he assured her that half the children in the world were having their adenoids removed daily, and that the other half would be the better without them.

In the end, he appealed to her vanity, as he hinted that a muffled voice detracted from a woman's charm. Mrs. Learoyd gave way, but she made him promise that he would perform the operation himself.

"I want you to hold my hand when I go under, doctor," she said. "And I want you to be the first person I see when I wake up again."

"With a clear bell-like voice," he reminded her, lying in a good cause.

Dr. Lawrence had given her his word. He was sincerely sorry that his engagements had clashed; but as Wednesday afternoon was early closing day, it was the most convenient time to operate, at home, upon a tradesman's wife.

As he took Miss Vine's hand, with the exaggerated homage that he always displayed towards her, he did not see the froth of her honeysuckle wrapper, which she was wearing for the delight of his eyes. He saw instead, little Mrs. Learoyd, with her dark, childish fringe, and her scarlet dressing gown, which suited her so well.

When he had written off her date, it seemed expedient to give in to his influential patient's whim; he had to consider his own interest before the fancies of an hysterical woman, who, in her time, had taken too large a dose of Valentino.

But, even as he smiled back at Anthea, he had a clear vision of the large bedroom in High Street, with the new Axminster carpet and the twin brass bedsteads, of which Mrs. Learoyd was so proud. He saw the empty shop below, with its sides of bacon and boxes of crystallized fruit, in the unfamiliar shuttered gloom.

A little pang rent him at the thought of his broken promise, and he had a sudden mad impulse to make some excuse to Anthea and dash back to High Street, to keep his appointment.

A glance at his watch restored him to prudence; it was past three. Mrs. Learoyd would have taken the anæsthetic, and, if the going was good, the operation would be nearly over.

But Mrs. Learoyd was not unconscious. At that moment she was crying, and screaming, and swearing by all her gods that Dr. Williams should not touch her throat.

For many hours past, she had been working herself up to a fever-temperature of fright. In every incident or object, she had seen a presentiment or omen. Only last night she had dreamed that she was back at the Crown, pulling away at a black draped beer-engine, and the customers had given her white camellias, instead of money, as payment for their drinks.

She had made up this dream, as well as the other about a ride in a coach, which was not the Rolls of her secret ambition; but they frightened her just as much as the realities. It was in vain that her husband scolded, the doctor argued, the nurse soothed. She declared that she would not have her adenoids removed.

In the end, she got her way, as women will; for Dr. Williams did not operate on her throat.

Anthea was swift to notice the slight abstraction of Dr. Lawrence's manner.

"Car running well?" she asked casually.

He threw her one swift glance from under his heavy lids; but the next second he was again her flattering courtier. In those three words she had him to heel.

Downstairs, in the library, there was open mutiny. Iris sat with her knees drawn up to her chin, as she stared into the fire. She wore a tawny pull-over, which matched her hair, and a string of amber beads in which the firelight glowed.

"Our position here is utterly degrading," she declared. "We ought to clear out—and save our souls."

Francis took his long nose out of his book.

"Where?" he asked.

"Anywhere."

"That's just where I went. And I came back again."

"We aren't like you," flashed Charles, taking sides with Iris.

"No," agreed Francis coolly. "The difference between us is that you would come back when your money was gone. But I came back *after* my money was gone."

Iris looked at him curiously, as though she were seeing him from a new angle. She reminded herself that this supercilious young man, with the polished hair, had actually rebelled against Anthea. He had been lost for several months in London, before he sent a request, on a dirty unstamped post card, for a return ticket. She remembered, too, that he had been very thin, on his return.

"When I am a parson," continued Francis, in his pedantic voice, "I am, naturally, going to preach on the beauty of high thinking and empty bellies. No, I'm not being coarse, Iris. I prefer the purity of Anglo-Saxon. But starvation ennobled me only to this extent. I made a solemn vow that I'd lie, steal or kill, before I went hungry again. It's too unpleasant. And I'm proud to add that, such is the strength of my character, I've kept my vow, dear brethren."

"Oh, shut up, you big stiff," growled Charles. "Can't you see we're serious. Iris and I are fed up. Every time, of late, that Anthea sticks her painted mug up to mine, I feel I'd rather clear out, and break stones."

"Only there's very strong competition for your stone-breaking job," Francis reminded him.

Then he turned to Iris.

"What I can't understand," he said, "is why *you* stick it. With your picturesque looks and wandlike figure, you could get a job as mannequin."

Iris bit her lip at his suggestion.

"Don't expose your ignorance," she said. "Don't you know that mannequins are only in seasonal demand?"

"Then what about the stage? Of course, I'm not ignorant enough to suggest that you try for the chorus. But why not try to wangle a job as leading lady? You're sufficiently inaudible, and you can play at playing golf."

"And why are you so anxious that I, alone, should preserve my self-respect?" asked Iris.

"Because you are a woman, and women are our mothers. True, you are not my mother; but I was born first, and my father preferred blondes."

Iris tossed back her hair impatiently and stared again into the red heart of the fire.

"I'm not being funny," she said. "Of course, I can understand why Anthea hangs on to you two. In view of her special complex, that is an easy one. But—why me? She loathes me, really, because I'm young."

Both the young men burst into a shout of laughter.

"Cut out the modesty, Iris," advised Charles. "You know, perfectly well, you're the decoy-bird."

"Not I." Iris laughed scornfully. "The boys come for the free bar."

"But what about Lawrence? He knows that Anthea only has him because he looks like Valentino. If he had no ulterior motive it would be playing the game too low. Even for him."

Iris turned on him, like a fury.

"Oh, you make me sick. I tell you, I'm desperate. I must do *something*. Soon."

"Same here," muttered Charles. "Only 'soon' is not quick enough. I want it *now*."

Francis opened his book again.

"You funny little people forget that, while you furiously rage, like the heathen, the faithful Lawrence is upstairs, putting Anthea through her paces. He may have some hopeful news for us yet. You can tell that is his step by the light in Iris' eyes."

"Hush," commanded Iris.

The gloom of her face was dispelled as the door was flung open, to herald Lawrence's entrance. He was his usual calm, elegant self, but a close observer might have noticed the tiny beads of moisture which dewed his upper lip.

"I wonder if I might ring for a cocktail?" he asked.

"Earned it?" asked Charles, with a wink.

Dr. Lawrence nodded and pulled down his mouth. Then he smiled at the three upturned faces.

"Sorry to disappoint you people," he said lightly, "but Anthea is going to live to ninety."

"Don't talk as if we were a pack of vultures," implored Iris. "I don't *want* the poor old thing to die."

Dr. Lawrence's smile faded as he looked at her.

"I was only pulling your leg," he said. "Honestly, I do sympathize with all of you."

"Like hell you do," growled Charles. "It'll pay you to keep her this side of the daisies for another twenty years."

The doctor twisted his lip.

"I wonder?" he queried. "One can pay too high a price. There is such a thing as a limit."

"And we've reached it," said Charles. "We're going to chuck it."

Dr. Lawrence's enigmatic face gave no clue to his feelings, but his voice grew persuasive.

"Don't play the goat now," he urged. "Not *now*."

"What d'you mean—exactly?" asked Francis.

They all stared at Dr. Lawrence expectantly, but he took refuge in vague generalities.

"You've stood it for so long that it is futile to throw up the sponge, now," he told them. "After all, any moment, something may happen."

"What?"

The young doctor shook his head.

"You must not expect me to betray professional secrets. I can only say this: Anthea's not quite so young as she's been led to believe—by herself. And organs can't last for ever. Be patient, just a little longer—do."

His glance held no contempt, for he understood the position better than an outsider. These young men stood to gain much, and to lose more. At any time Anthea might tire of them and want fresh victims to supply her daily diet of flattery.

In that case, she would either buy their freedom, or turn them adrift.

His lips set in lines of disgust, as he thought of the scene he had just been through, and the claims of her insatiable vanity. As he looked at Iris' unhappy eyes and the sullen faces of the young men, he saw Anthea as a painted leech, draining their youth.

In turn, his own thoughts drew blood.

"It's a crime to keep her alive."

At the entrance of a servant with a tray of cocktails, he recovered his composure. Glancing at his watch, he crossed over to the desk.

"Mind if I telephone?" he asked. "I want to hear how Mrs. Learoyd's op. went off."

"That's right," said Charles. "I used to be fond of little Dutchy, when she was at the Crown. Sad when good barmaids marry and get lost to us."

In idle curiosity, they all listened to Dr. Lawrence, as he put through his call, for he was one of those who perform on the telephone. Unconsciously, he assumed his professional smile.

"Hello. Dr. Lawrence speaking. Who are you? Come up the wire, please. Operator, please clear the line. Hello. Oh, is it you, nurse? Very fit, I hope? Well, everything gone off all right? Is the little lady very sorry for herself? Tell her I've rung up, and I'll be round—*What?*"

As he listened, his smile faded, and he wiped his face.

"This—this is a terrible shock," he said. "I'll be round."

"Bad news?" asked Charles, as the doctor rang off.

"Very bad!" Dr. Lawrence spoke with some difficulty. "She's dead."

"Now that's too bad," remarked Charles with feeling. "Have another cocktail, old chap?"

As he ministered to the doctor, he took the opportunity to fortify himself. Before he drank, he raised his glass.

"Poor little Dutchy. Here's luck."

He gulped with sentiment, as Francis, attracted by the tray, strolled across to the group.

"Cocktail, Francis?" Charles spoke to his cousin with rare cordiality. "Better have one, too, Iris?"

Iris' lip curled.

"As I'm not a member of the Learoyd family, I hardly need to be sustained," she said.

Still hugging her knees, she watched the group around the tray. Suddenly her face shaded with anxiety.

"Glyn," she said, "did Dr. Williams bungle the operation?"

She noticed that Dr. Lawrence wiped his lips before he replied.

"No. As a matter of fact, there was no operation. She died under the anæsthetic."

He put down his glass and spoke with emotion.

"Her heart was a bit weak. I barred chloroform, on purpose. But there was no risk. It ought not to have happened. But the nurse said she was in a terrible state beforehand, because I let her down. It—it makes me feel responsible."

"Of course you're not," said Iris quickly. "It was just pure bad luck."

"I know." The doctor ran his hand over his hair. "All the same, I feel that, indirectly, I've killed her."

"Not you," corrected Francis. "Anthea."

They looked up to see Anthea Vine standing in the doorway.

CHAPTER X

Account Rendered

MISS VINE HAD DISCARDED THE FROTH OF HER BEDROOM fascination for the tight satin gown, which signified business. Her mouth was drawn and her eyes sunken in their feathery pit of lashes.

"What are you saying about me?" she demanded.

"I'm saying that you are responsible," said Francis calmly.

While his companions gasped at his audacity, he finished his explanation.

"I mean, responsible for our consolation. In other words, we are drinking your cocktails. Have one? Just to brace you over the shock of Mrs. Learoyd's death."

"Mrs. Learoyd dead? How?"

She listened attentively to Francis' explanation, but her eyes never left Dr. Lawrence's face.

"Well, this lets you out," she remarked. "You see, there was no question of an operation."

"I wish I could see it like that," he replied. "I feel a bit responsible, although, really, I am not to blame. She was nervous and excitable, and, of course, her heart wasn't too strong. I'm going to see Learoyd and explain that it would have happened, just the same, if I had been there."

"If you are not to blame, why trouble to put yourself in the right?" asked Anthea sharply.

"But—he may think——"

67

"Rubbish. *Never* explain. And never excuse your actions. It is a confession of weakness."

Her voice was cutting in its contempt, and Dr. Lawrence rallied immediately, even while he looked thoughtful. The change in Anthea involved a dislocation of his mental values. Only a few minutes before she had been his absolute dupe; responsive to his professional advice, pliant as a reed—almost servile in her surrender to his will.

He had taken her for granted, because women had always made things too easy for him. They were a permanent element in his life, and he accepted them without enthusiasm, or special interest. He had never made an effort to pursue, or hold—only to break away.

"Perhaps you are right," he said. "But I must see Learoyd, to offer professional condolences."

"Don't. One can say too much." Anthea's tone was curt, as she issued her commands. "Write instead. Just the usual things—deeply regret, and so on. Make it short."

Then her mouth twisted in a crooked smile as she looked at her relatives.

"Why doesn't Iris have a cocktail, too? she asked. "To celebrate."

"Celebrate?" repeated Iris.

"The death of a woman. That grocer will be married within six months."

As she turned to the door, Dr. Lawrence made a bid to assert his old supremacy.

"You ought to be resting," he said. "I forbid any work today."

"*You* forbid? My dear little doctor—yes, I know you tower over me—open the door."

At the threshold, she turned round. Francis looked benevolent as a bishop as he raised his glass to her. Iris uncurled herself, and smiled languidly. Charles was nodding with the amity of drink.

Dr. Lawrence laid his fingers tenderly on her arm.

"I wish I could persuade you for your own good, dear lady," he murmured.

Suddenly, Anthea remembered her dream of the lions. Four of them—playful, friendly, submissive. Her domestic cats.... And the one who caressed his trainer, had been first to spring.

Her eyes were like flints as she dashed away the doctor's hand.

"Wait," she said. "I shall have something for you."

Dr. Lawrence escorted her across the hall, to the study, where the clack of the typewriter announced the fact that Sally Morgan was hard at work. Then he lit a cigarette and began to stroll about the vast area of the marble-pillared hall.

He wanted to readjust his ideas about Anthea, for his brain had received a severe jolt. It might be expedient to revise his policy. Like many an ambitious young professional man, he was the victim of economic pressure, and, therefore, pledged to study diplomacy.

Iris looked after Dr. Lawrence, and then, languidly got up from the rug.

"Follow on—follow on"—sang Francis—"And remember, you follow the Light—not Lawrence."

"I'm leaving you two mourners to the sanctity of your grief," Iris told them.

"Well, it's always a jolt, hearing anyone has croaked," mumbled Charles.

"Personally," remarked Francis, whose clear articulation was unaffected by his numerous cocktails, "I dislike death, because of the attendant detail of dissolution. So untidy. I've decided to adopt Elijah's method of transport. He went up in a fiery chariot, and I propose to come down in a blazing airplane. Same method—reversed—and same results. Neat, eh?"

He was still talking, when Iris slipped out into the hall. Although she interrupted his train of thought, Dr. Lawrence's heavy Eastern face lit up as she approached. He met her so frequently that he had grown to accept her attraction. Self-interest told him that while he could fall in love with Miss Vine's heiress, he must not pay undue attention to Miss Vine's adopted niece.

He always felt rather sorry for her, because Anthea understood the value of window-dressing so well. This was evident in her first humble venture—the forerunner of the chain of the "Dahlia" lingerie shops—where scraps of lace and ribbon were sold at prices ridiculously disproportionate to their value, by virtue of their attractive combination.

Ever since Iris had been acquired, through the adoption society, Anthea had dressed her like an expensive doll, and —following the traditions of the trade—her price was not marked in plain figures.

Lawrence shrewdly suspected that she was not for sale— but merely a show-specimen, to attract customers. At the end of the season she would be given away at sacrificial value, or thrown out, as shop-soiled lumber.

While Iris looked a typical modern society girl, the only society she knew was Anthea's set of spongers. She was a model of the moment, displaying the newest line, the newest eyebrow, the newest lipstick; yet she was without the physical or mental freedom of youth.

But even while she appeared to droop through the empty hours, she sometimes revealed glimpses of startling vehemence, like a salty wind blowing through the silken curtains of a stuffy room.

As she spoke to Lawrence, her glance was as enigmatic as his own.

"Are your eyes opened at last?" she asked.

"Am I your blind puppy, mistress?" he countered.

Iris looked away, down the vista of pillars.

"I think," she observed, "that one of the reasons why we dislike Francis specially is because of his fatal knack of hitting the nail on the head. He was right about Anthea. She *is* to blame for this death."

He interrupted her.

"I tell you, no one's to blame."

"You mean, *she* told you no one's to blame. And, in any case, it's not going to end here. All this will do you no good. And it's only the beginning. You will end by losing every patient."

The doctor shrugged his shoulders.

"My dear girl," he complained, "why pick upon me now? I—I've felt this."

"And I've felt it, too."

"Why? What have my affairs to do with you?"

His inscrutable long eyes under their drooping lids, forbade her to trespass; but after a second of hesitation, she tossed back her hair with her familiar gesture of despair.

"It *is* my affair," she cried. "We are all of us in this. Listen. You must break with her, Glyn. You *must*. While there's still time. It's too late for us."

He laughed at her vehemence.

"Do you seriously suggest that I'm to give up my best patient? Fantastic notion. Miss Vine is worth more to me than the rest of my practice put together."

"Don't I know that?" Iris bit her lip. "You're too dependent on her. Suppose—you should want to marry?"

"Well, I shall have to do as other men placed like myself, and marry for money."

"An old woman?"

"Not necessarily an old one."

Iris' released breath was almost a sob.

"That's something," she said. "All the same, it might come hard on you if you cared for another girl."

Dr. Lawrence whispered in warning at the faint sound of an opening door.

"Hush. Miss Morgan is coming. Besides, life is hard on you and me, Iris. We're drifters. It's easier for people with backbones."

"Like Sally Morgan?"

"If you like." Lawrence smiled at Sally. "We were just talking of you."

"Something nice, of course," interrupted Iris. "By the way, Miss Morgan, we want a little job done, and you do all the jobs in this house."

"Yes?" asked Sally, attentive and ready.

"We want Miss Vine murdered for the general good," drawled Iris. "Will you do it for us, please?"

Sally smiled discreetly as she shook her head.

"If you don't mind, not now. I want her to sign some papers."

Turning to the doctor, she handed him a note.

"From Miss Vine," she said.

Her business transacted, she went back to the study. Although she knew the contents of the note, she felt no special sympathy with Lawrence. She had been trained in business principles, and she considered Miss Vine's action justified.

But it was plain that Lawrence received a blow, when he tore open the envelope.

"What is it?" asked Iris.

"Nothing."

Before he could protest, she had snatched the note from him.

It was a statement of account, with a request for prompt payment; and it concerned his car.

When Lawrence first came to Oldtown, he made his rounds in a second-hand two-seater; but, shortly after he began to attend Miss Vine, he was better suited with a new Daimler. Local gossip, which coupled the facts, was not in error. Miss Vine had bought the new car on the understanding that she should be repaid in easy instalments.

She allowed him to suit his convenience in the matter of reimbursement; and, as he became gradually her favorite courtier, she protested, every time he gave her his check.

The last few months, he had allowed the payment of the instalments to slide, on the tacit understanding that the car was her gift.

As she had done nothing to disabuse his mind, it was a severe shock to realize that Anthea's memory was better than his own. Every month, a fresh item had been added to his debit-account; and the total, up to date, represented a sum which he knew himself unable to pay.

He regained his poise at the sound of Iris' anxious voice.

"Can you pay?"

"Of course," he replied.

"But, have you anything?"

"Yes—an overdraft. Don't look so worried, my dear. It'll be paid."

Iris shook her head fiercely.

"No, it won't," she cried. "She'll let it slide again, and so will you, because it's the easiest way. Oh, can't you see? She wants the debt to grow and grow, until you're completely in her power? You don't know what she is like *then*. Glyn, you must pay her somehow, and break with her."

He took her hand and kissed it lightly.

"Sweet," he said. "I must go now. And if you really want to help me, encourage Anthea to send for me. The only way I can clear this, will be by a cross-account."

She walked with him, in silence, to the car; but as he was about to drive off she spoke in a low strangled voice.

"I *hate* her. And it's so frightening to hate."

"Why?" he asked.

"Because one is so helpless. It's another person that thinks the awful thoughts, and does the terrible things. Sometimes, I'm so frightened of that other person."

"Iris, you're hysterical. The truth is, you think too much of yourself."

"Spoken like a doctor. Bravo. But you only show your ignorance of human nature. When one hates, it's never for oneself. I'm not afraid of anything Anthea can do to me. But I'm afraid for others."

"Surely you don't mean Charles—or Francis?"

She gave a hard little laugh as she shook her head and ran into the house.

Later, as Superintendent Pye was tramping home along the white dusty road, flooded with the white sunshine of early spring, a girl on a motorcycle scorched by him, as though to escape the torment of her mind. He had a glimpse of a beautiful, passion-marred face, with stormy eyes and compressed lips.

It was Iris Pomeroy.

"Flo's right," he muttered thoughtfully. "There's a mighty ugly state of things up at the Court."

CHAPTER XI

The Shadow Grows

THAT NIGHT, MISS VINE SAT ALONE IN THE MOORISH library, surrounded by her papers. She was feeling drained of energy, for the day had left its mark on her. While she told herself that she was reaping the aftermath of the board meetings, she knew that her depression had its roots in a dream.

She was glad that Dr. Lawrence had not come to dinner; she shrank instinctively from him, although she missed the stimulus of his presence. Without it, she had been unable to summon up her usual coquetry, but had drooped, glum and moping, at the head of her table, taking no part in the forced conversation.

She passed her retinue in review, as she stared at her papers, with sleep-filmed eyes. Charles was her darling—the apple of her eye. He was an admitted scamp, wherein lay most of his charm. She liked him the better because he tried to dislike her; he might break away, but he would return. She held him fast.

Lawrence? He was always charming and flattering. Her vanity whispered that she had not worn her most attractive wrappers in vain. If there were danger in her association with him, it was only added spice. Meanwhile, he was in her debt, and, today, she had turned the knife.

Iris? She was a girl, so did not count. An arrogant chit—

a typical example of a beggar on horseback. Probably she hated her, even while, sometimes, she dared to look sorry. Flick. Away with her. Mere rubbish.

Francis? Sulky and cynical. She held him only by the power of the whip, although, so far, she had only shown it to him. Still—she held him.

"Which is my real enemy?" she wondered. "Is there one among them who would stand by me, in crisis?"

Then she forced herself to look over the first rough plans of the new hotel for Timberdale. The scheme was still so fragmentary and indefinite as to be little more than a rumor. At this stage, it floated in her brain with the perfect symmetry of seaweed in an ocean pool; withdrawn, it would only be a handful of slimy string. The time had not come when she could present it, as a clear-cut business proposition, to her board of fellow-directors.

But, in her own consciousness, she was sure of its consummation and ultimate triumph. She banked on a building boom in Timberdale and intended to reap the advantages of a monopoly. Much of her success had been due to her uncanny instinct of location, allied with avoidance of any strong competition. To attack only the timid and defenseless, was part of the ruthless policy which also dictated the merciless scrapping of all worn material—human and inanimate.

Presently, the figures began to swim over the paper in the familiar way. Her head sank lower on her meager, scented chest. And, while she dozed, the lights of Oldtown were pricking through the darkness, and the shadows were stealing abroad.

The most brilliant cluster of illuminations advertised the local cinema, where, last night, little Mrs. Learoyd had been an earnest student of the star film. She had sat in a two-and-fourpenny seat, with a packet of chocolates, soft from the heat, on her lap.

Tonight, she lay on one of the twin beds, in the bedroom, which was strongly perfumed with white narcissi; and her hands would never warm anything again. She wore her best nightdress, while her features were set in an unfamiliar waxen mold. No longer a cheap, colored doll, she was mysteriously withdrawn from her counterfeit world of flickering shadows, which she had exchanged for reality.

Downstairs, in the dining room, Mr. Learoyd made the funeral arrangements; his marriage had been a failure, but he never owned it even to himself, and never would. In six months' time, he resolved to marry again, and he knew who it would be.

Miss Vine had a horrible talent for an accurate forecast of human frailty. The Learoyd affair had passed entirely from her mind; and whether the price of her caprice was a human life, remained one of the mysteries.

Suddenly she started and blinked, at the sound of her name. A young man, in evening dress, stood by her side. Tonight, Francis was the herald of bedtime; for the young people, in their mutual distrust, divided all duties and privileges.

"Close on eleven, Anthea," he said, putting his finger in the catalogue he held.

She made no movement to rise, but sat looking at the sheen thrown by a swinging lamp on his hair, and the fastidious set of his too-small mouth.

"What are you reading?" she asked.

He showed her a catalogue from the British Museum, and pointed to an illustration, ringed with pencil.

"See this vase?" he asked. "Ugly object, isn't it? I saw one like it, as far as I could judge, the other day, so, out of curiosity, I looked up its price. It should be valuable. Prices always interest me."

She watched the unusual flicker of interest on his impassive face, and laughed scornfully.

"Always money with you, Francis. If you are so keen to acquire some, why don't you begin? I was younger than you when I laid the first fagot on my pile."

Francis narrowed his eyes.

"I was only waiting for your perennial reminder about your age," he said. "I've always wondered how you got the nucleus of your fortune. You can't have chicken without an egg. But—of one thing, I'm certain. It was not the price of virtue."

Her eye beat down his insolence.

"A cheap sneer, Francis. I will take it on its surface value as the highest compliment a woman can receive. And, as usual, clever child, you are right. I received some valuable shares, as the price of my brain."

He shrugged his shoulders.

"Well, I cannot emulate you. Wren is still safe. Why did you make me an architect, of all things?"

"Because you were always drawing plans of houses, when you were a boy."

Francis laughed.

"Yes, I did that, on purpose, to take you in. I wanted you to waste your money, later on."

Anthea echoed his laugh.

"I can't swallow that. I'm not in my dotage, Francis. You were a little icicle, but you were not an abnormal child. Do you know you are my one failure? And yet, sometimes, I feel I could count more on you than the others, who are gentler. You've something of me in you."

"That should make you distrust me. Look into your own heart, and you'll know why."

Anthea smiled.

"On the contrary, I'm going to trust you—Heaven knows why—and tell you a secret. Do you see these papers?"

"Yes. Even a rotten architect like myself can recognize tracings."

"Well then, Francis, I propose to build a Munster at Timberdale. More money for jam for you."

He frowned reflectively.

"They've a pub there already," he remarked.

"I know. But it's only ghost opposition. I'll soon have the ground cleared."

"Ruthless woman. You'd make the Duce jealous. Ah me, many's the glass of ale I've had at the Timberdale Arms."

"And you'll have many more, if the landlady knows her business better than I know mine."

"D'you know who she is?" asked Francis.

"No, except she's the widow of an officer."

"Yes, Law. But she's also the sister of Superintendent Pye. Well, Anthea, since the speculation is to my future gain, I'll drink to the new Munster. But I'll drink at the old Timberdale Arms, to square things. Notice the barmaid there?"

"No."

"Then ask Charles about her."

Although Anthea was on guard, the cloud of jealousy settled on her face, for she resented any hint of rivalry to her absolute monarchy.

"I sometimes think you hate me, Francis," she said.

He was silent while he stared at her little glittering eyes—colorless as drops of rain water—the tight rose-tinted mask, and the scarlet curves painted over the merciless slit of her mouth.

"Then why not form a defensive alliance?" he asked. "Let me in on your schemes, Anthea. You'll find me no slacker, where finance is concerned. And I can promise you, I've no sentiment about business. Widows are nothing to me. In me, you may behold yourself in trousers, with a damned long nose to spoil your beauty.... No, don't speak yet. Just think a moment first. I'm proposing something which is to your ultimate advantage."

Anthea stared at him in surprise. Although nothing could slur his ice-clear enunciation, his eyes were shining, and he paced the room, in his excitement.

For a minute or two, she hesitated. A partnership with youth might be better than this eternal underground mutiny. She could relax in consultation and shelve some part of her burden of responsibility. And it would please Francis. She had never seen him before so propitiatory, or so anxious for a boon. In him she might find a friend.

"Friend." At that tepid word, her coquetry awoke. To gain a friend, she would lose a courtier—a slave. It was this conflict and surrender which reminded her that she was a woman, with power to foment and to soothe.

"No, thank you, Francis," she said. "I made my money, and I propose to keep it. You can reopen the question when you've something tangible to offer me."

"That will be too late," said Francis quietly. "For you will be dead."

He had grown white around the nostrils, so that, for one moment, she was afraid.

"Are you going to murder me?" she asked, with a quiver in her voice. "My dear, that will be a thrill."

"Not such a fool." He shrugged contemptuously. "I've no intention of swinging for you. No, I was referring to the course of Nature. Soon, you will have nothing to give away, for dead people possess nothing."

Anthea shuddered as she locked away her papers.

"What a cheerful little bedtime story," she said. "You mustn't keep me up any longer, Francis."

The court that awaited her at the foot of the great staircase, was smaller than usual. Because she missed Lawrence, Anthea took not the slightest notice of a guest—a pimply, but pleasant youth,—the son of a Colonel Ames. As his father was one of the few land-owners who exchanged hospitality with Jamaica Court, her discourtesy was marked.

She toiled up the marble stairs with a heavy tread, and, at the bend, never turned round to smile. At the back of her mind there was an elusive warning, telling her that she must remember something.

For the moment, it had escaped her. She was nervous tonight, for she felt the violent flutter of her heart, as the monstrous shadow rushed over her head, to lead her. When she entered the electric blaze of her blue-and-silver room, she felt heartsick at the thought of the terrible drudgery of her toilet.

Without a pause, wherein to weaken, she set to work with grim determination. However weary or disillusioned, she could not relax, or shorten the process of reconstruction by a single minute.

As she steamed and massaged, she thought of Francis' question as to the origin of her capital.

It was an old story, and dated back to the pre-war era of prosperity, before one of the most powerful companies in the City had made financial history by its defalcations and crash. Anthea was employed in their palatial offices, as a shorthand-typist—of which there were two distinct grades; the ornamental, who resembled the ladies of the Gaiety chorus—tall, graceful, with perfect figures and piled masses of hair—and the workers.

At that time, Anthea possessed the youth whose loss she so resented; for the rest, she was a sallow, flat-chested little nonentity, with a bun of depressed, mousy-hued hair. No one noticed that she was a glutton for work, with a genius for figures and a photographic memory. She came early, and stayed late, and never lost an opportunity to read a private paper, when she was alone, for a minute, in a principal's room, or to listen-in to telephonic conversation. Little by little, she put bits of her puzzle together, spending hours of research, to find a missing link.

But, still, she was overlooked, personally, and also on the salary list, although the chiefs, who took her diligence and competence for granted, had got into the habit of ringing for her.

One day they received the shock of their lives. During one of their involved transactions, certain shares had been registered in Anthea's name, after a common practice in business.

Intuition told her that it was the moment to strike. It was at this crisis that she revealed her quality and showed a courage and tenacity of purpose that almost redeemed her sordid tactics. The plain, shabby little typist, in her blue serge skirt, shiny from wear, her cotton shirt and man's tie, her woolen stockings and stout Oxford shoes—faced those high lords of finance and told them that, since the shares were nominally her property, she proposed to keep them for herself.

She was a little pike, defying the swollen sharks. Taking advantage of their uttter consternation, she gave them suitable reasons for complying with her demands. Her little speech was an admirable example of compression, for, in two-and-one-half minutes, she gave them all the points of the two hours-and-one-half address afterwards delivered by the counsel for the prosecution.

It was her first essay in blackmail and had a happy ending. Instead of taking her for a ride, after the manner of a crime film, the directors recognized her business acumen, and, since she had raised some very nasty points, they made suitable acknowledgment. She was allowed to retain some of the shares, and was also promoted, in order to identify her interest with those of the firm.

After this start, she forged ahead on her own merits. She took advantage of every opportunity offered her by the company, and was in the first flight of City women who received men's salaries.

With infallible rodent instinct, she left the company, when its reputation for prosperity and solidity was at its zenith—knowing that when it has reached the top of its flight, the rocket must fall. She had her chain of "Dahlia" lingerie shops well started when the crash of her late employers shook the city.

She read the details of the trial with keen appreciation, deepened by her own cold fury when she learned that one of the directors had fled to the Continent in the company of the most useless and ornamental private secretary.

In the depths of her heart she hated and envied that girl. Francis' jibe about her lack of attraction had opened a wound that was still green. Although she knew the destructive quality of temper, she worked herself up to a rage to remember, that, exposed to the loose morality of that office, she had been safe as in a cloister.

One of the directors blew out his brains—a second died in Paris, and left his mistress in poverty. The others served their terms of imprisonment, to emerge in the world, broken men. Anthea followed their misfortune and exulted over it, feeling that, in some measure, it avenged her insult.

Yet, even while she worked herself up to a passion over the old story, in the splendor of her blue-and-silver-room, she was aware of the buried reminder picking away at her memory. *Something forgotten.* She grew more nervous, starting at every sound, wincing at her shadow, and scared at the sudden sight of her own reflection in the mirror.

At last, she remembered. The heavy curtains of blue satin were still drawn over her windows.

Every Wednesday night her maid went to her dancing class. Although she made all the preparations for her mistress' toilet before she left, Miss Vine elected to draw the bath water and pull the cord of the draperies herself. Swayed by the subconscious policy of protection, she liked the Court to resemble a fortress by night, darkened and impregnable, so that she could not allow the light to blaze out in advance; and she would not permit another servant to penetrate the secrets of her bedroom, although Eames gossiped about every detail of her toilet, and her own appearance talked still louder.

Lately, her memory was failing. It was not until she drew her water that the one duty reminded her of the other. The porters at the station had noticed a slight deflection from the time-table of the Jamaica Court beacon. Although the light still never failed to go out, at the stroke of twelve, it was variable in its appearance, on a Wednesday night.

Miss Vine trembled like a leaf, as she stared at the window curtains. Although her room was on the first floor, she was sure that mocking spectators were lined up outside the glass, with flattened noses and half-moon eyes, staring— laughing.

Laughing at *her*. Her legs felt boneless, as, with an effort, she forced herself to cross the carpet. But directly she had pulled the cord, she was restored by the blankness of the outer darkness.

"I'm a fool," she told herself. "I must gain control. When everyone is against me, I must expose no loophole to the enemy."

But after she had put out the light, she could not sleep.

Dr. Lawrence had made her pay for her insistence, that afternoon, for in the intervals of her desperate flirtation, he had waved the red of danger signals. It is true that he had wrapped up the truth in half-playful admonitions; but he had given her the impression of her heart as an ancient clock, whose rusted mechanism might stop at any moment.

She was afraid of death; and as she tried to count the irregular beats of her pulse, her mind slipped away to her dream of the lions. Both Lawrence and Francis had shown their teeth today. She was surrounded with treachery—a rich woman, whose wealth was bait for the rats.

Presently, her senses dulled as her lids grew heavy, but she only counterfeited sleep. Her heart thumped and her brow grew damp with fear, as strange things began to happen in her room. The walls contracted and expanded, and her bed spun slowly round. When the movement ceased, she heard footsteps and whispers. People whom she could not see, because of her bandaged eyes, stood at the corners of her bed, and laughed softly.

Then fingers began to grope their way across the satin quilt, stealing towards her throat. She knew that she was in the grip of nightmare and struggled violently to awake. There was something in the bed with her, a great cold shape, like a stone image. She tried to push it away, but it rolled over on her, crushing her under its weight.

She awoke, to the realization that Nature was sending in her bill for the overstrain of the day. Her heart attack had passed, its fury blown out in the terrors of her imagination; but it had left her prostrate with weakness and deadly cold.

With the last remnants of her strength, she managed to reach the hand bell by her bedside; but, even as it rang, she gave herself up for lost. Although Iris slept in the next room, she knew that she would not answer the signal, even

85

if she heard it. She hated Anthea. It was her chance to let her flicker out in the darkness, alone, like a farthing dip. No one would blame her, wrapped in the heavy sleep of youth. And she would be free.

Anthea felt herself slipping down into the shadows and silence.

Then she became aware of a flood of light and of a girl's face, pressed so close to her own that, even in her weakness, she envied the smoothness of the skin and the unlined eyes. Iris supported her with strong young arms, as she held a glass to her lips.

Poison. She tried to push it away, but Iris persisted.

"Come on, Anthea, drink it, and you'll be all right. Nothing to be afraid of now."

There was a note in the voice which won her confidence, so that she swallowed the draught, recognized it for her own special restorative, and felt revived.

"Shall I send for Lawrence?" asked Iris.

Instinctively, Anthea felt the strips of plaster which crisscrossed her face.

"No one's to come in," she panted. "Promise."

"That's all right." Iris opened the door and spoke to someone in the corridor. "You two, rouse the servants and get all the hot-water bottles you can. But don't come in. I can manage by myself."

Anthea lay back on her pillows and surrendered herself to safety. All the shadows had fled with the light. She felt she could trust Iris. She was youth, and strength, and friendship.

She also displayed unexpected resource as she reheated the warm water from Anthea's own rubber bag in the electric kettle.

"This'll help," she said, as she slipped her hand between the blankets.

Delicious warmth began to steal over Anthea and the
violence of her shivering lessened. Everything was growing
dim again, but she felt comfortable and purged of fear. She
was vaguely aware of Iris as a slim, reedlike figure, in
creamy pajamas, moving about the room.

"I'm going to sleep," she whispered. "Don't leave me.
Things might get in. Don't let anyone see me—not even
Eames. Promise. Listen, Iris. Tomorrow I'll make my will."

As she began to doze, she heard a buzz of voices outside
her door, like the sounds of a hive, on a mid-summer day.
Above the whisper rose a clear-cut voice.

"Someone's giving away what isn't hers to give."

CHAPTER XII

A Business Test

ANTHEA REMEMBERED FRANCIS' WORDS, WHEN SHE awoke, next morning. They rang in her head, as she mechanically reached for the mirror and powder puff, by her side. Although she felt heavy, she was otherwise, little the worse for her attack; and she peeled the plaster from her face and applied the customary rouge before she rang for her maid.

Eames found her mistress in her most exacting mood. Her wave of softness and generosity had ebbed with the night, leaving her ultracritical and suspicious.

"Francis is right," she thought. "He always is, the bright boy. It's not to their interest to let me die intestate. That girl took me in with her fawning ways. But I'm myself again. And I've had my warning. Silas and his brats shall not burn the money I've slaved to make."

Her lips were like twisted vermilion wire, as she imagined the scene in the corridor, while she lay in drugged sleep, lulled to false security by the treachery of a girl. There would be bursts of smothered laughter and heartless jokes. Perhaps, even, Iris had let them peep at the Sleeping Beauty.

If this were true, she would turn her out of the house, this very hour, with nothing but the clothes on her back.

She shook her head as saner counsel prevailed. "That would only create scandal, and put me in the wrong. Besides, it might force Lawrence's hand. . . . No. I know a better way. They shall all pay. *Pay*."

She peered up at her maid over the rim of her cup of chocolate.

"Eames," she asked, "what happened last night?"

"We none of us got much sleep," replied Eames, anxious to advertise the loyalty and devotion of the staff.

"I didn't ask what kind of night *you* had," snapped Anthea. "Do you imagine I'm interested in you? Answer my question. What happened?"

"Lizzie and I got your hot-water bottles just as fast as we could," said Eames nervously. "We brought them to your bedroom door and gave them in to Miss Iris. She told us to go back to bed, and not to worry, as we'd done all we could."

"Worry? You? But, of course, wages such as I pay, are rare. Did you come inside the room?"

"No, madam. Miss Iris told me to try to get some sleep, seeing as I'd have to be up my usual time in the morning."

Eames' voice still dripped with conscious virtue, but her mistress was not impressed.

"Where were Mr. Charles and Mr. Francis?" she asked.

"The gentlemen, madam?" The maid's voice was prim. "I didn't see anything of them, as it was gone twelve. I concluded that they had retired and were in their own rooms."

Slightly reassured, Anthea finished her chocolate.

"Bring me the lingerie that came, last night," she commanded.

Eames hastened to bring the mauve-and-silver boxes, with the purple "Dahlia" label on the lid, for Anthea patronised her own wares. Very soon, the satin quilt was strewn with diaphanous garments of palest tints, like shreds from a sunrise.

Anthea chose set after set, with such acquisitive rapidity that Eames concluded that her mistress' eye was greedier than her judgment. Knowing that she would be held responsible for any mistake, she ventured to remonstrate.

"But, madam, you'll never be able to wear them out."

Anthea suddenly flinched as though an icy finger had plucked a nerve of her heart.

"What d'you mean?" she cried. "Has the doctor told you something—something I don't know? What are you hiding from me?"

"Oh, no, madam, indeed, no," protested Eames. "I've heard nothing at all about your health. But, really, *no one* could wear out all those, in a lifetime."

"But they can be ripped out," snapped Anthea.

Picking up a pale-green chiffon nightgown, she tore it from neck to hem, rolled it into a ball, and tossed it to the horrified maid.

"Here you are, Eames. Your perquisite. As you've already decided, a French hem will put it together again. And you needn't worry. I'll make it my business to leave none of these behind me, for others to wear after I've gone. Show me more."

Yet even as her eyes glittered at the sheer beauty of the garments, she glanced from them to the chestnuts on the lawn. Their leaves were still folded up in tight fans, and she pictured them in dark and bushy foliage, lit up with the white candles of flowery spikes.

"Where will I be then?"

She thrust aside the fear and gave Eames a sharp order.

"Get Miss Morgan."

Sally obeyed the summons with her inevitable promptitude. Polished and immaculate, she entered the room, her notebook in her hand. On her way to the Royal Suite she had wrestled with a small problem.

90

"I wonder if I should say I'm glad she's better. But I'm not supposed to know that she's been ill. Better feel my way."

Seeing no invalid signs, she gave her customary respectful greeting. Then, at the sight of the lingerie spread on the bed, the perfect secretary turned, suddenly, into a natural girl, full of envy and gush.

"How perfectly marvelous. Gorgeous. Are they 'Dahlia' stock?"

Miss Vine almost smiled at her enthusiasm.

"Yes, Morgan, they're 'Dahlia.' I wear them myself. If they're good enough for me, they're good enough for the public. They reflect my own taste. If I cannot claim to have my finger on the nation's pulse, I have it on its garters."

Sally's eyes grew thoughtful as she noted her employer's form of address. "Miss Morgan" foretold a spell of nigger-driving, while she had learned to distrust "Sally," which meant that Miss Vine had laid a trap for her.

As she knew the difference between the wholesale and retail prices of "Dahlia" goods, she scented the chance of a bargain.

"If you have any to spare, I wonder if I might buy them?" she asked.

"Certainly, Morgan," agreed Miss Vine. "You may have two sets. You may choose the colors."

"Oh, thank you. May I have pink and mauve?"

"Cyclamen and wistaria. Take them. You can deduct them from your check. And, Morgan, since you are in my employment, I will allow you a discount of five per cent. And now I'll dictate a letter."

"That pays me out for trying to get a bargain out of *her*," reflected Sally, as she unsnapped the elastic band of her notebook. "But, thank goodness, I'll look better in mine, than she will in hers."

Then she pricked up her ears at the substance of Miss Vine's note, which was to her lawyer—Mr. Waters.

Miss Vine looked keenly at her to see if she betrayed any sign of human interest, but was reassured by Sally's absorption in her outlines.

"Seen Iris or the boys this morning, Sally?" she asked.

"No, Miss Vine. I had breakfast alone."

"So they're late *again*."

Sally fell into the trap.

"But they were up in the night."

"Ah." Miss Vine paused, before she pounced. "Then you knew I was ill. Pray, why hadn't you the common decency to inquire after my health?"

"Because I hate inquiries myself," replied Sally. "They always make me feel worse than I am."

"And do you compare your mentality with mine?"

Sally thought rapidly as she framed her reply so as not to allude to the difference in their ages.

"There's no comparison, of course. But it's my ambition to be an important woman of business, too. At present, I'm only the raw material, while you're the finished article."

Anthea smiled at the homage.

"I'll make something of you yet, Morgan. Only—you must never marry."

Sally's face fell.

"I thought I would combine marriage with business," she said. "It's a fuller life."

"Fuller than mine?" Miss Vine's voice was shrill. "Fuller than affairs? One man for a dozen—or a score? How can a married woman boast of experience? No, Sally, take it from *me*. I know. And now since you want to follow in my footsteps, I will tell you a little tale. Cigarette."

Sally ministered to her as she lay back propped against satin pillows.

"When I was your age," began Miss Vine, "I was having tea, one day, in my sitting room, when a man climbed past my window, on a ladder. He was mending the slates on the roof. It was bitterly cold and he looked so chilled that I wondered if I ought to offer him a cup of tea. But I decided that since it was not my roof, it was none of my business. Not half-an-hour afterwards he slipped, and broke his neck, Sally."

"Oh, yes," murmured Sally brightly, too alert for sympathy, for she had noticed the danger signal of her name.

"Can you imagine what my feelings were?" demanded Miss Vine.

As there seemed but one possible reaction to the tragedy, Sally spoke quickly.

"You regretted a lost opportunity. Terrible for you."

Miss Vine broke into a shrill laugh.

"Aha, I thought you'd say that. No. I was glad that I had not wasted my tea."

As Sally stared at her in amazement, she was conscious of a sudden rush of antipathy.

"My point of view was the correct one," went on Miss Vine. "But your remark only shows confused thinking. You fall to bits at the first intrusion of sentiment, instead of seeing things in their true proportion. You have many good qualities, Morgan, but you will never rise, like me."

Sally set her lips with determination.

"I've time to learn," she said.

"Indeed? How old are you?"

"Twenty-two."

"Ah," Miss Vine pounced on the admission. "I was younger than that when I started to work."

"So was I," was the quiet reply.

They exchanged a long steady look, in which they met on common ground.

"She's not negligible," thought Anthea. "A sharp tool may prove a sharp weapon. I must be on my guard against her, *too*."

"Scrap that letter," she said aloud. "Ring up Waters, instead, and tell him to come here, at once."

CHAPTER XIII

Prelude

WHEN IRIS ENTERED THE MORNING ROOM FOR BREAKFAST, she was greeted by the two young men with ironic cheers.

"Here comes the Lady with the Lamp," called Charles.

Iris failed to find the cynicism which the occasion demanded. She was conscious of being false to her generation which forbade any plunge into sentiment.

She had not the large-hearted nature which spills its overflow on every subject. Imprisoned within herself, she could only respond, if the right note were touched. All her life, she had been starved of personal affection. At the orphanage, and later, at an expensive snobbish school, she had fought for her own hand.

Last night, for the first time, she had felt a warm rush of pity at the convulsive clasp of Anthea's cold fingers, which had clung to her hand, like the claws of a bird. Anthea had shrunk to an old child appealing in her helplessness. Someone had wanted her.

It was a novel sensation, making her aware of widened landmarks. But she tried to laugh flippantly, as she helped herself to a breakfast dish.

"The poor old thing was really rather pathetic," she said. "You know, she just clung to me."

"A crab once clung to me," observed Charles. "But I didn't find him pathetic. I know I ate him for tea."

"Don't be fatuous," admonished Francis. "You don't seem to realize that if old Anthea had croaked, last night, we'd all be on the Parish today. We're saved by our thoughtful little Iris. I'm inclined to think that Anthea has sized up the situation, this morning. The lady has such a pure mind."

Iris turned on him in a gale of temper.

"I never thought of anything like that," she declared. "You cheapen everything. After all, whatever she is, or isn't, she's a life."

Pushing away her plate, she hurried towards the door.

"Coming back?" asked Charles.

"No. I've finished."

"Ah," chimed in Francis. "Once more you've given your-self away. Whenever I study you, at meals, the mystery of your origin is revealed."

"What d'you mean?" demanded Iris.

"Only that, like every orphanage girl, you imagine your-self to be the illegitimate offspring of the nobility. But it's clearly indicated that you're the sixteenth child of a respect-ably married traveling tinker. Only the poorest evince ex-travagant traits, when raised to affluence."

"I hate you."

As Iris banged the door behind her, Charles turned to Francis.

"Why did you bait the poor kid?" he asked. "Can't you see she is edgy after being up all night?"

"I can't bear seeing food wasted," explained Francis pi-ously. "I'm the only person in this house who knows what hunger really is. I mean, the sort that drives you to dust-bins."

"Oh, dry up. We've only your word for it."

As he spoke, Charles rose from the table, and looked at his cousin, who was wearing the kind of gorgeous dressing gown which is usually associated with a film star.

"You'll be late for the office," he said.

Francis serenely blew a ring of smoke.

"I'm not going there today," he said. "Nor tomorrow. I'm not going there any more. I want to annoy Anthea. I am so afraid she does not realize how much I dislike her."

"Catching the cat, are you? It's been tried before."

"But never by me," remarked Francis calmly.

Meantime, Iris rushed upstairs to Miss Vine's bedroom. The memory of last night was still sufficiently strong to make her anxious to disprove Francis' assertion.

Her knock was answered by Eames, while the murmur of Sally's voice told her that she was interrupting business.

"Is Miss Vine better, and can I see her?" asked Iris.

"One minute, Miss Iris."

Eames glided away, to return with a message.

"Madam thanks you, and is better today, but is very sorry that she is engaged at present."

Iris gave a mirthless laugh.

"I see. What a lady ought to say. Thank you for the tip, Eames. Now, tell me, word for word, what Miss Vine really said."

"She said, 'Sorry to disappoint her, but I'm not going to die yet.'"

Iris was surprised by her surge of disappointment. But she managed to shrug her shoulders at the rebuff.

"From that remark, Eames," she said, "I conclude that she is herself again."

"Just so, Miss Iris. Madam is herself."

Iris drooped rather forlornly down the corridor. As a spoiled, thwarted child, she had been content to remain interest-bound, enwrapped within herself. But, lately, tendrils had broken from their hard sheath, and were feebly fluttering in the air, seeking some support around which to twine.

She knew that she was reaching out to touch Glyn Lawrence's heart; but those groping tentacles still hung limp and empty. He stood aloof, even while he seemed to want her; or else he wounded her by some sample of his wholesale love-making.

"I suppose I've been a vegetable," she reflected, "and I'm beginning to be alive. It's going to hurt. But experience should be worth the pain."

Through the staircase window she saw Charles, pipe in mouth, trudging with dogged determination through the grounds. Although he was on his way to his office, his appearance was not professional. He wore plus-fours with an old shooting jacket, and was without cap or coat, in spite of cold weather.

Outside the front gates, he stopped to whistle to a dog— any dog that would answer his appeal. It was one of his chief grievances that Anthea positively forbade him to bring a dog into the Court; for he craved a companionship which could only be supplied by the loyalty and devotion of an animal.

As dogs have a regrettably lax code of morality, they always made Charles feel his popularity with themselves, whatever the prevailing local opinion of his reputation. On this morning, two appeared, magically, from an empty road.

Both were anxious to have the privilege of accompanying him to the town. One—an Alsatian—was the property of Superintendent Pye, and had always a problem how to work off his surplus energy; while the other—a fat Sealyham— had probably been advised exercise, for the sake of her figure.

They greeted Charles according to the measure of their stature—the Alsatian putting his paws on his shoulders, and the Sealyham leaving white hairs upon his stockings. All the way to the office he whistled to them and kept them to heel, with a spurious sense of ownership.

His office was in a side street and faced the Cattle Market. It was a dingy room, with a mottled wallpaper and brown wire blinds. Its chief furniture was a clogged typewriter, a desk with a revolving chair, and one upholstered in leather, for clients.

His staff—a fair youth, who was much neater than his master—was doing his best to coax a sulky fire to a blaze.

"Hello, Rogers," called Charles. "Any post?"

"Only a bill and a circular," replied the youth.

"Good. That's the way to make life easy for us. Well, carry on as usual. Any luck with your football forecast?"

"The usual. Nowhere near it. Two chaps tied."

"Dirty dogs. What are you on now?"

Charles picked up a paper which was thoughtfully placed on his table.

"Cross-word," replied Rogers. "Hundred pound prize, and must be won."

"That's not the tone to take with us, Rogers. We can be led, but not forced. All the same, we'll have a shot at it. But our puzzle, Rogers, would be, what to do with a paltry hundred."

Charles spent most of his morning over the puzzle, although he left his work occasionally, to visit the "Bull" for a toothful. These visits were the outcome of boredom, rather than any positive craving for alcohol, or the society of a barmaid who was too refined for his taste.

"It's a mug's game," he remarked to Rogers, on his third return. "Don't you acquire the habit, my lad. It means nothing but a hole in your pocket. I'm forced into it, for the sake of business. Might make a useful contact in a pub, you know, and pick up something. True, I've picked up nothing but fleas—but it's my duty to study humanity."

Although the forenoon was a fair sample of his usual day, the afternoon brought a surprise, for Rogers opened the door to a lady. It was Sally Morgan, anticipating the spring in a green suit, with a few violets in her buttonhole.

"I saw your name on your plate," she said, "and I simply had to peep inside. So this is where you work?"

"This is where I rot my brains," corrected Charles.

Her eyes roamed over the shabby linoleum, the dusty law books and the choked fire.

"Does no one ever dust?" she asked.

"A woman is supposed to clean through. But I'm used to it. You're not to waste your sympathy on me."

"I don't mean to, when you've two hands of your own."

"Good. I hate sloppy people." Charles shook his handkerchief over a chair. "Sit down, do. Sorry I can't offer you tea. Anthea won't allow it. She's afraid I shall invite ladies."

Sally looked at the choked fire, and then, impetuously, seized the poker.

"She's rather fond of you, isn't she?" she asked, as she raked the ashes.

"Rather," grinned Charles. "I'm her white-headed boy."

"But she has more respect for Mr. Francis?"

"Naturally. He's the bigger scoundrel. Besides, he bilked."

Charles spoke tonelessly. On the whole, he had accepted life easily, unlike Francis and Iris, whose mutiny was static. When Miss Vine had adopted her cousins she had undertaken to make herself responsible for their futures. Her action had been construed into a promise, not only to prepare them, but to start them in their profession.

But although she had followed a general policy of slide, she was ready to smooth away signs of rebellion by hints of secret negotiations for partnerships. Again and again, she dangled golden bubbles before their eyes, but the bubbles always burst. She was an adept at this form of jugglery, to which she added an inexplicable fascination.

While the town only saw her as a repulsive painted old woman, the two young men felt the pull of a stronger personality than their own. She held them with some strange, perverted charm. In spite of broken promises and economic slavery, they stayed at the Court.

But, lately, Charles had been surprised by his own eagerness for freedom, as though the fires of unsuspected volcanoes had burst through their caked coating.

As he gloomed, staring blindly through the grimed window, he became conscious that Sally was speaking.

"That's a better fire. It only wanted air at the bottom. Why did Mr. Francis go away?"

"Fed up."

"Oh, I do wish it had been *you.*"

"Why? He came back again."

"Yes, but even if it was futile, it was a gesture. It would have shown you were dissatisfied."

"Does that fact need demonstration?" asked Charles bitterly. "Look at this hole. I've got to stick it from ten to five."

"Do you get any work?"

"An affidavit or two. Have a cigarette?"

Now that the blue dusk was falling, the leaping flames of the fire made the office appear less gloomy. They smoked in friendly silence, until Sally spoke reflectively.

"How did all this start?"

"I was farmed out to Miss Vine," replied Charles. "Father's a parson with eleven kids. After a bit, he started to name us by our number—Septimus, Octavia, Nonna, Decima. He called the last, and eleventh, 'Una,' and my grandparents, who have to help pay the piper, had the fright of their young lives, because they thought he was beginning all over again. Rather amusing."

But Sally did not laugh. Her young face was very grave as she frowned at the fire.

"Do you ever see your family?" she asked.

"Occasionally. We're just like other strangers when we meet, except that we catch the name, first time off."

"Well," said Sally grimly, "I'd like to meet your family."

"Gosh—why?"

"They might explain you."

"Do I need explaining?" asked Charles.

"Yes." It was plain, from her frown, that Sally made an effort. "I can't understand why any man, who's young and has his faculties, can stay planted in such an impossible position."

Charles gave a mirthless laugh.

"I was waiting for you to say that. But it's so difficult to explain. Unless you back outsiders, you can't understand. The fact is, we're all playing for time. We've taken on the most desperate gamble. The Calcutta Cup is pi to it. If Anthea had gone West last night, her cash would have gone to her brother. On the other hand, at any moment she might cough up a partnership, or something solid. She's always stringing us along with promises, but she's the unknown quantity. Don't you see we can't afford to throw in our cards now? We're too deep in."

As Sally said nothing, he kicked the fire.

"I suppose you despise me," he said.

"I can't," replied Sally. "You see, I'm rather in the same boat myself."

"You? How?"

"Well, I was so bucked up at getting this post. I'm ambitious and I want to hold down some big executive billet, some day. It seemed a steppingstone. And I admired Miss

Vine so tremendously. But I'm not so keen on the job now that I find myself criticizing—— Well, I mustn't say anything, even to you. A secretary must be absolutely confidential."

"Go on," urged Charles, in a low voice. "It's to *me*."

Sally shook her head.

"I can only say this. The time is coming when, for the sake of my self-respect, I must give in my notice. And—I don't want to."

Charles looked up quickly.

"I hope you won't leave us," he said.

"Why?"

"Because there are only two people at the Court, who count, with me. You are one."

"And the other is—Miss Pomeroy?"

"Gosh, no."

"But she is so beautiful."

"Is she? I'm too used to her to see her. Besides, she hasn't a rag of real character. Rather choice that, from me, eh? No, believe me, or believe me not, the other person is old Anthea."

Although Sally raised her brows incredulously, she was suddenly acutely conscious of the dingy office, the blue dusk and the firelight, as though she were viewing them from some other plane. She felt held in a moment of suspense, in which she waited for a curtain to be rolled up, or for a melody to begin.

The next second, she was her usual practical self, as she tossed the stump of her cigarette into the grate.

"Time to go," she remarked.

"All right, I'll see you part of the way," said Charles.

He turned back, at the doorway, at the sound of the telephone bell.

"It's from your cousin, Mr. Francis," announced Rogers. "He says it's important."

Suspecting an attempt to impress Sally, on the part of his devoted staff, Charles turned listlessly to the instrument.

As she waited, Sally heard his voice grow suddenly sharp.

"Sure?" he asked. "Look here, this isn't spoof? You're not trying me with a new version of the Spanish Prisoner? Oh, I will, and may Heaven bless you for those kind words."

His eyes were bright with excitement, as he rang off.

"That was Francis," he said. "We're all to be in tonight. The lawyer's been with Anthea most of the day, and, after dinner, he is going to tell us the terms of her will."

104

CHAPTER XIV

The Will

FEW SITUATIONS ARE MORE CHARGED WITH DRAMA, TO THE spectators, than the reading of a will. That evening, the atmosphere in the dining room, of the Court, was electric with suspense.

Sensitive to every impression, Dr. Lawrence was conscious of the general tension—of human nature on guard, to keep its secret, yet betrayed by glimpses of unexpected passions.

The room, in common with the others, was a replica of what was fine and historic, but there was no cohesion between the different periods and styles. Jamaica Court advertised the lack of taste of an owner who was without originality, yet greedy of perfection, like one who sees a highly priced model in a shopwindow, and poaches the brains of its creator in a spurious copy.

The walls were dark with paneling, scooped from a West Riding mansion, and hung with dim oil paintings and weapons. The chairs and oval table were new in the reign of George I. The carpet had been woven in the East, and the electric illumination simulated candlelight.

Anthea—in her most regal mood—sat at the head of the table. She wore a yellow Empire dress, and short ostrich plumes waved above her golden curls. A wisp of daffodil gossamer scarf kept slipping constantly from her shoulders, to be retrieved by one of the attentive young men.

With the exception of the doctor and secretary, it was a family party. In his role of spectator, Dr. Lawrence noticed that each member was keyed up to the utmost pitch of nervous expectancy. Charles was flushed and his laughter rang too loud. Francis was pale and silent, while Iris' eyes were brilliant with excitement.

Sally Morgan was the only person who ate a good meal. Charles kept glancing at her, to see if he could detect any flicker of the feeling she had revealed to him in the office. But she had reverted to her usual discreet imitation of the perfect secretary.

The doctor shook his sleek head as the hostess had her glass filled for the third time.

"It's no good making faces at me, doctor," she announced. "This is an occasion to be celebrated. Already I feel a disembodied spirit. Everyone, look at me."

She drew in her chin and peered up at them from under her lashes while they paid her the tribute of their close attention.

Well pleased with her effect, Anthea raised her voice.

"Again, look at me. I am the ghost of Anthea Vine. Last week, I died. Tonight, my youthful relatives are gathered together to fortify themselves in their sorrow and loss. Presently they will go to the drawing room, where the deceased so often sat, there to listen to the Last Will and Testament of Anthea Vine."

"No," protested Charles. "Hang it all, Anthea, we can't do it."

"But, darling," pouted Anthea, "surely you would not cheat me out of my last pleasure? This is a dip into the actual future. All this will happen—some day. I've always wanted to be present when my will was read. I've so often tried to picture your faces and forecast your feelings. I've seen your eyes glisten. I've wondered if one—at least—of you, would be grateful to me? Or even sorry."

"But, Anthea, you are making it impossible for us," cried Iris. "I—I simply don't know what to say, or how to look."

"Look as you do at this moment, darling—dewy-eyed with grief and radiant with hope. ... Isn't she adorable, doctor? Francis, isn't she a young man's dream?"

Anthea noticed the interchange of angry glances between the two young men and the flush of annoyance which spread over Iris' face.

"Mr. Waters is coming after dinner," she said, "to read you the rough draft. You won't mind doing without the trimmings, darlings? I mean, the hereinafters and the afore-saids. I shall sit in a dark corner and watch you all. And, when you hear it read, again, after my funeral, you will remember this dress rehearsal, and you will know that I am there, invisible to you."

Her words broke down their guard. At a vision of prison doors swinging open, they exchanged involuntary shamed glances.

"No good, Anthea," remarked Francis. "You won't get your effects. We shall simply play up to you. Remember, we're moderns. No feelings."

"Oh, you all of you have feelings—of a kind. Believe me, I shall see."

The doctor hastened to change the conversation.

"Have you people heard of the famous robbery?"

"Whose?" asked Anthea quickly, as though jealous of a distinction denied to herself.

"Mrs. Antrobus."

"That? Has she anything of value to lose?"

"Yes. A pair of Dresden china figures."

Everyone gratefully seized the opportunity to laugh.

"Absurd," declared Francis. "As if anyone'd risk going to quod for the sake of a pair of parlor ornaments."

"The Super thinks it's a practical joke," announced Charles. "He asked me, on the side, if I knew anything about it? I told him I'd want something more worth while."

"Like these pearls?" interposed Anthea, holding up a loop. "Aha, his eyes glittered then."

"Considering I get the job of putting them to bed every night, I'm too used to them to register emotion," snapped Charles. "And, Anthea, do get the agony over."

"So. He can't wait, this iron man of no feelings. Well, follow me, children, and hear your fates."

She led the way into the vast drawing room, a white-and-gold Empire apartment, gleaming with lights and mirrors. As she seated herself on a yellow brocade settee, her daffodil gown blended into her background—like a gilded butterfly alit on a sunflower—so that she seemed lost in the light, in lieu of shadow.

She uttered no word as coffee was served, but her deep pitted eyes watched the young people as they hung about in groups, turning on the radio, only to turn it off, and lighting cigarettes to throw them away.

She smiled at every movement symptomatic of nerves as she slowly sipped her coffee and liqueur. Presently the footman, obedient to his directions, announced the lawyer, Mr. Waters.

He was a big, pear-faced man, with a ginger spadebeard, and a honeyed voice. He wore dress clothes under his topcoat, and seemed prepared for a social evening.

"You won't have coffee," said Anthea, glancing at the bulky envelope in his pocket.

Obedient to her inflection, Mr. Water declined the invitation, even while his hand was outstretched for his cup.

"Is that my will?" continued Anthea.

"Only the rough draft. Directly it is put in proper shape, I will bring it for your signature."

"Good. Now, Mr. Waters, I wish you to acquaint my young relatives with the contents."

The lawyer raised the light fluff of his eyebrows.

"At once," commanded Miss Vine. "Give the gist. Leave out all legacies to small fry. Tell them exactly what concerns them."

In his turn, the lawyer became influenced by the drama of his position. He took up a commanding position in front of the carved Adam fireplace and collected eyes.

"To begin with," he said, "it may interest you to know that no one in this room can witness this will. For you all benefit under it."

Dr. Lawrence, sitting apart, nursed his chin with his long supple fingers. His Eastern eyes were inscrutable, but he was conscious of a need to screen his lips.

Anthea's eyes flickered from face to face.

"Tell them the value of my estate," she commanded.

"At the present time," replied the lawyer, "it is worth more than a quarter of a million."

"All of which I made myself, when I was younger than any of you."

Anthea's voice was vibrant with scorn. Iris broke the uneasy silence.

"I think it's marvelous of you," she said.

Miss Vine turned to the lawyer.

"For those kind words, tell her what her own share will be," she commanded. "She's waiting."

But the lawyer could not be diverted to give a direct answer. He consulted his draft.

"There are certain legacies to servants, which are inconsiderable," he said. "So I come to the sum of one thousand pounds, bequeathed to Miss Morgan, provided she be in Miss Vine's employment at the time of her decease. There is also the sum of ten thousand pounds bequeathed to Dr. Lawrence, provided Miss Vine lives for another ten years, and is his patient at the actual time of her decease."

" 'Death,' " corrected Anthea. "Give it them neat."

Her eyes ferreted out the emotions of her two legatees, and so missed the unconscious interchange of glances between Charles and Francis.

"Older than we thought," said their significant eyes. "She can only count on another ten years, as an outside limit."

Ten years. It seemed a lifetime to youth, spilling itself, drop by drop, in futility and waste.

With his usual courtly grace, Dr. Lawrence bowed acknowledgments to the slim figure posed on the golden couch. The lawyer cleared his throat for the final thrill.

"The residue is divided in three equal shares between Miss Vine's adopted children—Charles and Francis Ford and Iris Pomeroy. Lucky young people."

He beamed on the principal legatees, who appeared too overwhelmed to speak. A fortune was dangled before their eyes and they felt dazzled, as by a blinding light.

Iris was the first to find her voice.

"It—it's wonderfully generous of you, Anthea. Thank you."

"Wonderfully," echoed Charles.

"And now, there's only one thing to be done," said Francis smoothly. "That is, to forget about it, and hope it will be a very long time before we hear the *real* will."

"You can count on that, if I've anything to do with it," laughed Dr. Lawrence, intent on introducing a lighter note.

"It will be not only my pleasure, but my interest, to keep my patient alive."

Finding himself neglected, the lawyer turned to the company.

"My heartiest congratulations," he said. "And—that is all."

He was arrested by Anthea who had risen from her couch and was pointing to Iris.

"Look at her beautiful frock," she said. "At her age I never had a frock like that, so the men didn't roll in for me, as they do for her. Sex appeal is only a matter of window dressing. Could I sell 'Dahlia', lingerie if I didn't understand layout? But I missed all that—and the money I was slaving to earn has bought this frock for her."

She put her hand to her throat, as though she were choking, and burst into a torrent of speech.

"The lawyer has said that is all. *All?* But you, none of you, know what my quarter of a million means. A starved youth. No holidays. No amusement. No men. My enemies say I employ sweated labor. Why not? *I* was sweated—and it drove me to work harder, and to drive others harder. I've never yielded an inch to anyone. Why should I? And today I stand worth a quarter of a million. Let those I sweat do the same."

Dr. Lawrence stepped forward and took her gently by the elbow.

"I prescribe bed," he said. "All this has been too much for you."

She looked at the clock.

"No, it's not eleven," she said. "But you shall take me to have a cocktail. I'm tired of being dead."

When she was out of earshot Francis spoke.

"A third part of a quarter of a million."

"And we've got to *wait* for it," Charles reminded him.

"Years and years of dependence on her. She's got us tighter than ever."

Iris was looking down the long vista of the room at a dwarfed golden figure.

"How she hates us," she said. "She must have had a terrible youth. I'm sorry for her."

CHAPTER XV

Immortality

AS THOUGH HER ILLNESS HAD BEEN AN ALARM CLOCK,
which warned her of the passage of time, Miss Vine plunged
feverishly into the business of the new hotel for Timberdale.
Her mind was like a mosquito, giving her no peace, and
stinging her to realize the necessity of building yet another
landmark on the road to prosperity.

She lost herself in the details of the project, goading
her fellow-directors to agreement, and overdriving her
executive. But, although Sally Morgan was made to work
the round of the clock, Miss Vine's obsession was a relief to
the rest of the household.

With her, money was the ruling passion—and love, merely
the distraction. She took no notice of her school of young
men, sweeping them off the board like so many pawns. Although the routine of her night toilet was unbroken, she
grew careless about her appearance, during the day—not
allowing Eames proper time for the application of rouge and
powder, and wearing the red-and-white raddle of haste.

During this period the only exercise she took was in the
grounds of Jamaica Court. She realized that she could not
concentrate on details of financial policy and, simultaneously,
drive a car so as to satisfy her mania for speed, while she
intrusted her life to no chauffeur.

After pacing the terraces and red-gravel drive, until she

113

was tired, she always made her way to a far corner of the ornamental lake. At this end it was ten feet deep, under the shadow of the willows, and spanned by a frail bridge.

It was here that Anthea had discovered a mirror which was always kind to her. It took desperate courage to face the cruelty of her own looking glass; but she had only to grasp a stout bough of willow, and lower herself to within a few feet of the surface, in order to see, reflected in the dark pellucid water, the alluring oval face of a girl.

All lines were smoothed out by the flattery of Nature; the raddle of red and white was converted to delicate flesh tints, and her eyes were enlarged by the same illusive medium. Miss Vine could always think best when she held communion with her own face; she drew inspiration from the smiles and nods of her submerged double.

One keen March morning, when the sky was bleakly blue, and every crocus tightly closed, she paced the terraces in her usual morning promenade. Charles passed her, on his way back to the house, and, although she was deep in her revision of the situation, she threw him a fascinating smile.

To her surprise, he nodded in surly fashion, and passed her, with sunken chin and shoulders hunched up to meet his ears.

For a second a corner of her mind registered anger at this sign of mutiny from a courtier. It was one of the moments for which she lived—a signal for her to crack her whip and force him to subjection. But the Munster Hotel was rising, story by story, in its awful terra-cotta magnificence within her brain, so she walked on and forgot him.

Charles turned and looked after the small figure, with its huddle of magnificent furs. He was powerless to prevent a thought which flitted through his mind.

"Suppose she overbalances, and falls in the lake."

He was in a furious temper against Fate, for he had just received a letter from Higgins. Higgins was his hero, and the person who had power to unloose the floodgate of his envy.

It was one of those extraordinary attractions, dating from schooldays. Higgins had been an utterly undistinguished boy, average in every respect of looks, health and intelligence. But, although he had no more than his share of measurable luck, he possessed the supreme gift of a perfectly contented mind, so that he was always satisfied with his own property, and pleased with his surroundings.

Although he did not know it, what Charles really coveted was Higgins' happiness, which he thought must be attributable to some quality or belonging. He was the more popular of the two, for he had a superior brain, and was better at games; but he copied Higgins as faithfully as a sedulous ape, in a stumbling endeavor to strike his secret. An abortive ambition, for the temperamental Charles could never resemble the placid, unimaginable Higgins.

When Charles went up to Oxford, and Higgins got employment in an insurance office, Charles—who would have thrown up the job within a week—envied him steady work and a salary. Presently, Higgins married a girl at whom Charles would not have wasted a second glance, and went to live in a small bungalow, at Purley. When he heard the news, Charles moped for days, brooding over the happiness which he, himself, had missed.

This morning's post had brought a letter from Higgins, which was the usual happy recital of small events. He enclosed a snapshot of a bald scowling baby, wearing only a vest. On the back he had written, in his neat clerkly script, the grandiloquent words: "My Immortality."

It is certain that Charles did not want a baby; he wanted

a dog. But at the sight of Higgins Junior, he was over-powered by a sense of frustration and loss. He told himself that while Higgins was reaping his destiny, and going forward into the Future, striding over the stars, for ever and ever—he, himself, hung as a shriveled leaf on the Tree of Life.

He kicked loose red gravel up the steps of the terrace, in an attempt to work off his fury. As usual, he traced back the source of his failure to Anthea, who had chained him to her side with a share in a quarter of a million.

"Now, why are you looking so pompous?" asked a gay voice.

He raised his eyes to see Sally, minus a hat, but wearing a yellow cardigan over her official black satin frock.

"I don't like your coat," he said crossly. "You look like a circus van."

Sally merely laughed at his rudeness.

"I'm glad you hate it. Now I know it's all right. You've rotten taste. Besides, men don't understand the psychological value of bright color. You ought to wear yellow yourself."

Charles shook his head.

"Can't be done," he said. *"I've* nothing to be cheerful about. But I know a chap who has." He whipped out the snapshot and thrust it into her hand. "Here, just look at *this."*

He expected Sally—as a woman—to be overwhelmed by the infantile beauty of the photograph. To his surprise, however, she only laughed heartlessly.

"What a queer little chap. I hope he's not like his parents. If so, it's too bad of them to have done it."

"His father's the finest chap in the world," declared Charles. "There's no one I admire or envy so much. He—he's got all."

116

"I don't call this all," laughed Sally, returning the snapshot. "Just something to go on with—and better luck, next time. What are you sulking about? *Your* baby is bound to be lots better-looking."

"Mine?" Charles almost groaned. "Yes. *When?*"

"Oh, don't be so silly. You're not a patriarch. Lots of time yet. The trouble with you, Charles, is that you think yourself pathetic. But you're not."

"No. I'm unlucky."

"Unlucky in being yourself. You have chances and you fail to cash in. You don't use your brain, you have no ambition, and you don't work."

Charles, who was too used to flattery, and to girls who invited his kiss, felt strangely braced by Sally's criticism. Suddenly she appeared to him as the perfect wife, someone who would keep him severely up to the mark, but who would know how to reward good behavior. And he told himself that her kiss would be worth while.

"If you married a chap like me," he ventured, "and if I was a bad boy, you'd give me a black eye, wouldn't you?"

"Two," corrected Sally. "You'd be lucky if you could see the primrose path again inside of a week."

"I'd probably see two also," chuckled Charles. "Well, I suppose I must hike." He twisted Higgins' Immortality into a spill, as he added, "Where are you going?"

"To find Miss Vine," replied Sally. "There's someone who wants to see her, and what's more, I want her to have an interview. She is vaguely pathetic."

"Not like me then."

"No. *She* laughs all the time. Don't keep me. I must find Miss Vine."

"When you do, advise her for me, to take a dip in the lake. The deep end, for preference."

"A joke?" asked Sally. "You've all such a Russian sense of humor. Good-bye."

Her smile was so sunny, as she ran off, that Charles glowed with a sense of joyous comradeship.

"There's a wife," he muttered, as he trudged off to his office.

Sally was some time in finding Miss Vine, for she had not gone, as usual, to visit her looking glass in the lake. On her way, she met her head gardener, Simmons, and she stopped to catechize him about his last bill for coke.

He was accompanied by his small son, and in an interval of baiting his father Anthea noticed that he had cheeks the color of ripe apricots, and enormous black eyes.

Susceptible to masculine beauty, however tender the years of her victim, she proceeded to make a conquest.

"What's your name?" she asked.

"Horace, miss."

"And how old are you?"

"Nearly nine, miss."

"Too young, Horace. Do you like my beautiful garden?"

"Yes, miss."

He stared at her, fascinated by the contortions of her tight pink face, and by her trick of closing her eyes and then, suddenly, opening them wide. She mistook his interest for admiration, and became gracious.

"You have my permission to go wherever you like," she said. "Simmons, you can take him to the kitchen—back door—and tell cook to give him milk and cake. I advise the kitchen cake. It is probably richer than what she sends into the dining room. . . . Good-bye, Horace. You shall be my gardener, some day."

With a gracious smile, she turned to Simmons.

"I congratulate you on your beautiful boy, Simmons," she said. "He's a Murillo."

"Did she say I was a gorilla, dad?" asked Horace, as Miss Vine minced down the path.

"Yes, monkey-face," replied the proud father. "And she never said a truer word."

On her way to the lake, Miss Vine was overtaken by Sally, who was panting and flushed from running.

"Oh, Miss Vine," she gasped. "Someone—to—see you."

Miss Vine turned and noticed the carnation color in Sally's cheeks. She looked so attractive that her employer's snarl was her involuntary tribute.

"Really, Miss Morgan, I'd be better off with that boy as my secretary, if this is a sample of your discretion. You *know*——"

"But it's Mrs. Law, of the Timberdale Arms," interrupted Sally.

Miss Vine's eyes gleamed suddenly, and she nodded.

"All right. I'll see her," she snapped.

She walked back very slowly to the house, so that her victim should have plenty of time in which to cool her courage, while Sally ran ahead, as her herald.

The head gardener turned to his son.

"That's the lady that pays the rent and every morsel you eat," he said. "So mind your step."

"Is she a little girl?" asked Horace. "She's got golden curls, like Mary Pickford."

"Don't ask no questions. And don't throw stones near the glass. And don't cut the trees. And don't fall into the lake, for you'll have to find the way out for yourself."

Left to himself, Horace strolled round the grounds, but found little to interest him. There were few flowers, and no animals, while he could only gaze wistfully through the glass at the pots of forced strawberries in the conservatories.

Presently, he opened his new knife and drew down the bough of a willow, which hung over the lake, with the intention of getting a new fishing rod. He had cut only half through the tough wood when he heard his father's voice, calling to him, in the distance.

Awakened to a sense of guilt, he hastily released the half-severed branch, so that it trailed, once more, over the water.

CHAPTER XVI

Woman to Woman

MRS. DORIS LAW WAITED FOR OVER TWENTY MINUTES IN the enormous white-and-gold Empire drawing room, where she was shown by Miss Vine's orders. Its chill magnificence had worked its numbing effect, when Miss Vine—an insignificant figure, wrapped in furs—appeared at the door.

This unpunctuality was opposed to Miss Vine's usual procedure. She had none of the subterfuges of the small businesswoman, who wishes to impress her public. She did not hide behind a veil of invisibility and she kept her appointments to the tick, as though to demonstrate the value of every minute in a carefully mapped-out timetable. She was, also, above the threadbare device of sitting with her back to the light, and of reserving for her visitor the chair in the revealing sunshine.

This fall from her own high standard showed that some streak of tiger in her nature was awakened, and screamed for its victim. Her eyes were like points of ice, under her small cap, as she entered the drawing room.

Mrs. Law rose and walked to meet her, with a swagger which was pitiful, because it was so obviously assumed for defensive purpose. She wanted to appear as a wealthy woman of the world, completely at her ease.

She wore her smart black-and-white suit, decorated with a huge bunch of violets, and her face was smothered with powder, which failed to conceal the coarse red grain of her skin. Although its expression was foolish, it was also kind, while her eyes had the direct gaze which indicated innate honesty.

Mrs. Law could bluster, when driven into a tight corner, but she could not tell a lie.

Miss Vine missed no vulnerable point of the woman who had dared to challenge her to a duel. She made no sign of greeting, although she allowed Mrs. Law to hold her hand for a second.

The big, fair woman towered above her, as she tried to carry off the situation in a gusty laugh, to indicate her self-possession.

"What a perfectly charming room. Charming."

Miss Vine said nothing, but she continued to stand.

"What a charming day," remarked Mrs. Law.

"Very cold."

"Yes," agreed Mrs. Law, "I thought it was cold, too, but you see I ran over from Timberdale in my car. I left it outside in the road, with my dog, Sultan, in charge. I had no idea your drive was so long. Quite an estate. I've four dogs, you know, but Sultan is my special pal. Understands every word I say."

Miss Vine saw her chance to play with her visitor. "Do you like dogs?" she asked.

"I love all animals." Suddenly at her ease, Mrs. Law sank down again in her deep chair. "Anything that goes on four legs. I always feel there's something wrong about a person who doesn't like animals, you know."

In her turn, Miss Vine sat down and regarded her visitor through narrowed lids.

"Do you consider that a tendency to hold humanity higher than the lower forms of creation is a sign of inferiority?" she asked.

"I think it shows a nasty nature," replied Mrs. Law. "Of course, I was only a kid at the time, but when I read that Crippen had his wife's cats destroyed I knew, at once, he'd done it."

Miss Vine's painted smile became a sneer.

"I will not allow an animal inside the Court," she said.

Mrs. Law stared at her.

"Oh, well, if you're afraid of them, you can't get over your nature," she said quickly. "*You're* not to blame. I didn't mean that for one minute."

"Neither did I mean what you imply." Miss Vine's voice was a snarl. "I keep no animals because they're dirty and harbor germs of disease. They have no affection for anyone, but they fawn on the person who feeds them."

Mrs. Law felt suddenly at a loss.

"I wonder if I may smoke?" she asked helplessly.

"Do."

As Miss Vine made no movement towards the heavy silver box of cigarettes which lay, open, on a side table, Mrs. Law drew out her own case.

"I'm afraid I'm rather a heavy smoker," she apologized. "But smoking's matey, and my place is Liberty Hall. I always like men to feel at home—and women, too. It's good for business, I say. . . . Have one? Afraid they're only fags."

Miss Vine shook her head.

"Thank you," she said coldly, "but the state of my health will not permit me to join you."

She watched Mrs. Law as she tapped her cigarette and moistened the paper, and also when she threw the spent match on the carpet and hurriedly scooped it up again. Every time she flicked off her ash, Mrs. Law was conscious of raised brows. Feeling that she had committed some social blunder, the wretched woman was sorry that she had yielded to her impulse.

123

"It's so charming of you to see me," she said desperately.
Miss Vine showed her first sign of interest.

"Exactly what do you wish to see me about?" she asked.

"Well, it's like this," explained Mrs. Law nervously.
"I've had a proposition made to me about my hotel which
isn't going to pay me."

"Then, as a woman of business, I presume you will turn
it down?"

"Well, that's easier said than done. I can't afford to accept it, and I can't afford to refuse it. So, I appeal to you."

"In that case, I must refer you to my business represent-
ative," said Miss Vine. "I do not deal directly with subordinate matters."

Mrs. Law began to breathe heavily.

"No," she declared. "I appeal to you, on the human side.
As woman to woman."

Miss Vine licked her vermilion lips cautiously, as though
she foresaw amusement.

"I shall be glad to listen to you, as a woman," she said.
"One minute, please."

She pressed a button in the table, twice. A minute later
Sally Morgan made her usual prompt entrance.

"Miss Morgan," said Miss Vine, "this is the *present*
owner of the Timberdale Arms. As this matter concerns
business, I want you to make any notes that may be necessary."

Mrs. Law's face grew scarlet.

"Oh, Miss Vine," she protested, "please, not before this
young lady. What I have to say is personal. It's private and
confidential."

Thankful to be released from an unpleasant duty, Sally
was half way to the door when she was arrested by her
employer's voice.

"Miss Morgan, did *I* give you orders to go? This is my

private and confidential secretary, Mrs. Law, and the function of a private secretary is to be discreet and silent. . . . Now, will you state your case?"

Sally's face was as red as Mrs. Law's, as she sat as far away from the couple as she dared. She knew that Miss Vine retained her solely as a witness of Mrs. Law's humiliation.

As she remained silent, Miss Vine gave her victim a prod.

"Woman to woman, I'm listening to you," she reminded her.

Mrs. Law moistened her lips nervously, and glanced at Sally, out of the corner of her eye.

"Well, Miss Vine, it's like this. I'm so happy in my hotel. If I say it myself, I'm popular. Everyone calls me 'Ma.' People are always dropping in, for a glass, and a chat, and, sometimes, a bit of jolly. It's life, and I'd hate to give it up, and be private again. And I'd miss hearing the income rattling in through the cash register."

"Yes, we all like to hold what we have," remarked Miss Vine coldly, "if we can."

"Well," resumed Mrs. Law, "it seems that you can take it all away from me. You're a rich woman, yourself. I want you to *think*. I've had a hard life. My family's been in Old-town for generations. Really, we're landed gentry."

"Your brother is a policeman, I believe?"

"A Superintendent, Miss Vine. He's let down the family, but he really wanted to go in the Mounted Police, only mother wouldn't hear of his going abroad."

"I see. Won't you resume your story of hard luck?"

Sally bit her lip as the simple woman fell into the trap.

"Can't she see she's being drawn on?" she wondered. "Oh, the fool. Oh, the poor darling."

"Well, Miss Vine," appealed Mrs. Law, "you know how hard gentlemen-farmers have been hit by the new land taxes.

When Daddy died, I went to live with my elder brother and sister. It was no life for a young girl."

"Where were you educated?" asked Miss Vine.

"At the high school. I had to get up early, to ride in on my bike, and I only got sandwiches for dinner."

"Didn't you get any dinner at night?"

"Only a hotted-up one."

"Poor little schoolgirl," Miss Vine's lips writhed. "*I* went to a council school, until I won a scholarship for the high. My schoolmates—girls of your class, I imagine—showed their understanding of the situation."

Mrs. Law accepted the words, although she was puzzled by Miss Vine's metallic intonation. But the knowledge that the rich and powerful woman had been to a despised council school increased her own confidence.

"That would be long before my time," she said bluntly. "Well, when I left school, I had to take a job, so I went to the toilet saloon, at the Grand Hotel, where I thought I'd see life, and manicure gentlemen's hands, like the pictures. But did I? They set me on to wash heads."

"And how old were you when you started to work?" asked Miss Vine.

"Eighteen."

"Ah. I was fifteen. My first job was in a basement office, in the City, where I worked by artificial light. My hours were nine to six, but I prolonged them voluntarily, in order to make myself of value to my employer."

"Fancy that," gaped Mrs. Law. "Well, where was I? Oh, I know. The War. That was a godsend to me. I went as a V.A.D.—did my bit you know—and I nursed the Major, and married him. He was killed before his next leave."

Mrs. Law wiped her eyes which were suffused with facile tears.

"So you see, Miss Vine," she concluded, "my life has been a very hard one."

"But your tale's not ended," Miss Vine reminded her. "You've not come to the silver lining. You received a pension for your husband's sacrifice, and you bought the Timberdale Arms."

"That's right," agreed Mrs. Law, uneasily.

"And what have you done in the way of improvements? It is up to each one of us to leave things better than we found them. Have you made a speciality of quick lunches for motorists? Have you increased your advertisements? Have you put in central heating?"

"No," Mrs. Law laughed. "I left well alone. I'm not one of your greedy ones. I don't want a fortune."

"You differ from me." Miss Vine rose, to signify the end of the interview. "I consider you a lucky woman, Mrs. Law. You seem to have got something for nothing."

"Nothing?" gasped Mrs. Law.

"Certainly. What have you done to justify this gift from the taxpayers? Was matrimony such a sacrifice to you?"

Mrs. Law rose and threw back her head proudly.

"You don't understand, Miss Vine," she said. "You can't, for you're single yourself. But, when I married, I gave up my freedom. I gave the Major *everything.*"

"You mean, you gave up washing hair, in exchange for a fortnight's holiday with a man. And the sum that is now offered for the Timberdale Arms will bring in sufficient income to enable you to live in some boarding house, without washing any more heads."

"No, thanks," cried Mrs. Law, with spirit. "No tabby-cat life for me, playing patience with old maids. I'm not old enough for that. After all, my teeth and my hair are my own."

She spoke without any ulterior comparison or sneer. But

Sally caught her breath in dismay, as Miss Vine looked at the big woman's thick mop of guinea-gold hair, and her regular white teeth.

All her wealth could not procure for her what this fat, blowzy creature possessed. Her smile revealed the perfection of her denture, as she voluntarily held out her hand.

"Good morning, Mrs. Law. I've been so touched by your story of misfortune. I will present your case for the consideration of my fellow-directors, at our next board meeting. But I can't give you any hope. I am entirely in their hands. You must remember, I am but one woman against many men."

128

CHAPTER XVII

A Museum Piece

WHILE HIS FAVORITE SISTER WAS SWEATING IN THE drawing room of Jamaica Court, Superintendent Pye had an unexpected call for his professional services. Miss Pye's big face beamed with pleasure, as she brought him the message.

"It's from Colonel Bray. There's been a burglary at High Gables."

"Blow," grumbled the Superintendent, hiding his pleasure. "Another china robbery, I suppose. Jam pots, this time."

"I've just had a jam pot mystery myself," observed Miss Pye. "But I've solved it already."

"How?" barked Pye.

"I laid a trap for Betsy. I gave her soused herrings for breakfast, to which she is very partial—and at this moment —she is being sick. I've just said to her, 'Now, Betsy, you know herrings have never made you ill before, and wouldn't now, if you hadn't first lined your stomach with strawberry jam. And then she confessed."

"Your methods are too much like the third degree to appeal to me," remarked Pye.

Miss Pye's smile did not fade.

"I do wonder if this new case will be another mystery like the Dresden china robbery," she said.

"What d'you mean by 'mystery'?" demanded her brother. "I saw through that immediately. Clear as daylight."

"I mean the criminal is still at large," explained Miss Pye. "That is to say, you don't know who took them.",

Slightly annoyed by this reminder, Pye remained silent while his sister got the car out of the garage and ran it round to the front gate. His expression was bitter when she wished him good luck.

"According to you, it's simple," he told her. "All I have to do it to sit tight until the Colonel is sick."

He arrived at High Gables, in a grim mood, for the Colonel was a fellow-judge, whom he had fought, on points, at many a dog show. The house was a massive red-brick Victorian villa, set in thick shrubberies, and girt with the prickly protection of holly hedges. The lawns were cut up with small clipped trees, and gigantic monkey puzzles obstructed any view.

The butler showed him to the study, where he found the Colonel in a temper which exceeded his own. He was a survival of the Victorian type of soldier, with a face pitted like a pineapple, a white spiked mustache, and a very soft voice, which suggested the acme of ferocity.

"Sorry to hear you've had a visitor, Colonel," remarked Pye. "What did he lift?"

"He lifted a Chinese vase," was the soft reply.

"Valuable?"

"Only a museum bit."

"Oho? Where did you keep it?"

"In a locked cabinet in the drawing room."

"If it was so valuable, why didn't you keep it in a safe?"

The Colonel's face grew puce.

"Why the hell should I?" he whispered. "I pay rates and taxes for police protection. I don't expect cat burglars."

"And you don't get them for a ground-floor burglary," grinned Pye. "I'd like to see the cabinet," he added, with a change of manner.

The Colonel led the way to the drawing room, which was shadowed by the monkey puzzles, and was a chill apartment, crowded with Japanese screens and china, and slippery with willow-pattern chintz.

The lock of the red lacquer cabinet was intact, although the scratches around it told of an unsuccessful attempt to force it. A square of glass had been cut out of the front and lay on the carpet.

Pye inspected the aperture, and then examined the room, in impressive silence. His smile was superior, when, at last, he spoke.

"The work of a rank amateur," he announced. "He's plastered his finger marks all over the glass and woodwork. And the hole's very inexpertly cut. We'll soon have *him*."

"Has Mrs. Antrobus recovered her Dresden china ornaments?" asked the Colonel softly.

"No—and never will," was the sharp reply. "I wouldn't waste my time over that, because it was so plainly a practical joke."

"And how do *you* know?"

"In much the same way I spotted Williams' puppy for a winner, against your judgment, Colonel. You've heard he's turning out a champion. Three firsts and two seconds at Tewkesbury."

"We're not talking on *your* subject now," said the Colonel quietly. "We're talking of crime. I ask you how you know that the undiscovered robbery at the Moat House is the work of a practical joker?"

"Because he took only one figure, and had to return for the other. If he hadn't lost his nerve, he'd have done the job properly first go."

The Colonel laid his ace on the Superintendent's king.

"Then your joker's on this job, too," he said. "For he's left the lid of the vase behind."

Pye's jaw dropped.

"Let's see the lid," he said sharply.

The Colonel pointed to the bottom of the cabinet.

"There it is," he said. "I was showing it to a young feller, last night, and I suppose he put it down here while he was examining the vase, so it got overlooked. I remember, now, that he turned it upside down, to hunt for some mark."

"Who was he?"

"One of Miss Vine's sons or sweethearts, as the case may be," replied the Colonel. "One of the young Fords—the chap with the decent manners. My boy had some young people to dinner, last night—a cursed noisy crowd, too, and this youngster asked to see the vase. Said he'd spotted one like it, in the British Museum."

"And you found out then exactly how valuable it was," murmured Pye. "The question is, what value is the vase without the lid?"

"None to him," was the bitter reply. "And the lid is no value to me, *now*."

"I see," nodded Pye. "Stalemate." Then his eyes gleamed. "I can always get under the skin of a criminal," he asserted, "once I've a line on his methods. Now, this chap is safe to do exactly what he did before. He will come back for the lid."

"I'm damned if he shall get it," exploded the Colonel.

"So am I," agreed Pye. "This time we'll be waiting for him. He'll walk into a regular ambush. Would you like to be in at the fun, Colonel?"

The Colonel's red face puckered into a boyish grin.

"You bet. My man—Price—will sit up, too. When d'you expect him?"

"Tonight. Last time, he lost no time in paying his return visit. I don't suppose you're very early birds here?"

"Lights out about eleven-thirty, as a rule."

"Good. I'll be here, at eleven-thirty sharp, and let your man be standing by, to let me in quietly. I'll scrape on the door. Keep the place dark, and don't make any noise.... Well, good-bye, Colonel. I think you'll soon have your Chinese vase intact."

Restored to good humor, the Colonel walked with him to the hall where he suddenly grimaced.

"Excuse me," he said. "I fancy the game-pie I had for breakfast was a bit high. I feel infernally sick. Let yourself out, there's a good chap."

Pye kept chuckling, during the short run home.

"According to old Flo, the Colonel must have stolen his own vase. Won't I have her on?" he told himself.

His smile broadened at the sight of a familiar red roadster, parked in the road before the Cherry Orchard. To his surprise, however, a large Alsatian dog occupied the driver's seat. He recognized Pye immediately for a policeman, and growled at him when he tried to remind him that they had met before.

At that moment Mrs. Law came through the tall ornamental gates of Jamaica Court. She was puffing furiously at a cigarette, and her greeting was not so gay as usual.

"Didn't know the drive was such a dickens of a length," she grumbled, "or I wouldn't have left the car outside." She turned to the dog. "Stop yodeling, boy. Mother's here."

"He thinks I'm stealing your car," grinned Pye, as he patted the dog's head.

"Well, now you know what the poor devils you suspect feel like?" remarked Mrs. Law absently.

Pye looked sternly at his sister.

"I never suspect, Doris. I *know*."

"That's true," said Miss Pye proudly, as she appeared at the gate. "Adam never makes an arrest until he's dead certain of his man. And he never makes a mistake."

133

"Or many arrests, at that rate," remarked Mrs. Law.

Pye, whose pride had been soothed by Miss Pye's tribute, felt rubbed up again by his sister's tactlessness. But, as he looked at her eyes, he sensed her trouble.

"Been visiting in high society?" he inquired.

Mrs. Law blew out a mouthful of smoke, and hesitated.

"Meaning Miss Vine?" she asked. *"She's* no lady. Positively common, if you ask me. Been to a council school. And, my word, mean. Fancy, I had to smoke my own fag, and invite myself, too."

"Better than smoking hers," said Pye grimly.

Mrs. Law laughed loudly.

"If that's a hint, you've lost," she declared. "I'm here for dinner. Is it ready, Flo?"

She was very noisy all through the meal, as she described the glories of Jamaica Court.

"It's just like a furniture shop, with the tickets nipped off. Not one bit of comfort, or homeliness. I could sit in that drawing room, and read right through the *News of the World,* thinking it was *The Times* and that I'd been stung. It's that kind of starchy place. Very different from my old——"

As Mrs. Law suddenly choked over her smoke, Miss Pye exchanged glances with her brother. Directly the cloth was removed, and Betsy had appeared with a teapot, and three big cups, she turned to her sister.

"Shall I cut the cards, old girl?"

"I don't want the cards to tell what's coming to me," laughed Mrs. Law. "I know."

"A second husband with lots of money," suggested Miss Pye.

"All right, send him along. I can do with him."

"What's wrong, darling?" asked Pye.

134

"Nothing. Everything's merry and bright. It only looks as though I was going to lose my home."

Her family said nothing, but their faces grew grim as she outlined the situation.

"Miss Vine's little gang of thieves sent a smart aleck to make me a spot-cash offer for the Timberdale Arms. They're going to pull it down and sell the old stuff, I believe. It's a damnable price, but it's take it, or leave it. So I just went up to the Court, to see the old girl, and try if I could call her up. But it was no go. If she would give me a fair figure I could go into business again."

She frowned as she spoke, for she was conscious of being false to herself when she tried to impress Miss Vine with her imitation of a woman of the world. She had suppressed the true picture of an uneventful, hard-working girlhood, whose sole bright memory was the romance of a fortnight's honeymoon.

And she had no clear idea of herself as the genial hostess of an old country inn, which preserved the spirit of real hospitality, evident in many a basket of fruit and pot of tea, not charged for on the bill. But she had some confused feeling that her ruin would be a loss to the neighborhood. When a man was down on his luck, "Ma" saw that he had free bread-and-cheese, as well as a drink at the bar; while pensioners called for the crumbs, as well as the birds.

"What worries me most is the animals," she said. "I can't sleep at night, wondering what is to become of them."

It was Miss Pye who asked the first question.

"If you don't accept Miss Vine's offer, what will happen?"

"She'll go on with her building, and smash me."

Miss Pye caught her brother's eye, and nodded.

"You won't go?" she asked eagerly. "You'll sit tight?"

"What's the blooming good of that? I'll soon be broke. I couldn't hold out against the competition of a swagger

135

hotel. The trade's not what it was. No, I'll have to play for safety, and accept her blood money. It might bring in a quid or two. I shan't starve."

Miss Pye's eyes gleamed behind her big glasses.

"You'll never let her have a walkover?" she cried, aghast.

"Think I'm jolly and bright, myself, old girl?" demanded her sister bitterly. "It nearly breaks me to think of losing my old home, and it's being pulled down. A thousand bulbs from Holland coming up, at this minute. Serves me right for not sticking to the Old Country. And there's my contract for old sleepers from the railway company. Oh, my dear heart."

As her eyes brimmed over with tears, at last, Pye's great fist crashed down on the table.

"It's damnable," he shouted. "Don't give in, girl. Make a fight, and we'll stand by you."

"You'll have your chance to do that, all right, old boy," Mrs. Law assured him. "I expect I'll be often rolling in for a free meal. Bit of a change for me, that's done so much treating myself. Well, no one can bring it up against me that I didn't splash my money when I had it."

"No one can ever say one word against you," cried Miss Pye.

"Can't they, old dear? Wait till I'm broke. But here's a friend I can bank on. Think of *him* in poky quarters. Come to mother, sweetheart, she's making an old fool of herself."

As the great Alsatian put his paws upon her shoulders and licked her overpowdered face, Mrs. Law burst into tears.

"There's someone who may be in tighter quarters still," said Miss Pye ominously. "Six feet of cold ground. That old woman won't live much longer. It's in the cards. Why, at this very minute something may be happening."

Even as she spoke, Miss Vine was drowning in ten feet of water.

CHAPTER XVIII

Anthea's Mirror

WATER. UP TO HER NOSTRILS, BEFORE HER EYES, INSIDE her lungs. Iron bands clamping her temples. The roaring of seas in her ears. The flashing of lights—and a red blindness. An agony of choking. Then—darkness.

Miss Vine knew that she was drowning, but she could not realize her fate. In one second a solid world of terra-cotta hotels had flickered out. Such things happened to others—not to her. Even as her fingers fought for something to grip, so her whole being stretched passionately out to life.

Only a few minutes before, she had left the house in a fit of temper. Although she had pulped her opponent, Mrs. Law, in her turn, had drawn blood. It would have astonished the good-natured simpleton had she known that her unconscious sneers were already festering wounds in Miss Vine's brain.

She was obsessed by a vision of golden hair—thick as fleece and bright as sunlight—revealed by Mrs. Law's tiny black cap, and crowning her foolish red face. She would have given thousands for such a possession, and counted her bargain cheap.

The second shaft was barbed and went deeper. Miss Vine had never regarded herself as a spinster, because she dramatized herself as a queen. Spurred on by her rage, she walked yet faster, never glancing at the thick beds of crocuses—

white, purple and yellow. With their petals folded up into tight spikes, they were like trays of gay mosaic ranged on the different levels of the terraces.

She passed the mound, topped with the white classic temple, where the daffodils under the grove of trees, were still bound in their sheaves, and reached the lake. Her own private looking glass awaited her; it would soothe her, to see her own face, transfigured to illusionary beauty, rising up from under the dark water, like a pixie, obedient to a spell. Then her thoughts would clear, and she would be able to concentrate on details of policy.

Even amid the ferment of her venom-steeped brain, her personal interest was beginning to take control and direct the future.

"It might be a good plan to offer that fool some post in the new hotel," she thought. "She'd keep the local trade together, as she's popular in the district. And she might be a draw in the bar—fair, fat and forty. Good for me—humiliating for her. . . . *Golden hair*—and her own. She shall pay for that sneer."

The lake, which was mottled with patches of lily-leaves, reflected scraps of blue sky, in its clear stretches. Miss Vine walked around its edge, until she reached the deep end, spanned by the bridge. She minced along the plank, on her high French heels, and then stooped to grasp the stout bough of willow, which supported her whole weight, as she swung out over the water.

To her horror, it broke off in her hand. Her heart seemed to turn over from the shock, as she shot, head foremost, into the lake.

The cold took away her breath, so that she sank immediately. The green light rapidly dimmed to black, and the torturing fight for breath began. Because of a few bubbles in an air pipe, Miss Vine would soon be nothing but a waterlogged organism, with her active brain and complex personality reduced to less than the lowest form of pond life, and equal with the reeds and scum.

After the first unendurable agony, there followed relief, as her physical sensation was submerged in mental travail. Her mind cleared and grew lucid as a crystal, compressing a myriad reflections into one packed minute of retrospect.

At that moment she realized that life was sweet, and that she had wasted it. The limitation of wealth was its penalty. She could not spend all her money on herself. She could eat only a limited amount of food—wear out only a few clothes.

Her maid, Eames, was right. In her room were piles of new lingerie, which would become the property of others. Next week her will would be read, in reality, even as she had stage-managed it at her dress rehearsal—only her place on the golden couch would be vacant.

But her deepest regret was the rankling reminder that she had never married. She had missed one vital experience. Mrs. Law's fumbling thrust had driven home a shaft, barbed as a fishhook, tearing at her pride.

Her life had been too choked by the details and administration of finance for her to realize any loss. So long as she had shoals of courtiers—their lips primed with compliments —her vanity was satisfied, so that she was swollen with the power of conquest, and believed that the world was at her feet.

Now that it was too late, she lamented a lost opportunity. Fat foolish Mrs. Law, with her fortnight, had known more than she. The papers would print the contents of the will of Anthea Vine, spinster.

Even as the thought swam through her brain, something seemed to crack in her head, and the present broke up into a maze of disrupted lines and colors, spinning around her like a Catherine wheel. She distinguished sections of terra-cotta Munster hotels, slices of dainty "Dahlia" lingerie, strips of daffodils—tightly enclosed in their sheaves, fragments of golden hair, shreds of the faces of young men.

A pall of darkness fell and blotted out the distorted, blazing firework. And then the darkness slipped away. The roar of the seas died into silence.

At that moment Francis stood on the bank of the lake, staring, as though hypnotized by the widening circles of water. He had kept his word and stayed away from his office, only to find his act of mutiny ignored by Anthea, who was unconscious of his presence.

But the freedom from any show of responsibility was entirely to his own liking. He rose late, and led the life of a gentleman of leisure. The only flaw in his contentment was his empty pockets.

This morning, as he strolled through the grounds, which became his own, in his imagination, he was in time to see Anthea dive from the bridge and disappear in the lake, as though drawn under by some invisible hand.

In a dozen strides he was at the spot, where he stood as though rooted into the ground. Down below, somewhere among the weeds, lay old Anthea, leaking away her life.

The pupils of his eyes contracted until they appeared as a blaze of white fire in the sunlight. He had only to stand still and a fortune lay in the hollow of his hand.

The next second he awoke to the full realization of what had happened. Anthea was drowning. Kicking off his shoes and throwing off his coat, he dived into the lake, to reappear with a sodden bundle of clothes.

As he laid her, face downward on the path, and began to work her arms in the movements of artificial respiration, she stirred back to life. Spitting, gasping and choking, she was altogether a repulsive object to a fastidious young man's taste, as she pushed the dripping spikes of golden wig away from her eyes, and stared at Francis in incredulous surprise.

"*You?*" she whispered.

Francis hauled her to her feet, and patted her back in quite a genial fashion.

"I," he said, smiling down at the paint-streaked face. "Fished you out of the lake, you know. Shall I carry you back?"

"No. I'll walk."

"That's right. Good for your circulation."

As he took her by the arm, she twisted around, to look up at him.

"You saved my life?" she asked again.

"Yes. Sorry to appear heroic, but it was forced on me. Now, don't talk. Be a good girl, and run."

He dragged her, dripping and shivering, through the grounds, and back to the house. Although she looked like a drowned rat, he was astonished by her reserves of vitality. Still half-chloroformed by the laboring of waterlogged lungs, her eyes were sharp and bright with resolution.

When they reached the pillared hall, they were, almost immediately, the center of an excited group of servants. Francis, who appeared elated by his position, gave his orders.

"Now, don't gape. Don't press. Hallo, Miss Morgan, Miss Vine has fallen into the lake. She'll want a hot bath and brandy. Where's Iris?"

Eames appeared on the scene, and he relinquished his charge to the maid. As he did so, he spoke to her in a benevolent manner.

"Get into a hot mustard bath, immediately, Anthea. The sooner you're between blankets the better. And then try and forget you are a lady, and get drunk."

Miss Vine made no protest as Iris and Eames rushed her

up the great marble staircase, while her secretary was issuing the necessary orders. Then Sally turned away from the house telephone, and thrust a small glass of brandy into Francis' hand.

"Drink this," she said, "as a reward for your good deed."

"Is it such a good deed?" he asked. "I expect it will make me the most hated man in England."

As he spoke, he turned and almost ran into Charles.

"What are you doing at home, you slacker?" he asked.

"Forgot something," explained Charles, "so I came back. And how did *you* manage to get in the limelight, my little man?"

Francis looked down, as though he had been reproached for treachery.

"I—I just happened to be passing that way," he said.

"You would," murmured Charles, under his breath.

He was doing his best to fight the devil in his heart. But he had only just realized that he was in love, even while his eyes were dazzled by the light of Higgins' Immortality. If his cousin, Francis, had only chosen some other part of the grounds for his morning walk, at this moment, he, too, would be walking on air.

He tried to laugh naturally as Sally joined the young men.

"Another excitement for us," he said. "The second time, too. Anthea seems to have a charmed life."

Francis turned towards the staircase, leaving a dripping trail behind him, on the marble flags.

"I think a hot bath is indicated for me, too," he murmured.

Sally looked after him.

"Mr. Francis has come out in new colors," she said.

"Rather. Pleased as Punch with himself," agreed Charles. "He amuses me. We're told that this urge to risk our life for another is one of the finest impulses of mankind. I suppose Francis is surprised and pleased to find that he actually possesses it. Something he didn't know he had, like a rudimentary tail, or a third eye."

Sally patted his shoulder in a maternal manner.

"Don't act. I know what you're feeling. It's quite natural. As a matter of fact, I'm thinking much the same."

"How?" asked Charles, suddenly cheered by a link of sympathy.

"Well," frowned Sally, "I sometimes wonder if we are not too sentimental in this matter of the wholesale preservation of life. It might be better to concentrate on the question of *which* is the better life. Now, this is in confidence, of course, but I have just been a witness of an interview which has left a very nasty taste. Two women, you know. I liked the one, for you could see she was kind and spreads happiness. But, she's got to go under, just because she is cheese, and the other is wire."

Charles burst out laughing.

"I get you," he said. "You're thinking of Mrs. Law and the Timberdale Arms business. I won't give you away. But do you really think that if old Francis had done his duty he would have left Anthea to peg out in the lake?"

Sally echoed his laugh.

"Of course not, in practice. But I'm terribly ruthless in theory. Well, here we are, as we were. And it's good just to be alive. We mustn't grudge her that."

Charles felt the sense of comradeship that he always experienced after a chat with Sally. Her common sense was like a drop of strong vinegar, which cleared his mind, and sent the muddy sentiment to the bottom. He whistled cheerfully as he ran up the stairs.

"Poor old Anthea," he thought. "If she'd really drowned in the lake, I know that, at this moment, I should be feeling down in the mouth, and missing her like blazes. She'd leave a terrible blank. I'm not such a sweep as I thought."

Apparently Francis shared the same altruistic idea, for as Charles passed the favorite small bathroom, he heard his cousin's voice, raised in the jubilant strains of "Excelsior."

CHAPTER XIX

Vigil

PYE'S HEART HAMMERED WITH EXCITEMENT, THAT NIGHT, as he wheeled his bicycle into the thick of the shrubbery, and walked stealthily up the drive of High Gables. While he gave the impression of being strong and steady as an ox, his appearance was misleading, for there was an unsuspected nervous streak in his nature.

He often lay awake, at night, a prey to apprehension. Although he yearned for a chance to solve a murder mystery, in the small hours he was haunted by a fear that his brain might prove unequal to the test. He had wasted so many years judging the points of dogs, and deciding whether a motorist was drunk, or merely, not sober.

He felt he was on the right track in the matter of the second theft, for it seemed obvious that the same untrained hand had been at work. What worried him was the mentality of the unknown burglar.

While the value of the Dresden china figure was hardly sufficient to justify the risk, the Colonel's vase was, apparently, worth the hazard. But Pye did not altogether like the coincidence of another scamped job.

"Of course, it's possible that he did not know that there was a lid," he argued. "It probably looked all right, without it. The Colonel said it was at the bottom shelf of the cabinet, where anyone might overlook it, or not realize that the two things belonged."

In spite of this logic, Pye could not rid his mind of an uneasy suspicion that someone might be making a fool of him. The mere suggestion was enough to stiffen his resolution. His crest of hair was rampant, and his blue eyes very fierce, as he slid through the half-opened front door, and followed the butler into the drawing room.

The Colonel was already in ambush; his whisper was like a nest of disturbed cobras, as he outlined his plan of action.

"You sit here, Pye, facing the window. When you hear the chap, give a faint whistle, and I'll be ready to tackle him. I've reserved for myself the key position, facing both entrances. As an old soldier strategy is my own line. I've got my butler, in reserve, waiting in the hall, ready to enter, when I shout."

The fact that the Colonel had taken command was gall to Pye, who was a monopolist himself. He proceeded to put the civilian in his place by taking no notice of his orders.

"Good evening, Colonel," he said, in his natural voice. "All set for a night's vigil?"

"*Shush.*"

This time the Colonel's whisper resembled an engine letting off steam.

"That's all right, Colonel." Pye sat down on the easiest chair he could find. "He won't be coming for some time yet."

"How d'you know?"

"Because it would be too good to be true. I'm afraid our beds will go begging tonight."

In his turn, he issued his orders.

"When we hear him outside, we must take cover, and let him get inside the room. We mustn't give the show away, until he's well on the job. By the way, is the broken glass of the cabinet replaced?"

"Of course," rasped the Colonel.

"Well, let him get to work, and then switch on the light. I'll leave the time to your discretion, Colonel."

As the Colonel made no reply, Pye leaned his head against the cushion of his chair, resolved to be comfortable even if he lost his sleep. He was keyed up to the top pitch of expectancy and hopeful of speedy results.

The time passed quickly, at first. It seemed only a few minutes before the grandfather clock in the hall struck twelve.

At that moment the straggle of passengers off the midnight train were stumbling down the lane leading from the station. Francis Ford, who had gone up to town by the afternoon train, was among their number.

He laughed as he pointed to a light, set high up in a dark fortress, and explained it to the saxophone player.

"That's my juvenile cousin's light. Look, there she goes. Out to the tick."

As he spoke, the blazing star was suddenly swallowed up in darkness.

"Yes, I know that time signal quite well," remarked the musician. "You could set your watch by it. I suppose the lady is a regular old maid?"

"Anything but that." Again Francis laughed softly. "She's a time machine, indestructible, and wound up to go for ever. She's carrying on, as usual, although, by all the rules of the game, she ought to be in bed, dying of pneumonia. It was my good fortune to fish her out of her own lake, today. I'm anything but popular with my cousin, in consequence, so I cleared off for the day."

"You don't say so," murmured the saxophone player.

"I do say so. Well, gentlemen, our paths divide here. Good night."

The valley was speckled everywhere with tiny specks of light; but in High Gables the darkness was absolute. During the second hour Pye began to feel the strain of waiting. As habit asserted itself, he had to' fight hard to stay awake. He knew that if his lids closed for even a minute, he would fall asleep, and he regretted the impulse which made him choose the softest chair.

Apparently, the Colonel also resented the departure from custom, for, towards two o'clock, he spoke in querulous tones.

"What time d'you expect the feller?"

"The time I don't," snapped Pye.

"Hum. Seems to me mad dog's work."

Pye was beginning to have doubts himself.

"Look here, Colonel," he said, "this is my job, and I'll do it in my own way. *And* on my own, for preference. Suppose you cut off to bed?"

"I?" spluttered the Colonel. "Why, man, before you were born I've sat, perched up in a tree, tiger-hunting, and knowing there was a broken neck for me at the bottom if I closed an eye. *I'm* trained to keep awake."

"Sorry, Colonel. Have it your own way."

Pye chuckled to himself, a little later, when sounds of snoring announced the fact that the Colonel was fast asleep.

His own discomfort increased as the night wore on. He fidgeted in his chair, which had grown curiously springless and hard. Although he wanted to pace the room, he dared not do so, while the impulse to smoke was almost overpowering. He braced himself to stay the course by the reminder that, any moment, the unknown burglar might be stealing up the drive.

The place was full of sound—of squeaks and rustles outside, and of the creaking of furniture inside the room; but, while he started at every unfamiliar noise, gradually his conviction deepened that he had drawn a blank.

As the first wan signs of dawn appeared in the sky, Pye felt unaccountably depressed.

"Faulty deduction," he thought. "I've failed over a potty little job like this. Question is—how will I shape over a big one?"

It had grown bitterly cold, so that he felt stiff in every joint and utterly wretched. His sister would have made a new man of him within five minutes with hot bacon and coffee; but, as Pye did not know that he wanted breakfast and a fire, he suffered a concentrated inferiority complex. If, by some miracle, the genial Chief Constable of the County—Major Moore—had appeared at that moment, Pye would have immediately handed in his resignation.

When it was lighter, he coughed loudly, and the Colonel started upright in his chair.

"Well, Colonel, either the tiger's got you, or you've broken your neck," said Pye tactlessly. "Sorry to wake you, but I must be off. Business as usual, you know."

Both men looked yellow in the growing daylight, but the Colonel's eyes were set in deep pouches, and his expression was venomous.

"Bit of a washout?" he queried.

"Not at all," dissented Pye. "There are several reasons why we've drawn a blank. To begin with, the fellow probably knows that you sent, at once, for the police, while Mrs. Antrobus didn't call me in until after the second robbery."

"Why—then?" asked the Colonel softly.

"And there's another point," resumed Pye. "The fellow might not have discovered yet that the vase is valueless without the lid. Directly he does so, I'll stake my professional reputation that he'll pay you a second visit."

"Exactly when?"

"I can't tell you the date. But we'll force him to a time limit. The local rag comes out tomorrow. Get a small notice inserted that you're going abroad, and mention, casually, that your valuables are being stored at the bank, in view of your recent robbery. Make it sound natural, you know."

"Isn't that rather like showing our hand? He'll see we're laying a trap for him, if he has any brains."

"I'm not crediting him with much brains," said Pye. "This chap belongs to your own set, and loafs about all day, doing a bit of rabbit potting, perhaps. Haven't you tumbled to it, Colonel, that he's one of your own friends?"

The Colonel's face grew dangerously purple.

"Are you insinuating," he whispered, "that someone who's put his legs under my table has repaid my hospitality by robbing me?"

"I certainly do. And now, Colonel, you will be wanting a shave as much as I do, myself. Good morning. I'll be up again tonight."

He left the Colonel with his liver, and, consequently, his temper, upset for the day. When he met him, in the county club, he tackled the Chief Constable on the question of his subordinate.

"What sort of a chap is Pye?"

"Thoroughly competent," was the reply. "A good mixer, and knows his job from A to Z."

"Routine work, perhaps. But what is your opinion of him as Sherlock Holmes?"

Major Moore tried to shelve the question with a feeble joke.

"Nothing doing there. He's got a dressing gown, but he can't play the fiddle."

"I'm only asking," grunted the Colonel, "because I've got him on the job over the theft of my valuable vase, and, up to date, I'm not exactly—impressed."

"Your vase? Oh, come, man. One of the Bright Young People pinched that, for a joke."

This duplication of Pye's idea annoyed the Colonel intensely.

"I'd accept that," he said coldly, "were it not for the fact that my vase is a museum piece. Young Francis Ford told me so."

"Francis? But he's a liar. Always looks you straight in the eye when he speaks to you. All liars do that."

"An interesting bit of psychology," observed the Colonel stiffly. "When I held courts-martial, and, at home, on the bench, my own experience has proved the contrary. But, apart from this rubbish, I definitely want to see the return of my vase."

"You will, if Pye's on the job," the Chief Constable assured him. "Slow chap, and not exactly brilliant. But he's bulldog breed and he hangs on."

He burst out laughing, glad of an opportunity to change a vexed subject.

"His sister's the same. She was on the County Council Dairy-Class Committee with my wife, and they agreed to exchange family recipes for butter. Well, Miss Pye came down with hers, but my wife, like all women, has no sense of honor, and she wanted to hang on to hers. But Miss Pye gave her no peace. She just worried at her—day in, day out—until my wife kept her promise."

Major Moore paused, before he added impressively, "And that's typical of the Pyes. Once they get their teeth into anything, they hang on."

CHAPTER XX

Mirage

As though she possessed a charmed life, Anthea was none the worse for her accident. It was Francis who paid the penalty of his icy dip in the lake. The morning following his trip up to town, he awoke late, with a blind headache and a high temperature.

When she heard the news, Anthea paid a visit to his bedroom. Perching herself on his bed, and swinging her small feet, she could dimly see herself in the wardrobe mirror, as a golden-haired girl, in a simple white morning dress of white Kasha cloth. The picture appealed to her vanity, so that she could not resist the temptation of nodding and smiling at her own reflection, across the room.

To Francis, who saw her at closer range, she appeared as an ancient molting yellow bird; but he was still in the benevolent mood of her rescuer. He made no protest when she insisted on unbuttoning the collar of his pajama-jacket.

"There, that's better," she told him. "You look more like Shelley, and less of a pious choir boy."

Francis continued to look prim, in spite of his poetic bared throat.

"None the worse, Anthea?" he asked kindly.

"The better. I'm braced. I've not had a cold bath for years."

"Seen the faithful Lawrence, I suppose?" continued Francis.

"No. I've no time to be ill."

"Why—what are you so busy about?"

"I'm thinking of getting married."

He laughed at her joke, and then regarded her with faint admiration struggling through his surprise.

"You're an enigma," he said. "You ought to be dead, and you haven't turned a hair. But why this fatal passion for extinction?"

"Perhaps I want to do all a good turn."

There was mockery in her glance as she met his reproachful gaze.

"There is an old superstitious belief," he remarked, "that. if you save anyone's life, that person will do you an injury. You've struck back at me already, Anthea. I have an intermittent pulse, a galloping heart, and a high blood pressure. I diagnose incipient pneumonia."

"Oh, darling, all that because of little me? You shall stay in bed and be treated like a hero. Would you like the prettiest nurse I can procure?"

"Not on your life. I loathe ministering angels."

"Aha. The faithful heart."

Anthea was astounded and thrilled at the result of her experimental probe. Francis turned scarlet, and he glared at her in outraged fury, as though she had thrust a knife into a secret wound.

But, even while she gloated over his self-exposure, he regained his calm.

"I suppose my treatment will include a visit from the inevitable Lawrence?" he asked.

"Why not? I can afford to pay for my pleasures."

Their eyes met in a look of understanding. Then Anthea patted the sheet over his shoulder.

"I'm not forgetful of what you did, yesterday," she said quietly. "Or ungrateful."

She gave an involuntary shudder as she thought of her dream of the lions. Her fierce, intractable tiger had not taken his chance to spring. Yet, as she remembered the treachery of the broken bough, which had given way in her grasp, once again, in retrospect, her heart gave a leap of horror.

Her eyes grew suddenly shrewd.

"Francis," she said, "if you hadn't saved me, you'd have been a rich man, today. Don't lie to me. What was your motive?"

"You've a better brain than I have, Anthea," was the reply. "I leave you to make your own deduction."

"Then my deduction is—that you like me better than you will own. You realize, too, that we are like each other?"

"Are we? Then we both like money. What is my reward for saving your valuable life?"

Anthea shook her finger at him playfully.

"I'm sending for Waters, to alter my will," she said. "And I think you will like the new one better than the old."

"That's generous of you. But I'd have done it for nothing, of course. You shouldn't play human nature too low. No man can let a woman drown; even if he is a nonswimmer, he must, at least, accompany her to heaven or to hell. . . . Is it indelicate to ask what is my amended share?"

"You will receive one-half of the residue."

Francis' eyes glowed.

"Thanks," he said. "It's something for nothing, as I've just explained. But Heaven bless you for your kind thought."

Anthea slipped off the bed and crossed to the door.

"I'll send Lawrence to you, my heroic child," she promised.

As she opened the door, she nearly collided with Charles.

"I wanted to see you," he said. "Shall I make inquiries as to who cut that willow bough?"

"Yes," called out Francis, "you ought to hold an inquest on that. It practically amounts to murder."

Miss Vine's eyes flickered over the faces of both young men.

"What's the good?" she asked derisively. "No one would own up—and if he did, I'd sack him. I'll have no fools in my employ."

"I saw a strange boy about the grounds, that morning," observed Francis. "Probably, he had a knife, and had thought out his lie, and was looking for a cherry tree."

Miss Vine shook her head.

"No, that boy was a babe. Listen, Charles. I forbid you to say a word about the broken bough, to any servant, indoors or out. It might stir up mud and put ideas in their heads."

Charles grimaced. He was no fool himself, and he grasped the implication.

"She's washed out the servants, so she suspects us," he thought. "Francis is all right, as he fished her out of the water. Pleasant for Iris and me."

"Look here," he protested, "it's plain someone has done the dirty on you. You owe it to all of us to clear the matter up."

"Yes," chirped Francis, "why not emulate the schoolmaster, who punished the whole school to induce the guilty one to confess? Remember the fellow may want to come clean?"

Miss Vine flashed him a look.

"Francis," she said, "you have a sinister sense of humor, which frightens even me."

As she walked down to the study her painted lips were set in a cruel, triangular grin. Sally looked up from her typewriter in time to catch the expression before it faded.

"She's out for blood," she shuddered.

It was no surprise, therefore, when Miss Vine gave her orders in curtest tones of command.

"Get Waters on the phone. Say he's to come over, this afternoon, to alter my will. Not *now*. Will you kindly have the patience to wait until I have finished? Get Lawrence, first. Tell him to call and see Mr. Francis."

Conscious that Miss Vine's eye was fixed on her, Sally tried to be her usual cool and competent self, as she reminded herself that Charles's interests were not identical with hers. But, to her mind, Anthea and Francis represented a sinister alliance, and she felt hot with resentment as she delivered the message to the lawyer.

Dr. Lawrence obeyed his summons, partly in gratitude for work, and partly in trepidation. As Iris had prophesied, the Learoyd affair had done him no good in the neighborhood, and his engagement book was painfully bare.

In his extremity, he had let the matter of Miss Vine's account slide. Although he had been several times to the Court, for dinner, he had argued that a social occasion was not a right time for any allusion to business. When he had been alone with Anthea, after the reading of her will, he had confined himself to expressions of gratitude.

But he reminded himself, that, sooner or later, he must come to grips with her on the grim subject. The prospect was anything but pleasant, as he was deep in a financial morass.

It was a relief to realize that Francis was his patient, and not Anthea. He was his usual suave, confident self when he left the bedroom, and found Iris waiting for him in the corridor.

"Have tea with me," she invited.

"I will, if there's anything left of me," he whispered. "I've got a business interview with Anthea. Pray for the soul of Glyn Lawrence."

His first glance showed him that Anthea was not in her seductive tea-gown mood. She wore the black satin gown, which signified business, as she sat at her bureau, writing. Her greeting was friendly, but preoccupied.

"What's the matter with him?" she asked, extending her left hand for him to shake.

"He's told you that already," said Lawrence. "He has just informed me that he has incipient pneumonia. If he catches another chill, he may be right, ultimately. Keep him in bed and he'll soon be about again. He's a bit chesty, that's all."

"He shall be cherished," promised Miss Vine. "You've heard about my accident, of course?"

"I was shocked. Why didn't you send for me, to reassure myself and to enable me to—to work off part of my debt to you?"

Miss Vine raised the thin arch of her brows.

"What debt?" she asked.

Lawrence opened his pocketbook and drew out the account.

"I'm desperately ashamed of myself, dear lady," he confessed, "but there hasn't been a chance to mention it before. Of course, I will pay—but will you give me time? Some of my investments have turned out badly, of late."

Anthea glanced at the paper, and frowned.

"How careless of Miss Morgan," she complained. "This is the sort of thing she sends out to my usual debtors. I pay her to discriminate."

Dr. Lawrence experienced a sense of relaxed tension, as though a tight band, constricting his chest, had snapped. In his relief, he spoke at random.

"Perhaps she's in love."

"You mean with—Charles?"

Startled by the yellow glare in her eye, the young man shook his head.

"Aren't we all?" he asked carelessly. "With some one or other?"

"Are you?"

"Dear lady, I cannot afford to be. And now, suppose we talk finance. There's this question of my National Debt. If you are willing, I'd like to propose paying you off, in instalments, and in professional service?"

Anthea rose from her chair and laid her hand on his arm.

"Don't talk nonsense," she said briskly. "If I don't understand the financial problem of a young professional man in Oldtown, who should? I have to finance two beginners myself—poor dear boys."

She spoke simply, with no seductive pursed red lips or flutter of meretricious lashes. Her friendly smile invited confidence, as she continued.

"Surely you can trust me? I don't want to take advantage of your—need. I propose a moratorium. Meantime, you can't live on air. I'm owing you now for a professional visit to Francis."

The young man's thick, finely chiseled lips trembled slightly as Miss Vine sat down at her bureau and wrote a check.

As she flicked it across the table to him, his long eyes caught sight of the figure. Instantly he seized her hand and kissed it with a fervor that was different from his usual mock-homage.

"I can never repay you," he said, with a conscious double meaning.

Anthea merely laughed as she patted his shoulder.

"Oh, I'll find a way for you to pay me, presently. And now, you are not to worry any more. Run away and find

Iris. I have to see my lawyer, and then I have a young man coming to tea with me."

Miss Vine's young man was Charles. When Sally gave him the command invitation, over the telephone, he was only too glad of the excuse to desert his dingy office and come out into the spring afternoon. As he walked to the Court his spirits reacted insensibly to the stipple of green on the hedges and the piping of thrushes from the budding trees. The wet tarred road reflected the sky, so that a blue river rolled on before him.

On the threshold of the great pillared hall he met the lawyer, Mr. Waters, in the company of Miss Vine, who was graciously escorting him to the door. At the sight of Charles, she smiled.

"This is *my* young lawyer," she said. "He's come home, to take pity on my loneliness."

The big man looked bland and glanced down at his ginger beard. In the imagination of a scandalous small town, the fiction eclipsed reality where Miss Vine's relations with her young men were concerned.

"Ha," he remarked in his honeyed voice, "your young man is probably going to send me on the dole, one day. The younger generation, dear lady, is always knocking at the door."

"Then why not play for safety, and combine with the new generation?" asked Anthea. "Come, Mr. Waters—among friends—wouldn't you like to add a new name to your firm?"

At the words, Charles opened his mouth in a fashion that would have been ludicrous, were it not for the hunger in his eyes, as he stared incredulously at Miss Vine.

Mr. Waters stroked his beard.

"That's too big a question for me to give you an offhand answer," he replied. "As you know, we have practically all

159

the best business of the County in our hands. The practice is a legacy, as the name goes down, from father to son. I fear we could not include a newcomer, who would absorb another slice of yearly income, without considerable increase of capital, and some certainty of future revenue."

Miss Vine knew that he referred to her vast interests, which were spread out among several influential firms, outside the town. True to her policy, she trusted no person entirely. The local lawyer, Waters, only got occasional contracts and writs.

She thoughtfully twisted a ring with an enormous emerald, on her finger, before she spoke.

"That should not be too difficult for me. It would be merely a matter of readjustment. Naturally, I should place the interest of my own, before that of strangers. Charles," she placed her hand on the young man's arm, "is my own. He is my cousin."

"He is a very lucky young fellow," said the lawyer, dodging the subject of relationship.

As a sign that the interview was over, Miss Vine extended her hand, in queenly fashion.

"Good-bye, Mr. Waters. I shall expect my will, for signature, tomorrow morning. As for the other matter —sleep on it. I shall be prepared to consider a tentative figure as a basis for negotiation."

When the lawyer had swayed ponderously through the door, Charles enfolded Miss Vine in a gorilla hug.

"Angel. You don't know what this means to me," he said thickly.

"I do," smiled Anthea. "A big bite out of your legacy."

"Hang the miserable legacy. I don't get that till you croak. I'd sooner have this, and you, alive and kicking, at the same time."

He picked her up, like a doll, and held her, while she

kicked him daintily, after the fashion of a heroine on the screen. She was screaming with laughter and her face was flushed under its paint when he put her down again.

"And what will you do when you are a partner?" she asked. "Marry?"

"Even that is possible."

"My little Morgan?"

Charles pretended not to hear.

"Where's Lawrence?" he asked.

"With Iris," Miss Vine told him.

"Will you stand for that? Why don't you warn her off the grass."

He wanted to be alone, to think of his new happiness, but Miss Vine merely smiled.

"Lawrence? I've only to crook my little finger, and he'll come back to me. Do you think *I* am afraid of any girl? No, I'm giving *you,* his privilege—tea with me."

Dr. Lawrence felt no tug of the invisible chain of which Anthea had boasted, as he lounged on an Empire sofa, in the drawing room, his sleek black head resting on a yellow satin cushion. Iris, hovering over the tea things, was like a brilliant painted butterfly, with her exotic tinted face and fluttering hands. She seemed resistless and light as thistle-down, blown in the teeth of a gale, until she raised her eyes.

The intensity of her gaze roused and held his interest. At that moment, she looked hard and relentless as Anthea.

"Well?" she asked. "Are you going to pay her?"

"Ultimately," he replied.

"How?"

"My dear girl, is this your concern?"

Iris clenched her hands.

"I warned you this would happen," she said. "You're letting it slide—slide. You mustn't trust her. She's only playing you."

Dr. Lawrence shook his head.

"She was perfectly charming," he said. "For the first time, I understood her fascination. Her behavior, from first to last, was that of a friend."

Iris laughed bitterly.

"You don't know her," she said. "You will, when it's too late. I—I'm afraid. For she is always most dangerous when she is kind."

CHAPTER XXI

Castles in Spain

CHARLES AWOKE, NEXT MORNING, WITH A CONFUSED impression of a change in his fortune. As recollection rushed back, he rubbed his eyes open in incredulous wonder. It was altogether too good to be true—fairy gold, which, assuredly, had melted overnight.

But the hope persisted while he hurried through his dressing, and bolted down to the morning room, where Iris—in a wispy orchid wrapper—was languidly nibbling toast.

She stared at him with big eyes that were ringed with the traces of a sleepless night, but did not speak.

"Morning, Iris," said Charles briskly. "Been on the tiles? You know there's something wrong with a person who eats no breakfast."

"There *is* something wrong with me." Iris spoke in tragic tones. "Something wrong with you, too. There's something wrong with everyone in this doomed house."

"No, thanks, not with *me*, my angel of good cheer. Leave me out of your merry little list. Now, would you like to pour out my coffee and imagine you're Mrs. Lawrence?"

"Charles, you fatuous person. Will any of us here, ever marry? I can see nothing before us. No hope."

Charles helped himself plentifully from a hot-water dish, and spoke with his mouth full of bacon.

"Cheer up. I thought Lawrence appeared positively chirpy, yesterday. As if he'd stolen the baby's milk, or come into something."

"Oh, he's coming into something, all right. But he won't be warned. Blind as a bat. . . . Do you mind? I want to read."

Iris opened a French novel as her protest against further conversation.

Directly Charles had finished his breakfast he hurried to the study, where the click of the typewriter proclaimed the presence of Sally Morgan. As she looked up from the machine, her eyes held more welcome than her abrupt nod.

"Got any news for me?" asked Charles eagerly. "I mean —from Waters?"

Sally concluded that he was alluding to the alteration of the will, and she wondered from whom he had got his information.

"You must ask Miss Vine," she said. "You know perfectly well that I cannot mention her private affairs, even to you."

Charles burst into a jubilant hoot.

"That's good. Don't you know *I* am the firm of Waters? Any way, a bit of it—a little bit, like the parson's nose."

As Sally's mouth remained open, in her surprise, he told her of his future prospects. She listened with such gravity that he concluded she had breakfasted with Iris.

"Well—what's wrong?" he asked. "I've something definite to work at now, not a miserable farce. And I'll pay Anthea back every penny, honest, if I can lay my fingers on any trust money. Oh, Sally, you might be matey and laugh."

Sally complied with a ghastly forced grin.

"It's marvelous," she said, "if it's true. But I do so wish it wasn't coming from *her*. It seems just the same familiar old position, dressed up differently."

"Well—I'm hanged." Charles shook his head hopelessly. "What do you want me to do?"

"What do your brothers do for a living?"

"Let me see. The family fortune was spent on my eldest brother. He's a curate. The others have not done so well."

"But what do *they* do?"

"You shall know the worst. One is a cinema-operator."

Sally clapped her hands.

"Fine. He looked ahead and chose a coming profession. Oh, I'm so glad *one* out of your big family has intuition and enterprise."

"For a pure young girl, you think of remarkably nasty things," said Charles. "Just as I was going to ask you to marry me, too."

"Just as I was going to accept you, too," retorted Sally. "And remember, opportunity never knocks twice. You've lost your chance."

Charles stood his ground.

"Why are you crabbing this?" he asked.

"Because I don't believe in it. You've told me Miss Vine has done this sort of thing before."

"Nothing so definite as this. She's only thrown out hints about future negotiations, and so on. Why, she tackled old Waters under my nose. . . . Still—you may be right."

He stood staring out of the window, his hunched shoulders conveying an impression of utter hopelessness. Sunken in depression, he did not turn his head when Miss Vine, swathed in a fur coat, entered.

"Not expecting me?" she hinted, glancing at Sally's visitor.

"I'm always expecting you," was the quiet reply.

"Good. But remember, it's the unexpected that happens. You will have to carry on without me, today. I'm going down to the town, to rush through this little business about

Charles. If that gentleman will have the courtesy to look at me, I wish to say something to him."

Instantly, Charles swung round on his heel, as though he were her puppet, galvanized to life by her own vitality.

"I've little time to spare for you, Charles," said Miss Vine, "so I'm smashing through the law's delay. I rang up Waters, from my little bed, this morning, and extracted his hopeful idea of what I'm prepared to pay. There's a shock coming to him. Now, Charles, when I'm through with licking the agreement into shape, you must be prepared to come down to the office, immediately, to sign. Old Waters will be bristling with opposition, but I intend to sleep tonight knowing that your future is assured."

"I'll live at the end of the wire," muttered Charles shakily.

He had no words to express his thanks. The confirmation of his good news had stunned him to utter bewilderment.

Miss Vine shook her head with a benevolent smile.

"You needn't do that until the afternoon," she told him. "I suggest you run out to Timberdale in the car. Take Miss Morgan with you. I want a personal note delivered, by hand, to Mrs. Law."

Charles came to life.

"Shall we drop you in the town?" he asked.

"No," replied Miss Vine, "I trust no one to drive *me*. Besides, I'm going first, to make my morning reflections."

"Do you mean to tell me you are actually going to hang over the lake again?" asked Charles.

"Certainly. Now that the rotten bough is removed, I can trust the tree."

"But—it wasn't rotten, Anthea."

"Do you think I've forgotten that? It is my most stimulating reminder that someone living under my roof, and eating my bread, has wished to murder me.... Miss Morgan, here is the note. Good-bye, Charles."

When Anthea had gone, Charles turned to Sally, his face beaming with happiness. He saw its reflection in her own radiant eyes, as she impulsively caught his hands.

"Oh, Charles, it's wonderful. She really *means* it. I'm so glad for you."

"And I'm glad for you. For both of us. For everybody. Now, Sally—what about it? You know what I mean?"

Sally ran her fingers distractedly through the accurate lines of her permanent wave.

"I can't be quite certain," she said. "Of course, I like you better than anyone. But I'm not sure I can trust you. Too many other girls."

"And there always will be. I won't lie to you—not now. But I will, afterwards. It will be up to *you*. Oh, Sally, those other girls meant nothing to me. There's only one I ever wanted to marry. You're the one that can hold me."

"I'll keep you on the chain, all right, my bright young lad," Sally promised him. "I just couldn't bear to lose you to another girl. You're not the answer to a maiden's prayer —but you're something better. You're *you*."

Outside the door, Miss Vine watched their kiss, through the keyhole. When she rose from her knees and walked slowly between the pillars of the marble hall, only the dim portrait of somebody's ancestor saw the expression of her face.

The pale sun was shining when Charles and Sally motored out to Timberdale. In the fields, the green sea of summer was just rising through the winter dun, and lambs were racing each other over the grass. The catkins in the hedges and a sprinkling of celandines told that Nature was entering into her annual conspiracy with the future to lure lovers to their fate.

The car ate up the road only too quickly, and Charles stopped her before the Timberdale Arms. It was a low, long building, dim with age, with a lichened roof and a cobbled yard.

Sally pulled down her mouth.

"I see no special beauty in that old barn," she said. "It looks dark and damp and smelly. I'm beginning to think Miss Vine is a public benefactor to want to pull it down."

"Girls have no poetry or sense of beauty," objected Charles. "It's a glorious old pub. Makes you feel at home. Heaven knows how old it is."

"Then it's time it came down."

"That's the modern utilitarian spirit. I believe women would like to link up the world with Hell, for purposes of central-heating."

"If so, it would pay, for the first time," retorted Sally. "Men have failed to make sin a good business proposition."

Mrs. Law—her wonderful golden hair gleaming in the light—came out to meet them, with her usual suggestion of loud-voiced hospitality. Her laughter mingled with the barking of the four dogs that accompanied her; but sheer noise could not disguise the fact that her high spirits were assumed.

"I'd begun to think you'd forsaken us," she reproached Charles.

"Could I?" appealed Charles. "I'd as soon forsake my mother. That reminds me I *have* forsaken my mother, only she began it, when I was young. Fact is, Mrs. Law, I've been—as per usual—broke."

"And couldn't you chalk up your score like the rest?" demanded Mrs. Law. "You know quite well I'm not one of your pikes. You could take your own time to pay. . . . Well, come in. Someone's been missing you."

Charles glanced guiltily at Sally, as the barmaid—a sprightly brunette with an attractive Eton crop—smiled her welcome. But she noticed that, although he gave the charmer a surreptitious wink, his real interest was reserved for the dogs, who overwhelmed him with their attentions.

He apologized for his popularity.

"They always prefer low characters. By the way, you don't know Miss Morgan."

"Oh, yes." Mrs. Law spoke curtly. "I think we've met before. Isn't she Miss Vine's private and confidential secretary?"

As she remembered the humiliation of the interview, Sally forgave Mrs. Law's hostility.

"You've got to sample the home-brewed, Sally," interrupted Charles. "And make yourself at home. This"—he pointed to an earthen receptacle—"is where you spit."

"How thoughtful," said Sally, as she sipped her ale. "Everything provided. But I've really come on business, Mrs. Law. I've a personal note from Miss Vine."

Mrs. Law's face seemed to swell and darken under its coating of powder. She had the mentality of those who believe that every problem in life can be easily solved by the formula—"I don't know."

The plan had worked excellently as long as there were more enterprising spirits to accept her shelved responsibilities; but although she declaimed her present trouble to everyone in her bar, she collected plenty of sympathy, but no practical help.

Her hand shook as she tore open the envelope. But, as she read the note, her expression changed.

"Of course, *you* know what it's about," she remarked to Sally.

"No," replied Sally. "Miss Vine wrote it herself."

"Well—it's a—a sort of climb-down. She reminds me that, as I've done nothing about her offer, it may be all off. Come, Miss Morgan, *you're* in the know. Is she giving up the idea of building?"

"I'm afraid I know nothing," said Sally.

"I might have known *you* wouldn't," remarked Mrs. Law.

Sally remained silent, caution at war with her natural kindliness. She longed to reassure the big fair woman with some hint of the true state of affairs, as she understood it.

As a matter of fact, she was perplexed by Miss Vine's insistence on the new hotel. The economic factors seemed to indicate that it would not be a financial success, and the other directors were tepid, if not hostile, to the scheme. Only yesterday, a batch of new figures had been received, which, in other circumstances, would have caused Miss Vine to axe the whole concern.

But she held the controlling shares, and she seemed inspired by some curious personal animus in pushing on the new Munster. Her note, however, to Mrs. Law, seemed to hint at private surrender.

Mrs. Law heaved a deep sigh as she looked round her bar.

"Well, you can't help hoping," she said. "I suppose, it's the spring."

"Hope's in the air," said Charles, unable to restrain a hint of his own good fortune. "Why, even I might get married, one of these wet days."

"Then Heaven help the poor girl," remarked the attractive barmaid.

"Heaven will," said Mrs. Law unkindly, "for she'll be one of Nature's fools."

Charles grinned at Sally as he pushed Sultan away with a final pat.

"If I do get married," he said, "I know one thing. I'll keep a dog. I only want a home for that."

As he motored back with Sally castles were rising in the air, like the silver clouds piling up against the clear azure stain of the sky. Every kind of incongruous fancy frothed and rioted in Charles' brain. He saw himself working at dynamic pressure—burning midnight oil, to increase the fortunes of the firm—building a fine house—standing for Parliament—sitting on the Woolsack.

Dogs romped in and out of every dream, and Sally smiled at him, from every fresh castle; but it was the sad fact that he had completely forgotten to give his Immortality a place in the picture.

He spent the whole afternoon sitting by the telephone, feeling much like the faithful hound on his master's grave. When, at last the bell rang, his heart pounded so violently that he wondered if he were a victim of unsuspected disease.

"Will Mr. Charles Ford come at once to Mr. Waters' office?" asked the bored voice of a clerk.

Charles drove at sensational speed, on his way to the town, and disregarded a policeman's signal. He was worked up to such a pitch of excitement that he entered the offices of Waters & Son in a state bordering on collapse.

Dimly conscious of stately mahogany and Spanish leather, which advertised the prosperity of his new firm, and of Mr. Waters, beaming above his ginger beard, he wrote his signature, in a shaky hand, on a blurred document.

Anthea was the first to congratulate the new partner.

"I'm going to drive you back," she said, "in honor of the occasion. I've sent my own car back."

Charles came out of his dream as they passed through the gates of Jamaica Court.

"Anthea," he said solemnly, "if I can ever do anything for you, I will."

"You can do something now," she replied lightly, giving a dry scented cheek to kiss. "Take the car round to the garage. I'm getting out."

In the twilight, the lake looked dark and forbidding at its deepest end. As Anthea minced over the plank of the bridge, she shuddered at a memory of mud and reedy darkness.

A few feet below her lay a watery hell. Then she raised her eyes to the willow-tree, and stared at a raw scar on its trunk.

She had passed through all the agony of drowning. Not one pang had been spared to her. Francis had but awakened her from the rest of oblivion when he had restored her to life.

"I *was* drowned," she said. "They murdered me."

CHAPTER XXII

A Change of Heart

ALTHOUGH CHARLES WANTED TO BROADCAST THEIR engagement, Sally insisted on secrecy, for the present.

"Are you afraid you'll be stung?" asked Charles indignantly. "Haven't I signed the Deed of Partnership?"

Sally set her lips.

"You're going the right way to get a black eye, on account," she said. "And I want you to get this straight. I'd have been happier if you'd broken first with Miss Vine, and let your future prospects go hang."

"I see. So that you'd have a good excuse to chuck me over."

"No, in that case, I'd say let's emigrate. We'd probably only join the unemployed, but we could take our chance of luck."

"All this doesn't explain your hole-and-corner policy," grumbled Charles.

Sally's severe young face softened.

"I am so terribly afraid I might injure you with *her,*" she said. "Miss Vine will be furious at the thought of another woman."

"But she could do nothing—now."

"Can't she? There's still one thing that's worrying me. Has she signed the check for Mr. Waters yet?"

"No, and for a good reason. He was going up to Scotland,

by the night express. But she said the check would be waiting for him, on his return."

"I see," said Sally. "Now, Charles, don't you think we had better say nothing until the check is actually signed?"

Charles agreed, as the old misgiving returned. Even now, at the very last minute, a woman's caprice, or jealousy, might cheat him of his happiness.

He was not reassured, as he walked moodily upstairs, by the sound of Francis' voice raised in croaking jubilation. It was ominous of a secret understanding with Anthea, to his advantage.

"Oh, that will be—Glory for me——"

Charles looked inside the bedroom, which was so decorated with hothouse blooms as to resemble a prima donna's dressing room. Francis—sitting beside a huge fire, in his violet brocade dressing gown—explained the flowers.

"Anthea sends them. By the way, she's my only visitor. Why doesn't Iris come? I'm doing her a good turn by having Lawrence every day."

"You rag her so," explained Charles. "The poor kid's edgy. Too much reaction. Say a civil word to her, and she blasts."

"Perhaps she has reason," smiled Francis. "Woman's intuition, you know, although I'd back my own against any woman's. It tells me that Anthea's altogether too sweet. Before long her will will be as worthless as a curlpaper."

"What d'you mean?" asked Charles.

"Please don't talk," pleaded Francis sweetly. "It's sending my temperature up. And I want to be a little angel and sing."

Only a little later, Charles, himself, wanted to shout, for even as the new cloud appeared on the horizon, it shredded again into thin air. Sally Morgan—watchful and on guard —entered the study, to find Miss Vine writing at her bureau. The girl's heart leaped as she noticed that her employer was filling in a check. As she wrote the figures, she appeared to be swayed by impulse, for she held it out, so that her secretary could see the amount.

"Look, Morgan, it positively staggers me. All that money for my sweetheart."

She licked her geranium lips cautiously at the light that glowed in Sally's eyes. Afraid of betraying her joy, Sally turned quickly to her typewriter.

She had seen more than the total. Her hurried glance had assured her that the check was made payable to Waters & Son.

A minute later, Miss Vine gave her the sealed envelope, addressed to the lawyer.

"Post that yourself, Morgan. Waters will be home to-night, probably, and he will be expecting it."

Sally laid it nonchalantly on her desk, as though it were an ordinary business letter. Hugging her secret, she felt almost guilty of treachery when her employer spoke in a gentle voice.

"Morgan, I want all the figures of what Lawrence is owing me. Include the last check, and work out the interest. Five per cent will be enough. It's been hanging over his head too long, poor boy. I feel it is bad for his work, to keep him in suspense."

"Yes, Miss Vine," said Sally.

Her own happiness made her feel a little sorry for the unfortunate doctor, whose handsome face had proved too heavy a handicap. It was a welcome surprise when Miss Vine appeared to doubt her own judgment.

"Morgan," she said, "you have remarkably shrewd common sense, for your years. I wish I could have trained you from the beginning, for I could have made something of you. . . . Now, I want your truthful opinion on this Lawrence debt. Do you think I ought to write it off?"

Sally's brow puckered as she considered the problem. The knowledge that she was on trial made her anxious to justify Miss Vine's compliment.

"I am afraid that I shall sound ruthless," she said at last, "because, if one puts sentiment aside, I think Dr. Lawrence shows up rather badly. He must be mushy to have got into such a mess. I can understand, and forgive, the usual sort of debt. But, to my mind, it is rotten to accept an expensive car from a woman—which is what it practically amounts to."

"But I seem here, to be sponged on, Sally."

"You mean Charles—and Mr. Francis?" Miss Vine noticed that the second name was an afterthought. "But they wouldn't have gone as far as this. In any case, their position is quite different. They are your own relatives, and you assumed a definite responsibility."

"In fact, I've been a mother to them, Sally?"

In her earnestness, the girl failed to notice the double danger signal of the honied voice and her Christian name.

"I'm sure you have," she said heartily.

Contrary to her custom, Miss Vine did not spring, but continued to purr.

"Then would you advise me to enforce this debt? Remember, it would mean ruin to a young professional man at the beginning of his career. I've worked my own way up, Sally, so I know how hard life can be to beginners."

"Well, I've done the same," said Sally. "But I kept myself without any help, and I never got into debt. All the same, it would be a wonderfully generous gesture to reduce the debt to something he could pay without being crippled."

"Yes, but why should I do this?" asked Miss Vine. "Is there any moral obligation on my part?"

Sally hesitated, and then took the plunge boldly.

"Well, I feel that, perhaps, we were a little to blame for not making him understand exactly where he stood."

"But, surely, you—as my secretary—sent him the formal reminder, every month?"

"I did. But the payments were allowed to slip and slide, and nothing said."

Miss Vine half-closed her lids, so that her eyes were veiled by her preposterously long lashes.

"Thank you, Sally," she said, "for your youthful wisdom. You have given me something to think about. And now, go and post that letter to Mr. Waters. It means everything to Charles."

She had proved her secretary to be a model of discretion and reticence; yet, when she released her, it was equivalent to launching a herald of universal joy. Sally met Charles in the hall, where he hung about as though to gain some private information through staring at the study door. At the sight of his anxious eyes she slipped into indiscretion.

"One peep only," she whispered, showing him the envelope.

"S—Sally," stammered Charles, "is it the check?"

"I've seen it," she nodded. "It's far too much. You aren't worth it. And now, you're to forget you know."

"Quite. I'll detain you no longer, Miss Morgan, and waste your employer's time," said Charles formally.

It was quite a walk down the long winding drive, to the postbox, outside the gates, and Sally drank in mental vigor with the sharpness of the air. As she wondered at Miss Vine's unusual gentleness, she seemed, suddenly, to trace it back to its source.

"Her escape from drowning. Of course. No one could be so near to death and not think of—of what comes after. She's been hard to others all her life, but she wants to make it up to them before it's too late."

When she reached the house, Iris was lounging on the

177

terrace, drooping and exquisite as a fragile flower which had been denied water.

In her zeal as the perfect private secretary, Sally—who played, perhaps, rather too much for safety—had been careful not to endanger her business relations by personal intercourse with the other inmates of Jamaica Court. Iris, for her part, made no advances of friendship to Sally, and seemed rather to resent her attraction and capability.

But, touched by the sight of Iris' heavy eyes, Sally spoke impulsively.

"It's lovely out. Wouldn't a walk do you good?"

Iris laughed scornfully.

"What a hope. I—I'm so desperately worried. Fresh air can't set my mind at rest. But *you* could."

Sally regretted her first kindly impulse.

"Honestly, I would, if I could," she said. "But, I must warn you that, if it has anything to do with Miss Vine's affairs, my lips are sealed."

"Of course, it has to do with Anthea. Do you think I want a weather report?" Iris clasped her hand appealingly on Sally's arm. "Oh, Miss Morgan, do stop being a machine, and come alive. After all, we're both girls. And I'm in such trouble."

"Trouble?" repeated Sally.

"Yes. I'm really frightened about the money Glyn Lawrence owes to Anthea. Is she going to enforce payment? If she does, it will ruin him."

The pressure of Iris' fingers on her arm melted Sally's resolution, so that she slipped from the peak of her own high standard.

"I can tell you nothing," she said. "But Miss Vine seems —changed, today. Being so near to death must make a difference to anyone. They get a new angle on things. If I were you, instead of worrying, I should *hope*."

At the words, Iris' eyes grew luminous.

"You really think I can?"

"I do. And now, for goodness' sake, forget I've told you anything."

"I'm not the woman I was," reflected Sally, as she went back to the empty study. "It's as well I'm getting married, for I shall never follow in Miss Vine's footsteps."

At that minute those footsteps would have led her to the deep end of the lake, where Miss Vine stood on the little bridge staring at a torn stump of willow.

Sally would have been still more concerned at the effect of her indiscretion had she known that Charles was also assisting in the mass production of optimism. As he entered the "Bull"—the little public house opposite his office—he ran into Superintendent Pye, who was drinking at the bar.

His big face was a compound of doubt, bewilderment and gloom; for he was his own severest critic over his failure to recover the Colonel's vase. The physical discomforts of his nightly vigils, which his host insisted on sharing, together with the dislocation of his habits, was telling upon him.

Far worse than these, however, was the Colonel's skepticism, which got under Pye's skin and rasped his nerves. It took every ounce of resolution to persist in his occupation of a house where he knew himself to be an intruder.

Over and above his own humiliation, hung the shadow of his sister's trouble. His surly expression reminded Charles of some big clownish dog who has seen a proffered bone withdrawn within an inch of his open jaws.

"You look as if Old Man Worry had been sitting on your chest, all night, Pye," he said.

Pye's mouth drooped at the reminder of his forsaken bed.

"Matter of fact," he admitted, "I *am* bothered. My sister

—Mrs. Law, you know—tells me there's some talk of a Munster Hotel at Timberdale. That's not too cheerful news for a young widow with her living to make."

Charles looked round the bar, and then dropped his voice. "Cheer up," he said, "and have one with me, just to show you're not proud. I can't help my blooming relations, can I?"

"And they can't help you," grinned Pye. "Well—'Here's gravy with your bread.' "

" 'Here's bone in your stew,' " responded Charles, raising his tumbler. "And, Pye, under the hat, I was at the little old pub, yesterday, when your sister had a note from my beloved cousin, which sort of hinted that the new Munster is off."

Pye's big red face shone like a harvest moon.

"Now, is that really so? I've been away from home, most of my time, lately, so I've seen nothing of the girls. But, that's really fine news."

The wave of optimism went lapping on its way. When Dr. Lawrence called at the Court, to pay his daily visit to Francis, Iris met him outside the great gates.

"Why am I honored?" he asked, as he stopped his car. "It's sweet of you, but don't you think we'd better be careful? *Someone's* on the watch, and only waiting to pounce."

Iris laughed.

"Afraid of Anthea?" she asked.

"I thought *you* were, and on my account," fenced Lawrence. "Personally, I'm a fatalist. I feel I am doomed. But I am also reminded that there are many doors out."

"You mean—suicide?" gasped Iris.

"No. I merely infer that a doctor's life is a chancey one, with scratches and germs. But you had better not drive with me to the door, for I am also reminded that while there's life, there is hope. My snake tells me you've good news."

His eyes gleamed under their heavy lids as he listened to Iris' story.

"You got that from Miss Morgan?" he asked. "Then it's definite. She's not the sort of girl that tells fortunes in teacups."

His relief was evident in his manner when he entered Anthea's boudoir, after he had visited his patient. His graceful greeting proclaimed him the courtier paying homage to his lady. She was coiled on the divan, amid a pile of cushions, smoking a tiny cigarette in a ridiculously long scarlet holder. As she extended her small hand, he noticed that each nail was enameled with a different emblem—a crescent moon—a heart—a rose.

"Help me up," she said. "I've something to say to you, and it will come easier if I walk about."

Sunken deep in his low chair, he watched her as she paced the room, the wide legs of her black satin pajama-trousers flapping like miniature skirts. In the light of Iris' news, he believed that she was going to give him a formal quittance of his debt.

As he waited for her to speak, he felt the dreamy bliss of one who steeps in August sunshine, listening to the drowsy hum of bees over beds of mignonette.

"May I smoke?" he asked lazily.

"You may. Oh, I forgot? How is my beloved boy today?"

"Francis? He can get up tomorrow and carry on, as usual. Curious chap, isn't he?"

"Yes, he's prehistoric. He's lived many lives before, and remembers the evil and humor of them all. I'm glad he's well again."

Anthea heaved a sigh.

"That's the good part," she said. "Now for the bad. Glyn, I have something very important to say. Perhaps you already know it. I've just been informed, from a reliable source, that there is a slander in circulation about myself."

Lawrence's thought flew to Francis and Charles, as he blew out his match, to indicate that his cigarette could wait on her need.

"That's atrocious," he said. "Can you tell me what it is, dear lady?"

"I can," replied Anthea. "It is about—me and—you."

The young man's heart dropped a beat as she went on speaking.

"It is generally said, in the neighborhood, that I am *keeping* you."

Dr. Lawrence wiped the tiny beads of moisture from his upper lip.

"But this is preposterous," he said. "It's childish. Not worth considering."

"That is easily said, Glyn. You forget that *my* reputation is at stake."

"Of course. Your honor must be vindicated. Tell me who you heard this from. We must trace this slander back and make the original liar eat his own words."

"Trace it back?" Anthea laughed scornfully. "You—a man-of-the-world to suggest this. You know it's impossible. ... No. I mean to kill the slander myself."

"How?"

"In the only way. I'm sorry, Glyn, but I have no one to fight for me."

She held out a paper she had concealed in her palm.

"Your account," she explained. "I must ask you to **pay** it immediately, in order to protect my good name."

The paper shook in Lawrence's hand as he glanced at the total.

"That's impossible," he declared thickly. "My only chance is to work it off, as I've explained before."

"But, in the circumstances, I can no longer send for you," remarked Miss Vine. "Surely you understand that? I am an unmarried woman."

Dr. Lawrence pushed back his hair from his brow.

"Are you in earnest about this?" he asked.

"Perfectly."

"Then there's nothing for it but to file my petition. It'll break me completely. I'm afraid you will get nothing out of it, except the car."

"But I don't *want* the car," cried Anthea, like some fractious child. "It's secondhand. I've beautiful cars of my own."

Dr. Lawrence rose and stood looking down at her.

"What *do* you want?" he asked. "To ruin me?"

Anthea nestled among her cushions and blew a reflective ring of smoke.

"There are ways and means of settling," she reminded him. "Ever since I fell in the lake I've been passing my life in review. And it has struck me that, although I have achieved far more than the average woman, I have missed one experience common to my charwoman. Marriage."

Lawrence's face grew clay-color as he tried to laugh.

"I shouldn't try it, if I were you," he advised. "You're better off as you are. You have a marvelous position—wealth and freedom. Every man is in love with you. You couldn't be content now with one."

He scarcely knew what he said in his agitation and fear, so obsessed was he with a sense of his own weakness. Conscious of the stranglehold of a will power far superior to his own, he felt hypnotized as a rabbit before a snake.

Miss Vine watched his face while she smiled to herself.

"Although I am essentially feminine," she said, "I have a man's brain. I have learned my business policy from men.

I possess their grip of big problems and their ruthlessness. And—I've learned something else from them."

As he listened, Dr. Lawrence grew cold with foreboding.

"I learned," continued Anthea, "that when a director had an affair with an employee, he chose the youngest and most attractive. I see no reason why I should not do the same. The same rules apply to either sex. The only factor is wealth. Those directors were bald, fat, bandy, but they had only to sign a check, and they were suited. I can do the same. Only —I am far more attractive than them."

"You mean—you want to marry a *young* man?" asked Lawrence, in a low voice. "But it never pays. In the end, the woman always suffers—wretchedly."

"That's my affair," said Anthea. "Now, you must go. I am busy. But I hope you have grasped the position. I *must* protect my good name."

184

CHAPTER XXIII

Crisis

IRIS—HER EYES SHINING WITH HOPE—WAS WAITING FOR Lawrence, in the corridor.

"Well?" she asked. "Is it all right?"

He looked at her stupidly, like a man stunned by shock. Then, as he noticed the clear-cut corners of her mouth and the sheen of her leaf-brown hair, he caught her in his arms.

"I've got to kiss someone young," he said.

Instead of a caress from Iris, he received a blow.

"I don't want any of your wholesale attentions," she told him angrily. "You make me sick. Go back to *her*."

He laughed as he rubbed his cheek.

"Thank you," he said. "That's wholesome, and I feel better for it. . . . But you've got to listen to me. I've never kissed Anthea. I've only choked her with flattery. Only, just now, she—she rushed me."

At the sound of voices outside his door, Francis—looking like a tall, lean monk in his purple dressing gown—stole across the carpet, to secure the strategic position of the key hole.

He heard Iris laugh heartlessly.

"Don't palpitate. Men are absurd. Think of the women who have to put up with unwelcome attentions, for economic reasons."

"But women are tougher and coarser-grained than men."

Lawrence again wiped his lip at the memory of his interview. "I'd rather cut my throat than marry an old woman."

At his word Iris' lips quivered with fear.

"But we're not talking of *marriage*," she said in a sharp, thin voice.

"No. But *she* is."

"Repulsive," shuddered Iris. "Still, it has nothing to do with you."

"Of course not."

"You can't be married against your will."

"I can." Lawrence's voice shook. "Sally Morgan's sold us a pup. Things could not be worse. Anthea has me cornered, and I'm broke to the wide. I can see no way out. . . . But it's horrible. That painted scarecrow."

"Don't be emotional." Iris faced the crisis with unsuspected calm. "That won't help. Listen. You are not going to marry her. You have only to exert your will to resist her."

"That's all. But, when she looks at me, I feel like pulp. You have no idea of her deadly will power. It's like suction."

"So you're finding out, at last, what she really is?" Iris laughed mirthlessly. "I warned you, remember."

Suddenly Lawrence seized her in his arms, holding on to her with the grip of a drowning man.

"Marry me, Iris," he pleaded. "Then I'll be safe from her."

On the other side of the door, Francis heard the happiness bubbling up in the girl's exultant voice, and he guessed that her arms were around the doctor's neck.

"Of course, darling, I've been waiting for that. Oh, isn't this glorious? We're a partnership, now, against old Anthea, and we must win."

Francis' lips worked in silent laughter. All the evil and humor of those ancient memories with which Anthea had credited him, were concentrated in his grin. His mind was

186

always a leap ahead of the other person, but, apparently, Lawrence swooped swiftly on the same trail, for he gave a faint groan.

"No, darling, forget it. We can't marry. It would be sheer madness. Neither of us has a bean."

"Hush," commanded Iris. "Francis may hear."

"Not he. He's a complete example of a concentrated Ego. Interesting from a medical point of view, but not exactly an endearing character."

"But he has a sense of humor. I know him better than you. He loves to snoop. Hush. Now, listen to me."

She began to talk in eager whispers, which Francis had difficulty in hearing, even with his pointed ear laid over the keyhole.

The voices hummed on, as though marooned bees were buzzing towards freedom. Presently, Lawrence began to walked slowly away down the corridor.

"I must go. Bless you, darling. I feel an utter sweep for dragging you into this mess."

"And I've never been so happy before." Iris' voice was sharp with excitement, and unlike her usual bored drawl. "I've someone to fight for now."

"But you're not going to challenge Anthea? For Heaven's sake, don't. You're only asking to be eaten."

"I'm not afraid," declared Iris triumphantly.

Her boast was not an empty one, for, later that evening, she invaded Miss Vine's blue-and-silver bedroom, with the tempestuous sweep of a young whirlwind.

Anthea—resplendent in golden brocade—turned from the toilet table, one cheek crimson as a damask rose, and the other unrouged.

"What do you want?" she asked imperiously.

"To talk. Please send Eames away. I'll finish the job for

her, and my hand's in, through practice on my own face. *You* don't improve on Nature, do you, Eames?"

"No, Miss Iris," replied Eames primly, surrendering the hare's foot before she obeyed her mistress' nod of dismissal.

Iris, tall and slim in her billowing flounces of yellow tulle, looked like a daffodil swaying before the wind, as she stooped over Anthea and delicately pecked at her face.

"I've always yearned to do this," she said. "I sometimes think that Eames has lost her eye. She makes you look artificial, Anthea."

Anthea, simpering in the glass, was gratified by her own reflection, so that she felt a momentary softening towards the girl.

"I would let you do this for me always," she said graciously, "only it would mean more leisure still for Eames. I have not exactly a sluggish brain, Iris, but even my ingenuity cannot discover how to make that woman earn her wages."

"But you must have something for something?" asked Iris.

"I should like it, for the sake of novelty. I am used only to receiving nothing for something."

Iris was silenced by the thrust. She had come to demand fresh favors as a moral right, only to be reminded of unfulfilled obligations.

The strength of Anthea's hatred for her youth and beauty hung heavy on the air, like an actual force. She felt its pressure and remembered Lawrence's warning of the suction of Anthea's will.

"You don't like me, Anthea," she ventured.

"Why should I?" flashed Miss Vine. "*You* hate me."

"No, no."

"Don't lie. You are jealous of me. You know that men come for you, but they stay because of me."

Utterly staggered by the charge, Iris stared incredulously at the peaked painted face in the mirror. But it was not only caution which warned her not to flame into responsive fury. The pressure of Lawrence's lips was still fresh upon her own, stirring her to pity.

This derelict of her own generation actually wanted to wade back again into the sea of time, damming back the waters with her own indomitable resolution. She craved marriage, even while the tide of new life was flowing in, sweeping the wreckage of the past away.

Full of compassion, Iris made a fresh effort.

"You're hard and bitter, Anthea. Perhaps I've been to blame. I've taken your generosity too much for granted. But—I really have wanted to be friends with you. That night, when you were so ill, I felt nearer to you, and I thought we would begin all over again. But, the next day, you sent me away."

"Yes, my eyes were opened then," said Anthea. "You got me on my blind side, that night. But it wasn't difficult to understand your anxiety not to let me die, intestate."

"Just what Francis said," flashed Iris. "But I never believed that *you* would credit me with only the basest motives."

Anthea put her head on one side and looked up at the girl, like an ancient inquisitive parrot.

"So Francis said that, too?" she murmured. "Odd, how our minds chime. He has an impure knowledge of human nature, but he is the only one who has proved his loyalty."

"Charles would have done the same," said Iris.

"So you say. But it's hard to believe when I have the actual evidence that someone under my roof has deliberately planned to murder me. Someone who knew that I was in the habit of entrusting myself to that bough of willow." Her face crumpled up. "And it broke, in my hand, like a blade of grass. Shall I ever forget?"

Iris shrugged her shoulders helplessly.

"I see. You distrust me entirely. I can never convince you. I was mad to come."

"Then you had some object in coming?" asked Anthea. "What was it?"

"I won't waste your time, now. I was going to ask you for something. That's all."

"For yourself?"

"No, for Glyn Lawrence."

"Aha." Anthea traced an opulent Cupid's bow above her shrunken lips. "You want me to cancel that young man's debt, I suppose?"

"I was hoping even for that," admitted Iris.

"And why should you hope?" persisted Anthea.

Iris paused doubtfully, for she knew Miss Vine's talent for a lightning guess.

"I don't know," she replied lamely.

Anthea's eyes scorched her face, like a prairie fire.

"I suppose," she said, "that Charles has got wind of some of my private business, and has been circulating a rumor that old Anthea has repented her sins?"

"No, Charles has said nothing to me," protested Iris.

But the guilty flush on her face had betrayed her to Miss Vine. There was a triumphant glitter in her eyes as she swept from her room, and down the great marble staircase, followed by a cringing spidery little shadow.

Charles was smoking a cigarette in the hall, while he stared at the study door, as though expectant of seeing someone. At the sight of him, a cruel smile flickered around Anthea's painted lips. She left the door of the study open behind her, as she called sharply to her secretary.

"Miss Morgan."

Sally looked up from her typewriter, with a nervous start. Conscious of her lapse from discretion, her usual confident calm had deserted her.

"Miss Morgan," repeated Miss Vine, "I want an explanation of your conduct."

"Certainly, Miss Vine, I will explain anything I can," replied Sally meekly.

She was aware that Iris hovered outside, in the hall, and that Charles was standing in the doorway. Catching his eye, she shook her head, to signal a need for caution.

"If the fool tries to champion me, we're both lost," she thought. "But he will—the darling."

Miss Vine raised her lorgnette.

"That is an interesting bit of wireless, Miss Morgan," she observed. "But you forget that I, also, have graduated in telegraphic communication. I only needed that shake of your head to convince me that you are both in collusion."

Even as Sally had feared, Charles blundered into her trap.

"What the dickens is the matter, Anthea?" he asked. "What has poor Miss Morgan done to get your goat?"

Miss Vine's agile mind leaped, like an ape, to her conclusion.

"I am accusing Miss Morgan of showing you a private letter to my solicitor," she said.

"Not on your life, Anthea. Only the envelope."

"Then she showed you that?" Anthea pounced on her victim. "She gave away information, regardless of her duty to her employer. I do not expect brains or initiative in my so-called secretary. If I can procure a shorthand-typist, who can spell correctly, I have schooled myself to believe that I am suited. But, when I consider the high salary I pay, for two qualities only—loyalty and discretion—I feel I am entitled to those."

"I am very sorry, Miss Vine," said Sally.

It was contrary to her code, ever to defend herself. She did not care how much dust she ate, so long as Charles was not goaded to the imprudence of intercession. Yet she was puzzled by the personal bitterness of the attack, which was entirely different from the formal blame, accorded to and accepted by a private secretary, in the presence of a third person, in order to oil the wheels of business.

She saw that Charles, too, was perplexed, for he stared at Anthea as though he doubted his own ears. She looked at him out of the corner of her eye, and then spoke to Sally, in a voice which cut like a wire whip.

"Your sorrow comes too late to help you, Miss Morgan. I am disappointed and disgusted with you. Kindly take a month's notice."

"Yes, Miss Vine," said Sally.

Rising hurriedly from her chair, she walked out of the room.

"Keep quiet," she whispered to Charles, as she passed him.

To her dismay, he put his arm around her, and swung her round, so that they faced Miss Vine, together.

"If Sally goes, I go, too, Anthea," he said.

Iris—standing in the hall—watched the scene, as though she were the spectator of a drama. While she reproached herself bitterly for her own indiscretion, she was overwhelmed by the revelation of Miss Vine's treachery. It was evident to her that the whole scene had been leading up to her design to make Charles betray his secret.

Miss Vine raised her painted brows.

"May I ask what this young person is to you?" she asked.

"We're going to get married," replied Charles exultantly.

Miss Vine's eyes gleamed.

"May I be the first to congratulate you, Charles?" she

asked. "It is very noble of you to sacrifice your future for the sake of this young typist."

Charles glanced at Sally, and saw the dawn of fear in her eyes.

"I don't quite understand, Anthea," he said. "Honestly, I am sorry to go against your wishes. But a man must settle this marriage business for himself."

"But, dear Charles," murmured Miss Vine, "I have always looked on my past generosity to the three of you, as a thank-offering for my prosperity. So you owe me nothing and need not consider my wishes."

"But I do, Anthea. There's the partnership."

"Oh, that lapses, of course, if you marry against my wish."

As Charles pushed back his red cowlick, in utter perplexity, from his brow, Miss Vine began to laugh, on a high shrill note.

"You're thinking of that check?" she whinnied. "But, tonight old Waters will look at it and say to his son, patronizingly, 'Here's your super-businesswoman. She fills in a check, but forgets to sign it.'"

There was a pause, while the three young people stared at Anthea as though she were the presentment, in miniature, of some mighty malignant fate, which overshadowed their lives.

Her voice dripped honey as she spoke to Charles.

"You've always been very dear to me. So I offer you your choice between this girl and myself. When Waters returns my check, you shall tell me if I am to make it valid, in your presence. At the same time, you will sign a paper promising not to marry for ten years, under penalty of forfeiting a sum in excess of any possible revenue from your partnership. I will give you three days in which to decide."

193

"I have decided." Charles' voice was so husky as to be almost inaudible. "I stick to Sally."

"You'll do nothing of the kind," interposed Sally speaking with spirit. "You are all counting without *me*. I decline to marry your nephew, Miss Vine."

"You would not be marrying my nephew, merely an anonymous pauper," remarked Miss Vine. "I could have made something of you, Morgan. Your head's screwed on all right."

There was poison in her honey, which clouded Charles' eyes with doubt, and stung Sally to impotent anger.

Iris stepped out of the background.

"Anthea," she said, trying to make her voice sound casual, "I've been invited to spend a few days at the Rectory, at Crosskeys. As I don't feel we are in for exactly a pleasant family evening, do you mind if I ring them up to say I'm coming in time for their supper?"

Miss Vine inclined her head in permission.

"Do. I shall miss you, across the table, as an attractive picture in that charming, but extravagant tulle frock."

"I'm going, too," announced Sally, "if Miss Vine can spare me."

"Wire to town and engage a temporary secretary," directed Miss Vine. "Directly you have secured a substitute, you are free to go."

"Thank you, Miss Vine."

Anthea laughed.

"It seems that all my birds are leaving the nest," she said. "Francis will have his dinner upstairs, for a little longer, so, Charles, you and I will have to keep each other company. ... There's the gong. Good. I'm hungry."

Charles and Sally watched her small figure gleaming down the vista of the pillared hall. Iris accompanied her and exchanged conventional remarks. She seemed withdrawn within herself, so that she treated the situation with the detachment of a neutral.

Charles turned to Sally and spoke in an unfamiliar quiet voice.

"When you go, Sally, I go, too. That stands. But let things drift for a bit. It will all come right."

Then he passed his hand over his eyes.

"I can't think," he said. "I feel as if there'd been an explosion inside my head. It's Anthea. I can't realize *her*."

"But I can," whispered Sally. "And I know now where I stand."

CHAPTER XXIV

Flowers for the Police

MISS PYE WAS SMOKING TOO MANY CIGARETTES. SHE TOLD
herself that she wanted to accumulate coupons, in order to
obtain a watch for Betsy, but, in reality, she was worried
over her brother.

Pye had the nature which broadcasts its good fortune,
but shares its troubles with no one. He gave her no reason
for his nightly pilgrimages, and refused to admit that the
shortness of his sleep was affecting him. When Miss Pye
asked him if he were working on the High Gables robbery,
he held her with a choleric blue eye, as he demanded, *"What*
robbery?" as a hint for her not to trespass on his domain.

It never occurred to Miss Pye, that, during her father's last
illness, she had sustained similar conditions for over a year,
while she nursed him, and had still remained her placid
cheerful self.

It was obvious, however, that the strain was affecting her
brother's temper, if not his actual health. He returned, one
evening, to the Cherry Orchard, after a worrying day at
the station, caused by the fact that one of his men had been
over-zealous in dealing with a member of the sensitive
public.

He was ready to be soothed, as usual, by his sister's good
high-tea and her silence, when he saw that the last precious

requisite was to be denied him. Mrs. Law, with her shoes off, sat in his own easy chair, smoking like a furnace.

"Hullo, lad," she called cheerily. "I hiked over, and not for the sake of my figure, either. Got a chance, this morning, to sell the little old car, and I snapped at it. I might have to give it away, later on."

"What d'you mean, girl?" demanded Pye. "I thought the new Munster was off?"

"*And* on again," said Mrs. Law. "The old girl must have been drunk when she wrote that note."

"No," corrected Pye, whose sense of fair play overrode his own prejudice. "Miss Vine is abstemious."

"I believe you. She'd be a far better woman if she drank. Well, old boy, I'm here to ask favors. I've decided, when I leave the old place, to take a job, so I want you to have Sultan, for a bit."

Pye's jaw dropped, for he knew that his own Alsatian would resent the intruder.

"If it's the slightest bother, I'll find someone else," said Mrs. Law quickly.

"Not in the very least," declared Pye stoutly. "Course, he must come here."

But he was disproportionately irritated by his own promise. Although he was essentially a doggy man, he foresaw canine civil war, caused by the undisciplined Sultan. Miss Pye, who was watching him anxiously, noticed how the veins over his temples suddenly swelled and knotted into bunches of blue berries.

He smote the table with his open fist.

"Damn that woman," he shouted. "I'm going to tell her something she ought to know."

"What d'you mean?" asked Mrs. Law, as her brother snatched up his cap.

"I'm going to choke some home-truths down the gullet

197

of that painted Jezebel," he replied. "She thinks she's set high above us common folk, like a queen, with everyone smarming her and telling her lies. Well, she's going to hear, from me, that her name is *mud.*"

"All right, Adam, but have your tea first," urged Miss Pye. "Your kippers are getting cold."

"And so'll I get cold, if I wait," shouted Pye, as he stamped out of the room.

Mrs. Law looked doubtfully at her elder sister.

"Oughtn't we to stop him?" she asked. "In his position, he might make trouble for himself."

Miss Pye shook her ginger-gold head.

"No one can shake him, when he's set," she said complacently. "But he knows when to stop, so don't you worry. Look here, old girl, suppose you finish the kippers, and I'll grill him some fresh ones when he comes back. I've just got to slip out to the post."

Her big face was serene as a moon daisy as she went from the room. But, as she hurried along the twilit road, after her brother, she was panting, like a choked volcano, in her repressed agitation.

She told herself that Doris must not suspect, in case. Adam was in one of his rare rages and might go further than he knew. He mustn't see her following him, but she had better be near him, in case——.

Fortunately, Pye did not look back, but charged blindly forward, like a wounded ox. Although the curves of the winding drive of the Court hid him from her, Miss Pye could easily follow his progress by the sound of grinding gravel plowed up by his furious pace. When the terraces came in sight she hid behind a bush.

It was her boast that she knew the inside of every house in the neighborhood. In the case of Jamaica Court, her curious nature had caused her to visit it, several times, during its erection, and the foreman had taken her all over it. She had a photographic memory, and was positive that she could find her way amid its maze of rooms and passages.

"I'll slip into the hall, after Adam has gone in," she decided, "and try to locate where they are. No one would see me, with all those pillars, and then I'll snoop. The door won't be locked, until eight. It'll be on the latch, like Betsy always leaves it. Miss Vine's got far too many servants to have them properly trained."

Miss Vine was in her bedroom, about to dress for dinner, when Eames answered a footman's apologetic knock.

"William says it's the Super to see you," she announced, "and he *would* come in, madam," she explained. "Pushed him right back, he did."

Miss Vine stood, in hesitation. She did not know whether to wither this affront to her majesty by invisibility, or to respond to the human challenge. Then her eyes gleamed at the prospect of a duel. Pye would be terrific in a rage, and she welcomed the spice of danger. He had come prepared to bite off her head, but she would send him away, with filed teeth and pared claws.

"I'll see him," she decided. "Put him in the drawing room."

Taking off her ropes of pearls, she draped a lace fichu over the low-cut neck of her black satin frock. Then she passed a powder puff over her painted face and smiled maliciously at her dimmed reflection, as she wiped the rouge from her lips.

As she had foreseen, her changed appearance took Pye by surprise. The fierce expression of his face was momentarily clouded, and he stared at her shrunken figure, with sunken eyes and mouth, as though he beheld her ghost. Only the wonderful lashes and golden curls remained to remind him of the painted scarecrow of fashion, whose brazen manner and peacock scream made her always a public spectacle.

199

"Good evening, Major," she said, using the title of the Chief Constable. "Have you come to arrest me?"

"No, madam," he replied stiffly. "But my errand is unpleasant."

"Then I can guess what it is," said Miss Vine quickly. "I had a painful interview, a few days ago, when I was far from well, with your sister. I know I left her with a wrong impression, but the truth is, I was afraid of her. She's so tall—and big people have no idea how they seem to *dominate* a shrimp like myself."

She cast a wistful upward glance at Pye, who, unconsciously drew himself up, so that his massive form towered over her, like a rock.

"Please sit down, Major," she said.

"What I have to say, is best said, standing," he told her.

"Very well." Miss Vine heaved a pathetic sigh. "I suppose, I must go on craning. . . . What fine women your sisters are—both of them. You can't think how I admire them, and envy them their height, and their beautiful golden hair."

"Why?" asked Pye, staring pointedly at her wig.

Miss Vine ignored the implied sneer.

"No, Major," she said, "I am a platinum blonde, which is something quite different, as every woman knows." She glanced at her wrist watch. "I ought to be dressing for dinner, but when I heard it was you, I felt it would be discourteous to my King and Country—whom you represent—not to see you. But—it's getting late."

"Sorry to hinder you, madam," said Pye, "but I have come here, to point out to you, that you—as a member of society—are failing in your plain duty to a fellow citizen, and one who's got her own way to make in the world, and who is a poor woman compared with you. It's rank injustice, and sheer cruelty, for which you'll pay, in the long run, as sure as God made little apples."

He worked himself up, as he went along, so ended better than he began. Miss Vine drooped under the blast of his reproach.

"I should deserve to pay," she said, "if I were to blame, as you think. But you don't know the truth. I am not so—pink as I'm painted. As a man of the world, you must admit that we, who are in the limelight, have to wear a protective mask. When you take away my—my—trimmings, I'm just like any other woman, who's alone in the world, and timid of her own judgment, and—tired."

Pye twisted his mouth.

"All this doesn't explain the new hotel in Timberdale," he shouted. "It's a monstrous shame."

"I think it does," said Anthea. "Didn't your sister tell you that I'm placing her position before the Board, at our next meeting? And I told her, too—what you must admit, Major —that although women have advanced, all the real power still belongs to men."

"Hum. They say you've got all your directors just where you want them."

"And who are 'they'?" asked Miss Vine scornfully. "The poison-tongued women, who tear my reputation to tatters, over their teacups? What do they know of me? I've never been invited to any house in Oldtown, for fear I might infect the atmosphere? Rather galling to any woman of spirit. Do you think it justice to judge me on calumny? Why, it is actually said that I carry on a violent flirtation with my adopted sons."

Pye began to feel uneasy, as he reflected that his own suspicions were not supported by proof.

Miss Vine sank down into a chair and looked up at him with appealing eyes.

"I'm going to confess to you, Major," she said, "what I've been too proud to own to any living soul. I've failed horribly over those children I adopted. I've poured out money, like water, for them and I've met with no return but ingratitude. I do wish you'd tell me where I've gone wrong."

Hardly conscious of his own action, Pye dropped heavily into a chair.

"You went wrong from the start," he said, "for you took on a man's job, when you adopted boys. No woman could carry it through properly. They haven't the authority."

"No?" Miss Vine pressed a button in the table. "But what do you think I ought to do about it?"

"They ought to be in jobs, where they'd be independent and not hanging round on you," declared Pye.

"But my ultimate aim was complete future independence, Major. Only, it is difficult to begin. Francis is always so avaricious, that I was afraid I might turn him into a complete money-grubber.... And Charles is careless. When I gave him a car, it was in dock within the month. Who could entrust him with moneyed interests?"

The footman appeared with a tray of cocktails. Anthea took one, and then waved them aside, just as Pye was telling himself that he would choke before he accepted her hospitality.

"I'll tell you something, in confidence, Major," went on Anthea, as she sipped her cocktail. "I've just arranged for Charles to become a partner of Mr. Waters. But I'm still perplexed about Francis. What would you advise?"

Forgetful of his original mission, Pye puckered his brow, for he dearly loved to manage the affairs of others. The servant entered again, with a large tumbler of whisky-and-soda, which, obeying Miss Vine's nod, he did not offer to Pye, but placed it on a table, within his reach.

"Well, madam," said Pye, "since you ask me, I should advise extreme caution with that young man of yours. I always thought him barmy, when he was a kid."

Instinctively, his fingers closed around the glass and he took a deep gulp.

"Oh, Major, what do you mean?" cried Anthea.

"Well, it was always 'Please' and 'Thank you,' with him, and he called me 'Superintendent,' instead of 'Mince-pie,' like that young devil, Charles."

As he joined in Anthea's laughter, he told himself that he had been mistaken in his estimate of Miss Vine's character.

"She's just a plain body, underneath," he reflected. "Because she tries to hide that death's-head of hers under a pot of paint, we've been slinging mud at her, instead of pitying her for being such a guy."

As he drained his last drop of whisky, he felt refreshed and forgetful of the looming ordeal of his nightly vigil. He had also wandered far from his original theme, and Anthea was not disposed to let him remember it.

"Oh, Major," she cried, springing up from her chair, like a girl. "I do wish you would give me your opinion on my roof garden. I hear you are *the* authority, in Oldtown, on flowers."

He followed her willingly enough up the great marble staircase, and along several cross-sectional corridors.

"The woman's no fool to have made all this money," he thought, as his keen eyes noticed the thick pile of the carpets and the abundance of statues, paintings, and stained glass, which might have offended a less crude taste.

At this time of the year, the flat roof was enclosed with glass, so that it resembled a conservatory. The wealth of flowers really delighted him, because, besides admiration, he found plenty of room for criticism.

As they were leaving, Anthea absently broke off a spray of small white orchids, which, when she bid him good-bye, she put in his buttonhole.

When he turned back, at the door, for a last glance, she was running towards the staircase, in a frantic race to catch the minute—a tiny fleeting black figure, lost in the vast area of the marble hall.

He never saw her again, alive.

CHAPTER XXV

The Final Curtain

ANTHEA LAUGHED SILENTLY AS SHE RAN UPSTAIRS. HER heart leaped from exertion, but also from triumph. She had fooled the big policeman to the limit of credulity. When they next met, she would smile exultantly into his face, to remind him of his humiliation.

In a few days he would learn how she had pulled the wool over his eyes. Although she had no doubt that the new Munster would pay, in the long run, she was resigned to accept it as a parasite feeding on her capital reserve. The price of revenge might be crippling, but she was determined to pay it, so fierce was her resentment against the big fair woman, who had taunted her with spinsterhood.

Soon—very soon—that last sting would be withdrawn. Her next purchase would be a husband, the most superior article that her money could buy—handsome, graceful, young.

He was coming to dinner, tonight, at her special command. She saw excitement ahead of her, for all her lions were snarling at her, from their corners. Francis, now officially recovered, would no longer respect the truce of his invalidism. Charles had not spoken to her since she had dismissed Sally Morgan.

And Lawrence, the suave graceful beast, who fawned on her, was the most dangerous of them all. He had slunk out of her presence, scared at the thought of future bondage; and she knew that terror can madden the most timid creature to reprisal.

When he had spoken to her, over the telephone, his voice had been smooth, and his acceptance of her invitation, immediate. It made her wonder as to his present line of policy; and she welcomed any stimulus to her brain.

As she took her place at the head of the table, it was plain to the three men that she was in her element. There were no rivals present, to challenge her majesty with their youth. She wore a simple little-girl frock of white cloudy chiffon, which suggested the purity of the first snowdrop. Dewdrops, pendant from a narrow band, gleamed, whenever she tossed her golden wig.

Dr. Lawrence bowed over her hand, with exaggerated deference.

"You look Eternal Youth," he said.

In reality, he was reminded of a specimen preserved in spirits, and a hint of mockery flickered in his smile.

Anthea watched him from the corners of her eyes, noting the subtle change in his manner. It held secret triumph and veiled understanding, as though he had weighed the advantages of her proposal, and had decided to play for safety.

She asked herself why she should question his philosophy in a period of post-war landslide, when marriage—on either side—might be anything from a fifty-fifty partnership to an economic surrender.

"I wish to see you, after dinner, alone," she said imperiously.

He shook his head, but with no trace of his former uneasiness.

"Sorry, Anthea." For the first time, he used her name. "But I've a case in the country which will probably keep me out all night. I must start directly we've finished dinner."

"That sounds like a husband's excuse to a deluded wife, Glyn."

"Does it? Well, you may have the chance of comparing my fiction with your reality, later on. Who knows?"

Francis pricked up his ears. Now that he had exchanged his dressing gown for evening clothes, his face looked rather drawn, but he appeared to be in excellent spirits.

"Am I to infer, Lawrence," he asked, "that you actually consider Miss Vine to be capable of the idiocy of marriage?"

"I consider her capable of no idiocy, Francis. For the rest, I can only repeat—'Who knows?'" He hastened to change the subject. "Where are the girls tonight?"

"Iris is staying at the Rectory," replied Francis glibly. "Miss Morgan is dining in her room, owing to pressure of work. And Charles has lost his tongue."

Charles glowered at him, over his soup.

"You've heard, of course, that our Miss Morgan has got the sack?" resumed Francis, his eyes fixed upon his cousin's face.

"Nothing of the sort, clever," interrupted Anthea sharply. "It's only a temporary hitch. When things have settled down, I'm keeping her on. I couldn't do without my little Morgan."

To her own surprise, her voice rang true. Sally had certain qualities which appealed to her, and she credited her with others, which to her mind, counted higher—a lack of personal softness and squeamish scruple. Indeed, she saw herself again, as a youthful worker, in the girl, and had no idea of the enormity of her libel.

Charles stared at her, and then burst into a shout of laughter.

"Come on," he said, holding out his glass, to be refilled. "Let's drink and be merry, for tomorrow, we peg out."

"No, don't even talk of dying," cried Miss Vine, with an affected shudder.

"Too young? But why not? Don't you die, every night and twice, on matinées, and still continue to top the bill?"

Miss Vine was silent as she looked at the pool of candle-light reflected on the polished wood of the table. Her thoughts lingered on an agony of pain and darkness, which had changed, miraculously, to light and the warm pressure of Iris' arms. And she had but to close her eyes to feel again the icy lake-water lapping above her lips, her nostrils, her eyes, her head. Because she had tasted the bitterness of death, twice, a careless youth chose to make a joke of it.

Then she, too, like Charles, changed her mood. Shaking off her depression, she also signed to the servant to refill her glass. Abstemious, as a rule, by reasons of health, tonight she craved the live current in her blood and the sparkle in her brain which were bequeathed through alcoholic agency.

The young men exchanged covert glances and smiles, as she let herself go on the flood of her rising spirits. As though united by some bond of daredevilry, they competed with each other over the extravagance of their compliments.

"You're at the top of your form, tonight, Anthea," said Charles, as Miss Vine came to the end of a smoking-room story.

"Ah, I can let myself rip, because I have not to consider the virginal prejudices of the girls," she told him. "I'm always cramped by women. Men for me. All my life, I've had lovers, and I shall have them, till I die."

"But isn't three rather a crowd?" asked Charles, glancing round the table.

"No." Anthea shook her head so violently that the dew-drops tinkled. "I'm selective. I can always pick up and tune out."

Her eyes sought and met the responsive smile on the doctor's lips, so that she laughed too long and too loudly. While her blood raced and her head felt light as a bubble, she was conscious of a semi-submerged instinct which warned her not to make a fool of herself.

The doubt faded before the strong gush of her exhilaration. She had faced the danger of three mutinous courtiers and now, she had them hanging on her look and smile.

But the whisper in her brain persisted, warning her that she was only safe so long as she faced them. She held her lions by her eye, and the magnetism of her will. What—if she turned her back?

As she sat, momentarily silenced, Charles fumbled in his pocket.

"Oh, Anthea," he said carelessly, "I met Simmons, on the drive, just before dinner, and he asked me to give this to you."

Miss Vine tore open the envelope and skimmed the letter, as she held it at the length of her arm.

"DEAR MADAM," it ran, "As it is not my custom to gossip, it was only this afternoon that I heard of your unfortunate accident, and I now hasten to offer my regrets and assure you I am happy to know you have suffered no ill results. I had previously warned my son not to injure anything on the estate, so I questioned him, when he confessed that he tried to cut off a bough of willow, for a fishing rod. I gave him a sound thrashing, and hope this meets with your entire satisfaction.

"Yours faithfully,
"THOS. SIMMONS."

Miss Vine drew back her lips, so that her gums were exposed. She had believed that her household included a potential murderer, while the real culprit had been a lovely boy with dark liquid eyes.

She had made them all suffer, so that the guilty person

should not escape punishment; and now, like a tigress that had tasted blood, she did not want to release her grip of her victims.

With an angry gesture, she crumpled up the letter. Simmons was a fool. A man who would volunteer a statement to his own detriment could not be entrusted with a responsible post. Tomorrow, he should be sacked.

"Is Simmons stinging you for a rise?" asked Francis.

"He will get an Irishman's rise, Francis," she said. "But he writes an excellent letter."

She pressed her hand to her head, for the crystal clarity of her brain was beginning to cloud. Yet the old shrewdness snapped into her eyes as she realized that the boys were laughing at her, because she had drunk too much wine. The next minute she had forgotten everything, and was laughing, too, with a fresh story ripping from her lips.

The young men looked at the posturing, grimacing parody of youth who sat at the head of the table, with a riot of conflicting emotions. Crosscurrents of pity and hatred, toleration and amusement, disgust and sympathy, shook in the air, like heat quivering over the sea, or gnats dancing in a sunset glow. The atmosphere was tense as the hush that preludes an electric storm.

Suddenly Anthea rose unsteadily to her feet.

"I'm tired of all of you," she said crossly. "I've business letters to write. Francis, *you* may bring me my coffee."

As the favored courtier nodded indifferently, Charles winked at the doctor.

"Business?" he muttered derisively. "My eye. Forty winks." Then he raised his voice. "Pass the decanter—you. Come, Anthea, let's have a parting toast from our little Snow White."

Anthea turned back and raised her glass with a girlish gesture.

"Here's to our next merry meeting," she cried.

"All of us?" asked Lawrence.

"Horrors." She grimaced. "How discreet and dull. No, I drink to my next meeting, with *one* of you."

"Lights out?" asked Charles impudently.

"Of course." Her laugh was a peacock scream. "Good night, boys. Sweet sleep—and dream of *me*."

They all gazed at her rouged wizened face and slim white form, as she postured in the doorway. Her hands fluttered like moths to her scarlet lips, as she blew a shower of kisses.

It was her final curtain.

211

CHAPTER XXVI

The Dream

ANTHEA WAS GLAD OF THE SILENCE AND GLOOM OF THE Moorish library. She felt too dull and heavy to study the figures which Miss Morgan had placed, ready for her, on her desk. Her eyes closed and she sagged back in her chair, in a half-reverie.

Disturbed by the rattle of china, she looked up, to see Francis—his face impassive—standing before her, with a cup of coffee on a tray.

"Your coffee, madam," he said.

"Thank you, Francis." She smiled up at him. "Put in the sugar. No, one only. Surely you remember?"

"Yes, madam."

"Oh, don't be a fool. Leave that to Charles. Tell me, do you consider I drank too much at dinner?"

"No, madam."

"But I took more than I could carry?"

"Yes, madam."

Anthea marked the glint in Francis' eye, and knew that he would not relax his wooden expression, or vary his formula. She had made him her servant, and her servant he would remain.

"Have I your permission to go, madam?" he asked.

"Yes, curse you."

"Thank you, madam. May I send the second footman, Charles, to announce the hour of eleven?"

"No," snapped Anthea. "You are to come yourself."

"Certainly, madam. But the panel doctor said I should go early to bed."

"I shall expect *you*, Francis."

"Very good, madam."

Francis closed the door behind him, and Anthea gulped down her coffee, to quench her sudden thirst. With an effort, she took up a market report, and tried to concentrate on the figures. But they quivered like a cobweb shaken in a breeze, and, presently, they slid off the paper, and hung in the air, just before her eyes. She tried to brush them aside, but they still clustered thickly before her range of vision, like a curtain, so that she was compelled to close her lids, to get relief.

Almost instantly she drifted into a light fitful sleep, from which she awoke with a nervous start, and the sensation that someone was creeping behind her chair. She turned round quickly, to see nothing but the skull-like pattern on the Persian carpet.

"Nerves," she thought. "I'd better go to bed."

But habit protested against a dislocation of routine. Eleven o'clock was her bedtime, and her will dictated that she should endure until the appointed hour.

Again she rubbed her eyes, feeling as though webs were spun thickly all over her mind. Her brain was clouded, as though its cells were clogged with sticky filaments. Even while she tried to force her leaden lids apart, they fell, and she dropped off again, to sleep.

This time she had a horrible dream, which was so vivid that she appeared, for its duration, to be actually awake. She thought that Francis came to the door, and shouted, "Bedtime, Anthea," and then disappeared, before she could speak to him.

She wanted desperately to retain him, for she felt lonely. He seemed to be her last link with humanity, and his going left her alone in a dead world, under an extinct firmament.

Presently she dreamed that she was crossing the hall, which had grown to a colossal size, and was beginning to mount a precipitous marble staircase, on her way to bed. Once again she was conscious of someone stealing behind her. Turning her head, fearfully, she saw only a craven little shadow, dragging at her heel.

She realized that she was frightened of her own shadow. As she toiled up the endless flight of stairs, she watched the black shape riding the marble wall. Every second it grew taller, until it towered over her, like a titanic distortion, menacing and horrific.

At the turn of the staircase she shut her eyes, so that she should not see It hunch Itself, to take Its overhead leap. When she opened her eyes again she noticed that the white wall was blank.

She no longer cast a shadow. Even as her brain questioned where it had gone, the answer came in the terrified flutter of her heart.

It was inside her room—waiting for her.

She tried to turn back and go downstairs, but her feet refused to obey her will, and she knew that she must go on to her appointed fate.

When, however, she pushed open her door, she saw only the commonplace of her familiar surroundings. The dream blurred again, while she dragged herself through the protracted toilet of nightmare. But she knew, subconsciously, that the horror was still there, waiting to spring upon her.

Suddenly she saw a faint stir behind the electric-blue satin window hangings. It began to bulge and swell to the roughly blocked outlines of a human form. As she stood, rooted to the spot, she was aware of a hand, with groping fingers, creeping out from the folds of the curtain. Then everything grew black, and the dream died out.

She woke up, or, rather, thought she woke up, until she realized that she had remained inside her blue-and-silver bedroom. She knew then that she was still dreaming, for she retained the knowledge that, in reality, she was dozing in the Moorish library, as the aftermath of being slightly drunk.

Her terror had gone, and she felt composed, and even curious to find the explanation of a subtle change in the bedroom. It was now daylight, so that she could see into its every corner; yet, while each object was unchanged and in its usual position, she seemed to be viewing it from a strange perspective.

While she was pondering the problem, the door opened, and Eames came in. She moved noiselessly as she made a beeline to the drawers which were built into the walls. Opening them hurriedly, she began to pull out a quantity of new lingerie. It lay in piles on the floor, in palest tints of shell, turquoise, apple, daffodil, lilac.

Miss Vine watched her in surprise, which changed to indignation, when she noticed that the woman was hastily packing some of the garments into her own cheap suitcase. As she worked, she kept shooting furtive glances behind her, as though she were listening for footsteps.

"She doesn't know *I'm* watching her," exulted Miss Vine. "I'll let her finish the job. And then she shall answer to *me.*"

Even as the thought flashed through her mind, Eames put the remainder of the lingerie back into the drawers, closed them, and rose from her knees.

"Eames," called Miss Vine sharply.

The maid took not the slightest notice.

"Eames, are you deaf?" Miss Vine's voice grew shriller. "Why don't you answer, you fool?"

Still the woman paid no attention to her mistress. In a

215

royal rage, Anthea rushed across the room, and shook the woman violently by the arm.

"Eames," she shouted, "what is the meaning of this disgraceful behavior? You are discharged."

The maid merely looked at Anthea with blank eyes. Suddenly, however, her dull expression sharpened into apprehension. She shivered, looked around her uneasily, and then, almost ran from the room.

Anthea followed her, screaming to her to stop. She chased the woman right to the green baize door which led to the right wing.

"She's stark mad," she decided. "Morgan must deal with her. She'll soon clear her out. Where's Morgan?"

But there was no bell at hand, to summon her faithful secretary. Panting with baffled rage, she retraced her steps, until she reached the well of the great staircase.

Down in the hall, a footman leaned against a pillar, furtively smoking a cigarette. At this act of gross insubordination, Anthea's rage bubbled over, like a volcanic eruption. Forgetful of dignity, she rushed down the stairs, and violently struck the cigarette from the man's insolent mouth.

"You are discharged," she cried. "Go—at once."

The footman did not pay the slightest attention to her command, and she noticed, with a thrill of inexplicable dismay, that he was still puffing away at his cigarette.

Cold fear began to percolate through her fury, damping down its fires. These servants—who had formerly hastened to obey her glance—treated her as though she were a breath of air. She was no longer mistress in her own house.

Something was hideously wrong. But Morgan would tell her what was amiss. She would know how to deal with any situation. She must find Morgan. . . . Then she remembered that she had dismissed her secretary, merely to spite her for something which she had never done.

She had made them all suffer, and their future punishment would be still heavier. Charles would know the dull misery of unemployment and poverty, or else, barter Sally for a mess of pottage. Iris would see the man she loved become the legal property of another woman.

Standing in the hall, impotent as a spent match, Anthea regretted her own tyranny. When she had adopted three superfluous children, she had been given—as a bonus for her generosity—a wonderful chance to draw on the mighty force of their youth. And she had deliberately thrown it away, repulsing their every overture of friendship and making her hospitality only a form of bondage.

At this crisis she wanted their help and co-operation to stamp out the mutiny. Like a leaf drifting before the wind, she wandered from room to room, looking for them. The emptiness of the enormous house seemed to mock her wealth; she had built and furnished all these splendid apartments for no tenants.

"Too late. Too late."

She heard the words reverberating through the air, like the tolling of a passing bell. They rang in her ears, as she searched for Iris.

"I *must* find my little Morgan," she thought. "She will tell me the truth."

An atrophied seed of affection was actually sprouting in the darkness of her withered heart. But although she kept her finger pressed on the button of the bell, she rang in vain.

Utterly desolated, she passed down the deserted corridor. As she drew near to her bedroom, Dr. Lawrence and Iris came through its door.

"What are they doing in my room?"

Her instant suspicion was automatic, overpowering her softer mood. Then she noticed that Iris' eyes were heavy, as

217

though she had not slept and her lips drooped sadly. But Lawrence was smiling as he whispered in the girl's ear.

"We ought to alter the proverb," he said, "and say 'While there is death, there's hope.'"

Iris pushed him away, as he tried to kiss her.

"You sicken me when you say things like that. Go away, Glyn. I'm in no mood for you."

He seemed only too glad to obey. As he turned towards the staircase, with his graceful swing, Anthea stepped forward and barred his way.

"Glyn," she said imperiously.

He stared at her, but did not speak. With a backward glance at Iris, he sauntered down into the hall.

Anthea trembled from head to heel at this fresh humiliation, but she was also beginning to grow terribly afraid. She shrank back in a corner when Sally Morgan came out of her bedroom. Suddenly she was fearful to summon her faithful secretary. If Morgan flaunted her authority she would know, indeed, that she was no longer mistress in her own house.

Sally Morgan took Iris by the arm.

"You'd better lie down," she said. "Fretting will do no good."

"I know," faltered Iris. "But it's so ghastly. I keep going over it, again and again, and still I can't realize it. Not even, just now, when I went in to take her some flowers."

"Yes," said Sally quietly. "It's impossible to realize that Miss Vine is really dead."

As she listened, Anthea uttered a piercing shriek, but no sound disturbed the silence of the corridor. Even as she had foreseen, from her invaluable secretary, she had learned the truth.

She was dead.

The shock of the discovery awoke her, and she found herself huddled among the cushions of her chair. The green shaded light fell upon the market report, which lay upon the bureau. She was back again, in a world of stocks and shares; and although she was shaking violently, and her forehead was clammy with sweat, she laughed, in her relief.

"What a horrible dream." She spoke aloud. "It seemed to last for years. It must be very late. Has Francis forgotten me?"

Still oppressed with the memory of her dream, she began to worry at the threat of neglect. Owing to her own antipathy, there was no clock in the room to tell her the time. As she waited, her mind began to revolve slowly and creakily, like a globe in an unaccustomed orbit.

"That dream. Was it a warning?"

A note—written in excellent script upon cheap paper—lying on her desk, reminded her of her punitive policy, to avenge a nonexistent injury. In common fairness she should prosecute it no longer, while generosity dictated reparation.

Anthea was swept away on a flood of benevolent instincts.

"Charles shall have his partnership, and Sally too. But he must leave me a share in my little Morgan. She's ambitious, and she shall lead her double life. I'll give her a big executive post. Francis, too. Iris can have Lawrence, if she's fool enough to want him. I don't trust him after my dream. It was sent to warn me. . . . Francis!"

He did not obey her call, and, in spite of the absurdity of her fear, she was afraid to go to the door, lest she should see a footman smoking a cigarette in the hall. The house seemed curiously still, as she listened.

Then, to her deep relief, she heard footsteps, and Francis entered the library.

"Bedtime, Anthea," he announced.

She looked at him, without speaking.

"Now, he'll go away again," she thought.

219

Instead, he advanced to the bureau, and stood looking down at her in slight amusement.

"Sleepy?" he asked.

"Yes." She rubbed her lids apart, for she still felt heavy. "Francis, was I drunk at dinner?"

"You exceeded slightly," he replied. "But you remained a perfect little lady and told us carefully-selected anecdotes, from the parish magazine."

Then he sat on the edge of the table.

"Anthea," he said, "I'm going to ask you a favor. It hurts me more than it hurts you. I'm broke. A benevolent uncle wrote and offered to lend me any sum from a bob to a thousand quid. All I got was a bob, but it's a thousand pounds, now, so the gentleman kept his word."

Miss Vine's lips grew thinner as she listened.

"So you've got into the claws of moneylenders?" she cried. "You fool."

"All that. But I *must* have money, Anthea. I'm desperate. Remember, I saved your life."

"You merely obeyed a natural instinct, as you admitted yourself," said Anthea.

There was a terrific conflict in her brain as two forces clashed in warfare. While she realized that here was an opportunity to redeem the first instalment of her pledge to the future, her crafty lower nature reminded her of a way to evade her bargain.

"That dream was *not* a warning," she thought. "If Francis had gone away directly I should have accepted the omen. But he is trying to draw my teeth."

"I'll give you no good money, to throw away after bad," she told him. "You've been a fool, and I've no use for fools. Get out of your mess yourself."

Francis looked down at her intently, as he spoke in his

220

usual pedantic manner. But he used a curiously familiar phrase.

"You've had your chance. I *warn* you the consequences may react to your own disability."

He went out of the room, without waiting to hold open the door for her. When Miss Vine entered the hall its great empty space blazed with wasteful electric light.

She did not notice the growing shadow, which accompanied her, as she mounted the stairs to bed, because all her energies were taxed by the ascent. The shallow marble steps seemed steeper and more numerous than usual, as she toiled up, with leaden legs.

Her bedroom was empty, for Eames had gone to her dancing class. She made a grimace of distaste at the sight of all the lotions, creams, and astringents laid in readiness, on the glass slabs.

She felt so weary and confused that she was almost tempted to break through her rule, and evade the terrible drudgery of her toilet. But her will prevailed, forcing her to go to the bathroom and turn on the taps. As she left its glowing, grass-green glass luxury, she paused on the threshold, arrested by her own reflections in the triple mirrors of her dressing table.

She saw dimly three slim, golden-haired girls, in filmy white, all visions of youth and beauty. Thrilled by the sight, she stretched out her arms in her favorite affected gesture of appeal.

"Waste. Oh, send me a man."

She did not know that her prayer was granted. Her luck was in, for, tonight, she was not alone.

Too tired to be conscious of her own actions, she plodded through each stage of her toilet, omitting not a single grimace or hop. In a dream, she steamed and massaged her face,

221

and adjusted the strips of plaster, in key positions, over her shrunken cheeks.

And then, suddenly, the sleeper awoke. With a shock, engendered by her old inhibition, she noticed that her curtains were still drawn over her windows. Instantly her mind flickered back to a London shop while grinning faces pressed against the glass.

The conviction that they were still there, mocking her from outside, faded before her returning common sense. Only conscious that, at last, she was ready for bed, she crossed the room, to draw the cords.

As she did so, she noticed a stir behind the satin hangings, and groping fingers of a hand crept out of the folds.

Then the curtain billowed out, as though blown by a wind —and the rest was even as her dream.

CHAPTER XXVII

Ordeal

HAD MISS VINE BEEN REQUIRED TO FILL IN A CENSUS FORM, stating the number of persons present under her roof that night, she would have omitted one very reluctant tenant.

Miss Pye had placed herself, not only in a false position, but one of danger, where a single false step might lead to exposure and disgrace. After the first glow of action had faded, she bitterly regretted the impulse which had spurred her to play the part of Guardian Angel to her brother.

When she hid behind the bush, in the twilight of the drive, the situation seemed heavy with peril. As the great door was opened, she saw how Pye pushed back the man with the flat of his hand, and literally forced his way into the lobby.

It was plain that Adam was in a flaming temper and no longer master of his actions. Miss Pye, therefore, waited for a few minutes and then cautiously tried the handle of the front door. It turned easily in her fingers—a neglect of caution for which she felt she could not blame the servant, who must have been confused by the Superintendent's attack.

Inch by inch she widened the crack, until she, in her turn, entered the lobby. Peeping through one of its stained glass windows, she could see a section of the hall, which appeared to be empty.

It was a salve to her pride that her brother had not been left to wait in the hall; but, as she reconnoitered, the footman crossed her line of vision, accompanied by Adam. Even at that distance she could see that the veins still protruded on his temples, and this danger signal nerved her to further excess.

"He's not safe," she thought. "I *must* be near him. If nothing else, I can help him to make a getaway."

She was about to pluck up her courage to enter the hall, when she heard the tapping of high heels, and Miss Vine appeared, as a small black silhouette, in the distance.

"They've not met yet," reflected Miss Pye. "The man fetched her from another room. Oh, my dear life, I might have bumped into her. I must get my story ready, in case——."

She snatched at the first excuse for her presence which flashed into her head. If anyone found her, she would say that she had come to deliver an important message to her brother, from the Constabulary; and she hoped that it would be taken for granted that she had been admitted in the usual way.

Breathing heavily in her excitement, she pushed open the swing doors, and took cover behind the first marble pillar. To her relief, the hall appeared empty, although she could not tell whether eyes were watching her from the well of the staircase.

Even in her agitation, she was stirred to interest in her surroundings.

"What a barracks of a place. Coo, it's nearly as fine as the Victoria and Albert. Now, let me get my bearings. I remember the dining room's to the right. No, I'll concentrate on the rooms where they are most likely to be. Drawing room, library, or the little room. That's the study, and it's over there."

Treading lightly, after the manner of a heavy woman who was a featherweight dancer, Miss Pye flitted from pillar to pillar, until she came within ear range of the sound of clicking.

She shook her head.

"The secretary's working in there. Good. So long as I can hear her typing, she won't be nosing around. Now for the library."

Making a beeline in its direction, she knelt down and placed her eye and ear, alternatively, to the keyhole, only to be disappointed by silence and darkness.

"Not there," she decided. "Adam will be shouting fit to drown the Last Trump. They're in the salon. Well, I can't help feeling glad she's received him there, even if he ends up by murdering her in her own drawing room."

Once again she left the safety of her screening pillar, to embark on a series of little trips to her objective. But when she reached the door she could hear only the faintest murmur of voices.

Baffled by her ignorance of what was taking place inside, she determined to be an invisible witness of the interview. At this juncture the fidelity of her memory came to her aid.

"There's a cloakroom, over in that corner, that opens out to a corridor. From there I can get into the conservatory, and I *think* it has one door leading into the drawing room. I might be able to hear something from there."

Growing bolder with success, she crossed the hall, without taking cover on the way, and hurried through the unlighted cloakroom, praying the while that she might be in time to avert disaster. Even in the corridor she could smell the heavy perfume of forced blooms, and feel a current of moist hot air.

When she entered the conservatory she heard a murmur of voices, but although the muted pitch grew clearer, as she padded silently over the rubber flooring, she could not distinguish actual words.

"Never mind," she reflected. "I can get some line on what I see, and form my own conclusion."

Screened by an enormous bush of camellias, she peeped between boughs of waxen blossoms into the Empire salon. To her surprise, Miss Vine and her brother were sitting close together, in what appeared to be friendly conversation.

Miss Pye's initial relief changed to characteristic suspicion.

"She's talking him over," she thought, "and he doesn't know it, the big stiff."

The strong scent of forced lilac encircled her in warm waves, as she pressed her nose to the streaming glass. From where she crouched, she commanded a view of the door, and of the footman, who appeared carrying a tray of cocktails.

Miss Pye felt her scalp tighten, in spite of the sticky warmth.

"Coo, what an escape. If I'd stayed in the hall he'd have caught me, and I'd have to waste my excuse on him, and go away."

In spite of her distrust of Miss Vine's tactics, she grew hotter, without aid from the temperature of the conservatory, when she noticed that her brother was not offered refreshment.

"He wouldn't lower his dignity by drinking *her* rot-gut," she told herself, "but she might have asked him if he had a mouth."

Before her indignation could cool, the footman reappeared with a big whisky-and-soda, and Miss Pye became again a prey to the darkest suspicion.

"She's vamped him. There must be *something* about her, because of all her men. He's a masterful man, too, and they're always the biggest fools over women."

She quite forgot the peril of her position, as eavesdropper, as she tried vainly to catch the drift of their earnest con-

226

versation. Presently they rose to their feet, and she breathed a silent prayer of thanksgiving that the danger was over.

She hurried through the veils of flowers pendant in green walls of creepers, on her way to get out of the house first. But as she cautiously opened a crack of the cloak-room door, she realized that Miss Vine and Adam were already in the hall, cutting off her retreat.

She waited for them to pass, but, to her dismay, Miss Vine led the way towards the staircase.

Lurid episodes of the underworld, culled from the Screen, clouded Miss Pye's mind.

"Oh, the fool to go upstairs," she groaned. "He might know that, with a woman like her, he's only safe on the ground floor. She has laid a trap for him and he's fallen into it. She'll push him into a bedroom, lock the door and then ring the bell and scream that she's compromised."

Casting caution to the winds, she crept up the staircase, following as quickly as she dared, on the trail of Miss Vine and her victim. Fortune, however, came to her aid, for, although at this hour the house was populous with servants, she did not meet a single member of the domestic staff.

Her brother and Miss Vine seemed to be always just around the corner. She heard their footsteps and voices, but she rounded each bend, only to find that they were once more out of sight. Beads of moisture gathered round her mouth in the excitement of the chase, and she grew reckless in the risks she ran. But, in spite of her boast to carry the plan of any house in her head, she lost her bearings completely as she panted down the intersecting corridors.

Suddenly she heard the sound of brisk footsteps crossing a floor and the sound of a soprano voice singing a popular air. It was obvious that a housemaid was about to emerge from one of the bedrooms. In a panic lest she should be caught far from the safety of her base, Miss Pye opened the first door, and shut herself into a recess of pitch darkness.

She held her breath in suspense, as the girl passed by her hiding place; and it was not until the sound of her footsteps had died away that she dared to unfasten the catch, only to find herself completely baffled by its mechanism.

She tugged, pressed and turned with moist fingers that slipped on the metal. Unfortunately, a total lack of any sense of machinery was among her limitations, so that she could only wrench the door violently, in a blind effort to discover its secret.

"It's a spring lock, and I'm imprisoned," she told herself. "But where the dickens, am I?"

Exploring the darkness cautiously, her fingers touched the head of a mop. A smell of disinfectant and a painful encounter with the rim of a bucket confirmed her impression that she was in a housemaid's closet.

"Then there's no air," she thought. "Question is—how long can I hang on?"

Even as the question crossed her mind, she heard again the dull thud of footsteps over the thick carpet of the corridor. Rescue was close at hand. But, as she doubled her fist to strike on the panels of the door, fear for her personal safety was stifled by a stronger instinct.

If she were caught in this compromising situation it might injure her brother's official reputation. She might be accused of being on premises for an unlawful purpose—a phrase with which she was familiar, owing to her relationship to a member of the force.

The family trait of hanging on asserted itself in this crisis, as she spoke sternly to herself.

"Flo, old girl, you're no fairy, and can stand a little fug. Squeal now, and we're all in the soup. *No*. Stick it out."

In spite of her resolution, her ordeal increased in severity with the passage of time. She fancied that the air grew more heated, while it thickened so that she seemed to be swallowing it in repulsive mouthfuls. As a matter of fact, she suffered actual physical distress, as she was a big woman and used to open windows.

But she hung on, although her neck was damp and her clothes stuck to her in a clammy embrace. Whenever the grim idea of suffocation stirred in her mind, she forced herself to think of her brother's career. Presently her mind began to waver, and her head to nod.

Afterwards, Miss Pye liked to imagine that she lay, for hours, unconscious in a swoon; in reality, she dropped into a heavy drugged sleep induced by the close air.

She was awakened by a distant metallic chiming, and she knew, from its note, that it must be the Town Hall clock about to strike the hour.

"There's some sort of ventilation," she thought, as she began to count. "Heavens, how late. Eight, nine——"

The clock continued to strike, filling Miss Pye with consternation. She suddenly realized her position in a strange house, where she had no authentic business.

"I *must* get out," she muttered, tugging frantically at the handle.

This time, by sheer accident, she stumbled on the secret of its mechanism. She heard the click of a lever, and felt the door open before the pressure of her hand.

Her heart was hammering as she crept into the corridor and looked furtively, in either direction, to make certain that she was alone. The electric blaze was now dimmed down to a few isolated lights, an informative fact which lessened her fear of discovery. But although she knew that the servants had gone to bed, her position was of such acute peril that she felt as though she were in a waking nightmare.

"I must get my story ready," she thought.

But she could imagine no reason which would explain her presence on the first floor of a strange house, at such a late hour. Her only hope of salvation was to find her way out before discovery.

She knew that the young people in Jamaica Court often came home late, for she had heard their voices in the road, when she was in bed. Therefore, there was a good chance that the front door would remain unbolted, if only she could locate the great central staircase.

To her horror, however, she found herself completely lost in the maze of passages. The feeling of being in a bad dream increased in intensity as she crept along, scarcely daring to breathe, and expectant, every second, of an opened door.

Suddenly, the gruff notes of a man's voice sounded so close to her, that, in a panic, she sped round the corner of the corridor, like a coursed hare, and pushed open the nearest door, in the hope of finding another refuge.

To her horror, however, it was brightly lit, which made her fear a catastrophic encounter; but, as she flashed her big glasses over the room, she saw that it was empty. Even in that minute of mental stress, she noticed that it was too long for its width, and, also, the additional details of the cosmetics on the toilet table and the snapshot of Dr. Lawrence stuck in the mirror.

"It must belong to the Pomeroy girl," she thought, "or the secretary. Any minute she may be back. I'm not safe here."

Her knees were shaking from the shock of her ordeal. She seemed to be bottled up in a trap, for she dared not return to the corridor, lest she should meet the man whose voice had frightened her.

At this crisis she was saved by her gift of observation, for she noticed the outline of a door, which was covered with paper, so as to appear part of the wall. Pushing it open boldly, she saw, to her joy, that it led into an unlighted room.

"If no one's asleep in there, I may get out that way," she thought.

Then her spine suddenly crept at the sight of an unhuman horror. In the broad beam of light, she saw the huddle of a shriveled figure, whose face was, apparently, composed of wallpaper.

As she forced herself to approach it, she saw that the dummy was the body of an old woman, dressed in grotesquely juvenile white satin pajamas. Her face was almost covered with strips of plaster, but, in spite of this disguise, Miss Pye recognized the drawn features of Miss Vine. A thin trickle of blood oozed from a gash in her forehead, and she stared up at the ceiling with dead, sightless eyes.

Miss Pye's lips formed a word noiselessly.

"Murder."

Even in this moment of horror, her common sense reminded her of her own peril. It would be almost impossible to prove her innocence if she were caught in these compromising circumstances.

Although semiparalyzed with fear, she kept her head. Remembering to shut the door of the girl's room behind her, she groped her way through the darkness of the death chamber, by touching the wall with her fingers. Only too soon, however, she lost all sense of direction, and seemed doomed to perpetual blindness, forever tapping her way towards the vanished light.

The room appeared to have grown so vast that she wondered if she had overshot the door and were going round in a circle. It needed all her self-control not to break down at the thought of the dead thing lying somewhere on the carpet.

"Suppose it has moved." Imagination galloped away with

her. "Suppose it's creeping after me. Cold fingers clawing my ankles. Any second.... Oh, thank Heavens."

She gave a little sob of thankfulness as her fingers found the handle of the door. Very soon, she was outside in the corridor, but lower down, so that she was able to locate the glimmering outline of a nude statue of a woman holding up a cluster of lamps.

For the first time, Miss Pye picked up her bearings. She was close to the great central staircase. She ran along to the landing, and, trusting to luck, took the two flights in a mad rush, like Cinderella leaving the Ball. Sick with suspense, she hurried across the hall, to find that Fortune favored her still.

The door was unbolted, to admit some late inmate of Jamaica Court. But, although it was with a sense of miraculous freedom that she felt the night air on her face, when she was outside the house she tore all the way down the winding drive.

Across the road she could see a faint light shining through the fanlight of the humble Cherry Orchard, as though to welcome her home. The little hall, where the gas burned at half-cock, was like a haven when she let herself in with her latchkey. On the hall table was a note from her brother.

"Out. Breakfast, seven sharp."

The familiar message restored Miss Pye to a miraculous calm. At the rush of old values, her adventure faded to a fantastic dream. She went into the kitchen, to make tea, with the feeling of a storm-tossed mariner who had reached the safety of port.

CHAPTER XXVIII

The Light Goes Out

WHEN PYE RETURNED TO THE CHERRY ORCHARD HIS FIRST deed was to put the spray of orchids in water—an action prompted entirely by solicitude for a rare specimen. His second was to shout for his sister.

When Betsy told him that the mistress was gone out, he concluded that she had accepted an invitation to cards and supper. Although slightly aggrieved, he had to admit that Betsy filled the breach, for she had kept up a good fire, and soon cooked him a meal of ham and eggs.

"Now, *I*'ve made myself an Indispensable," he reflected, as he stretched his ungaitered legs to the blaze. "But old fat Flo has had the patience to train someone else to do her job. Hum."

When the clock struck eleven, he heaved himself regretfully out of his easy chair. His nightly vigil at High Gables had grown to be a test of his quality, for each successive failure left him more depressed, and, consequently, more vulnerable to the Colonel's irony.

Although his teeth were locked on to his job, so that he could not relax his grip, he was beginning to doubt the wisdom of his policy. He had an uneasy feeling that he was fastened to the end of a long string, while someone played with him.

It was a witched night, with a pallid gibbous moon that

scuttled amid tatters of cloud, and a raw moisture greasing the camber of the road. When he reached High Gables, he noticed that the weary-eyed butler was hiding his outraged feelings under the cynical mask of the well-trained servant.

"I don't think the master expects you," he said.

"No, I'm a bit before time," remarked Pye, advancing into the hall. "Don't disturb him. I know the way."

He was in time to detect the Colonel stealing up the stairs. When he saw that his retreat was known, he came down again.

"I'm calling this farce off," he said. "Sorry you had your ride for nothing."

"That's all right, Colonel," remarked Pye cheerily. "I'm glad you're taking a night off."

As he turned towards the drawing room, the Colonel's voice recalled him.

"Afraid that room is no longer at your disposal. We're locking up and all of us are going to bed."

Pye stuck out his lip at the opposition, even although his own neglected bed was pulling him.

"I can't intrude against your wish, Colonel," he said. "But I must tell you something which I have held back. When I examined the drawing room, the morning after the burglary, I could find no evidence as to how and where the burglar entered the house."

"You mean—there were no marks or traces of any kind on the door and windows."

"Um."

"Then you infer the feller was *inside* the house?"

"Looks like it."

"One of my servants? Then, why the hell didn't you question them?"

"Because, Colonel, I stick to my original theory. I'm sure that the vase was taken by the same joker that took Mrs.

Antrobus' ornaments. And I'm also sure that he will turn out to be not unknown to you. He's bound to come back for the lid. Will you give me just one night more?"

To Pye's surprise the Colonel barked assent.

"All right, Pye. I'll see it through with you. But—it's for the last time. That stands."

Through painful familiarity, Pye could find his way about the drawing room in the dark. Very soon, he had found his special chair, while a protesting creak in the corner told him that the Colonel had also located his station.

The first few minutes of waiting passed in the usual strained silence, which was broken by the hall clock striking the half hour after eleven. Pye was reminded that, owing to his unpunctuality, he would have to endure his penance for a slightly longer period, and he cursed both himself and his early-rising ancestors.

The chimes had barely died away when another faint sound was audible, outside the window. Pye thrilled in every nerve at the suppressed excitement of the Colonel's whisper.

"He's here. Take cover."

Silently, each watcher hid himself. As Pye waited in his alcove, it seemed to him that no hunter, perched high on his platform awaiting a tiger, could have vibrated with fiercer emotions.

His prey was just outside. The scraping went on interminably, until his own nerves seemed grated, in sympathy. Then the blood rushed to his head at the sound of a thud.

The intruder had dropped inside the room.

The watchers could hear his feet shuffling over the carpet. Presently a small circle of light danced over the cabinet.

Pye waited until the housebreaker had begun to cut into the square of new glass in the cabinet, in order to make a red-handed capture.

235

"Now," he shouted, switching on the light.

The Colonel guarded the window, while the butler stood before the door. Both gaped in consternation at the figure in Pye's grasp.

It was Francis Ford. He stood perfectly still, as though petrified by the shock of the assault, while Pye turned triumphantly to the Colonel.

"Well, Colonel, is this gentleman known to you?" he asked.

The Colonel made convulsive efforts to clear his throat.

"I believe," he said huskily, "that I had the pleasure of your company at dinner the other night?"

Francis bowed in silence.

"May I ask if you require anything in this cabinet?" continued the Colonel.

"Yes." Francis smiled slightly. "The lid."

Pye coughed uneasily as he remembered that, while county families were not what they used to be, big house still held together.

"Do you make a charge, sir?" he asked the Colonel.

"I do." The Colonel suddenly shouted with explosive effect. "This young cub has outraged my hospitality."

"I admit it," said Francis. "But the real responsibility rests on Miss Vine, whose life I saved; and yet she refused to let me have money. I *had* to raise it, somehow. . . . Do you mind if I sit down? I've been on the sick-list and I'm all in."

His voice failed, and he looked so pale that the Colonel pushed him roughly into a chair.

"Small whisky," he said to the butler. "And now, Ford, I want to hear what you have to say for yourself."

Pye coughed for the second time.

"It is my duty to warn you——"

"All right, Pye, I'm familiar with your bit of Bible,"

broke in Francis. "But I feel the least I can do is to offer the Colonel some sort of an explanation."

His surface politeness veiled insolence and indifference; but he seemed anxious to talk, as he slowly sipped his whisky.

"As I hinted before, I have been squeezed by moneylenders, and the value of your vase, Colonel, was my temptation. In fact, I was so determined to make a successful job of its removal that I made two trial trips of petty larceny, for the sake of practice. Housebreaking is a most stimulating pastime."

Pye caught the Colonel's eye, and held it.

"Do you mean you took Mrs. Antrobus' china figures?" he asked.

"Yes. Amusing, wasn't it?" Francis began to laugh. "I took them separately, on purpose, as I wished to take nothing of value, and most of her stuff is good or perishable in water. It goes without saying that, as I have the instincts of a gentleman, I left the lady's property on the premises."

"Where?" asked Pye eagerly.

"If you prod in the moat, close to the bridge, you will soon locate them among the rushes. And if there is a reward for their restoration, Superintendent, I resign my own claim in your favor."

"But how the devil did you get into my house the first time?" broke in the Colonel.

"I never left it," explained Francis. "When the others were going, I slipped upstairs, to wash my hands, and then I hid in the bedroom half-way up the stairs. I left, afterwards, from the same room, as an open window excites no attention, in a bedroom. Quite an easy descent, but I had to take care with the vase, so I left the lid for a future occasion, in case of accident. I want both of you to acquit me of forgetfulness. . . . And now, Colonel, what is the next move?"

Pye's lust of the chase fought with his sense of sportsmanship. While he felt that an ugly situation might be saved by the exercise of tact and forebearance, he was thankful that the responsibility was not his.

But he knew that the Colonel was hard as nails, and that he could not overlook any insult to his bread and salt. He was not surprised, therefore, when he barked an order to his butler.

"Car."

"Am I to rouse the chauffeur, sir?" asked the man doubtfully.

"No, you fool. Bring her round, and I'll drive her myself to the station."

He remained grimly silent until the Daimler glided up to the front door. Francis, however, appeared to find no awkwardness in the situation, as he seated himself beside Pye.

"At last I have some inkling of the sensations of a man who is taken for a ride," he remarked.

Then he, too, became silent, until a bend in the road brought them in sight of Jamaica Court. Blurred by the screen of trees, they could just see a light which shone through the darkness.

Francis laughed as he pointed to it.

"That's Miss Vine's room. A nice little scandal for her, but I warned her. Will you ring her up tonight?"

"Tomorrow is soon enough," replied Pye.

"It *is* tomorrow. That's twelve striking now."

Even as Francis spoke, the light went out.

CHAPTER XXIX

The Footman's Cigarette

PYE WENT TO BED IN THE MOOD OF A SPORTING SPANIEL who, after weeks of dozing before the fire, has caught his first rabbit. An undercurrent of triumphant memory ran through his dreams, so that he muttered and laughed, even in his sleep.

He had promised himself a late breakfast, so he was reluctant to open his eyes when he heard his sister's voice.

"Adam, wake up. It's official."

He blinked up at Miss Pye, who was standing by his bedside. She carried a tray, which held, not only his shaving water, but also a coffee pot and a pile of sandwiches.

"I thought you could eat while you dressed," she explained. "Dr. Lawrence has just rung up, from Jamaica Court, to say, come at once. Miss Vine is dead."

As her brother stared at her, she added in a tense whisper, *"Murdered."*

Although nothing could shake her calm, he could see that she maintained it at the cost of strain; but she poured out a cup of coffee with a steady hand, as he slid out of bed.

"Murdered?" he repeated. "Great Gosh. Why, I saw her light go out in her room, at twelve."

"Did you? Anyone with you?"

"Yes. Colonel and one of the Fords. Now, clear out. I'm going to dress."

As her brother spoke, Miss Pye's lips relaxed, and she glared behind her glasses no longer.

"I'll bring the car round," she said briskly.

Pye could hardly restrain his excitement as he drove up the drive of the Court, accompanied by a constable. After long abstinence from crime, the surfeit of a robbery and a murder was almost overwhelming. He had his chance, at last.

An unfamiliar Dr. Lawrence met him on the threshold. His face was pale and unshaven, while it was apparent that he had dressed hurriedly.

"She's upstairs," he said. "Her maid rang me up to say that her mistress had met with an accident. Of course, the instant I saw her I knew it was more serious, so I've touched nothing, so far as I could avoid it."

"Good," grunted Pye. "Can you take me up?"

The curtains were looped back from the windows, so that he was able to compare the dramatic contrast of the glittering blue-and-silver apartment with the crumpled scrap on the carpet. At first, like his sister, he recoiled at its unhuman appearance.

"Bless my soul, what's wrong with her face?" he muttered.

"Merely some kind of beauty culture," explained the doctor.

Pye snorted as he remembered that Miss Vine had decorated him, with the witching smile of a siren. So much effort for such a futile result.

"How long has she been dead?" he asked.

"After a certain time it is impossible to indicate the exact period," replied the doctor. "She has certainly been dead for nine hours, if not longer."

"That would be about it," corroborated Pye. "What is the cause of death?"

"She received a blow from some heavy blunt instrument, and died, at once, from shock. Her heart was in a terrible state."

"Where is the weapon?"

"I haven't seen it. Her maid was the first person to find the body, so, perhaps, she removed it. She persists in calling it an accident, which is absurd."

"Impossible, unless the body has been moved," agreed Pye, "and I'll soon find out about that. She's lying on her back, on a thick carpet, which would deaden any fall, while the wound is on her forehead. And now, doctor, I and my man will go over the room. Stay on the premises, as I may want you later."

The thrill of waiting for the unknown burglar paled before Pye's excitement as he subjected the room to a minute examination, overlooking no article in his quest for fingerprints. It was a long job, owing to the size of the apartment and his own conscientious standard, but his yield was barren.

Presently he left the constable on guard, and descended to the hall, where he rang the bell.

"I want to see a responsible member of the household," he told the man. "And no one is to leave the premises without my permission."

He felt the thrill of supreme authority as he was shown into the library, where Charles Ford was talking in earnest undertones to a pale, but composed young lady.

Like the doctor, Charles presented a slovenly appearance—unshaven, with swollen bags under his eyes, and rough hair.

Pye nodded to him and spoke curtly.

"Morning. Bad business, this. Sorry. Now, first of all, you understand the body is the property of the police, until after the inquest, when you may have it back for burial.

241

Until then, it will remain in the mortuary, where I am having it conveyed. No one is to enter the room until after its removal."

Charles winced at the speech, as he pictured Anthea's outraged majesty if she had heard herself translated to terms of the rubbish heap.

"Now," proceeded Pye, "I want to know who slept on these premises, last night."

"I did," mumbled Charles. "Miss Morgan, and, of course, the servants."

"How many servants? I shall want to take their statements, as well as your own?"

"Oh, quite a crowd."

The girl with the sleek waves of hair and the immaculate frock, interposed.

"I can give you a list of them," she said. "I'm better used to this sort of thing, as I am—*was*—Miss Vine's secretary."

It seemed to Pye that she wanted to protect and steady Charles, who was plainly a victim of shock. He noticed the young man's trembling lips with a keen eye that held no personal suspicion.

Nothing less than fact satisfied Adam Pye.

"Bit upset, aren't you, Mr. Charles?" he remarked.

Again he noticed that Sally Morgan looked apprehensive, as Charles plowed his hair into spiky furrows, with his fingers.

"I can't realize it," he said. "It's like some horrible joke. There was I, always saying rotten things about her being murdered. And now—she *is*."

"Ever threaten her?"

"Good lord, no. We had a bit of a roughhouse now and then, but I—I liked her."

242

"Um. You say that only you and Miss Morgan, of the family, slept here last night? What about the others?"

Sally answered for Charles.

"Miss Pomeroy is staying at Crosskeys Rectory for a few days. And Mr. Francis is also away."

Pye looked at the girl's calm face.

"Oho, I see you've heard about *him*," he remarked.

"Oh, you know, too?" Sally smiled faintly. "Yes, we were rung up, directly after we had the—the other news. We cannot understand it, but, of course, it seems nothing—now. I suppose he did it for a joke?"

"Unfortunately, the Colonel won't see it in that light."

"No, it looks to me more like spite work, to get even with *her*," said Charles bitterly. "When does he come up before the bench?"

"Tomorrow. Should have been today, but I shall be on the job here, so can't attend to testify."

"Well, I suppose I must see him," said Charles wearily. "He must have a solicitor."

"Not just yet, Mr. Charles. I want to know what time you went to bed."

As he hesitated, Sally began to make a concise statement.

"We both of us went upstairs at the same time, a little before eleven. The last time I saw Miss Vine alive was just before dinner, when she came into the study to give me some directions about work. She had dinner with Mr. Charles, Mr. Francis and Dr. Lawrence. She left the table before the meal was over and went into the library. That was the last time anyone in the house saw her alive, except Francis. The doctor went after dinner, to a case, and Francis took in her coffee, at her request. She liked to be waited on by the boys. He told us that she wanted him to call her at eleven, for bed. He seemed put out, as he said he had another engagement.

Her maid was out, at a dancing class. I imagine that Francis was the last person to see her alive."

"Thank you," said Pye. "Did you hear any unusual sound during the night?"

"No, my room is some distance from hers."

"You?" Pye swung round to face Charles. "Where do you sleep?"

"My room is in the same wing as Miss Vine's," was the reply. "But I heard nothing."

Pye sucked his pencil gluttonously as he saw a packed day before him, instead of his usual slack routine.

"I'd like Lawrence," he said.

"I'll fetch him," volunteered Charles.

"He wants something to do, to take his mind off," confided Sally to Pye, when they were alone. "Can you help?"

Pye nodded, as Dr. Lawrence entered the room. He had shaved, and now presented his usual smart professional appearance. His manner, too, had changed slightly, for, in spite of veiled eyes and decorous voice, it was not that of a mourner.

"This is a bad business for me," he said. "I lose not only my best patient, but a legacy of ten thousand pounds by her premature death."

"You're bearing up well," observed Pye bleakly. "I want to ask you a few questions, doctor."

"Delighted. One minute, first. I've just been on the phone, talking to Miss Pomeroy, who's terribly distressed by the news. I told her not to come over until I came and fetched her in the car. I want to get the body out of the house before she arrives. Is that in order, Superintendent?"

Before Pye could reply, Sally broke in.

"But she went in her own car. What about that?"

Pye looked alert, although he made no comment, as he turned to Sally.

244

"If you will make a list of the servants, I will take their statements, after I've checked up on the doctor's movements. Merely a matter of form, you understand, all of you." He turned to Charles and added, "I'll give you a permit to see Mr. Francis at once."

As Charles turned towards the door, Sally gave him a tender maternal look, but her voice held reproof.

"Better shave first."

Charles was grateful to get out of the house, whatever the nature of his errand. As he walked briskly along the road some of the nightmare load of oppression slipped from him. He soon found that he had grown sufficiently normal to dread his meeting with Francis.

His cousin, however, showed no trace of awkwardness at his position, when he greeted Charles.

"What about the will? Has Waters come over yet?" His voice was high-pitched with excitement. "Cursed luck, my being out of it, just now."

"Whose fault?" asked Charles gruffly.

"Well, what of it? I'll soon be out of here. I want to talk of the other. I can't keep still since I heard about it. Charles, we're both rich men. Amazing good luck, isn't it?"

As Charles remained silent, he began to laugh.

"Why are you looking down your nose? You're just as glad as I am. The only difference is that *I'm* not a hypocrite."

Charles felt too confused to defend himself, for underneath his ferment of horror and shock, a faint exhilaration was beginning to stir.

At last, he was like other men—free, and possessed of a future.

"Well, it's a bit thick to hang out bunting, in the circumstances," he said gruffly.

"Ah, I forgot the actual circumstances. By the way, was

it you who helped her to shuffle off this mortal coil? If so, I'll stick by you, as a matter of policy and gratitude. You left no incriminating clues, I hope?"

"Oh, chuck it. . . . Who'll you have to represent you tomorrow?"

"No one. I mean to plead 'Guilty.' It has always galled my pride to be the subject for scandal, and I want the whole neighborhood to know the truth about us and old Anthea."

"Not *now*. Look here, I am a lawyer, although the town forgets the fact. Let me see what I can do."

"No, thanks, my dear Charles. I want to get as light a sentence as possible, and I count on getting an acquittal. I'll conduct my own case. I'm safer so, as Browning says."

He persisted in his intention, in spite of Charles' arguments.

"Before you go," he said, "and this affecting interview must end, I want you to take back the Colonel's vase. It will look better for me, tomorrow. It's in a suitcase, under my bed. Remember to ask for a receipt."

When Charles returned to Jamaica Court he was dismayed to find Sally's luggage in the hall. He had forgotten that a temporary secretary was due to arrive from London that afternoon, according to the arrangement made by Miss Vine.

Pye, too, was sorry to hear of her departure, for he had been struck by her coolness and competency. She had been of great assistance in his task of interviewing the household staff, and also in the tactful removal of Miss Vine's body.

"I've left everything in order for my successor," she told him. "She is thoroughly experienced and she is elderly. There's been too much scandal about this house, and I'd better not stay on, in the circumstances. Here is my address and telephone number, so that you can get in touch with me if there is any point you want cleared up."

Although he knew that he would miss her, Pye was most glad to see her go.

"That young lady's altogether too cool a customer," he decided. "I shall be able to get a better line on Charles, when she's no longer here, to spoon-feed him."

When the car took Miss Morgan to the station, the spirit of anarchy seemed to enter the domestic staff. Their mistress was dead, and the secretary was gone.

She had not left five minutes before the door of Miss Vine's bedroom was opened by her maid, Eames. She looked cautiously around her before she entered. The spring sunshine streamed in upon the glittering silver walls—sterile of all emotions, now that it was but an empty shell, from which the life had departed.

Treading lightly, the woman crossed to the built-in drawers, and took out piles of unworn lingerie—pink, mauve, blue—which she threw on the carpet. Making a hasty selection, she packed them into her suitcase and went to the door.

On its threshold, she gave a violent start, and then, seized by sudden panic, rushed along the corridors until she reached the safety of the right wing.

Pye spent a busy day, conducting a thorough search of the premises, to find the missing weapon, and also, in consultation with Mr. Waters, who brought Miss Vine's will for inspection.

Apart from his authority, the household was in a state of demoralization, so that a bored footman, as he lounged against a pillar of the marble hall, took the opportunity to enjoy a surreptitious cigarette.

CHAPTER XXX

The Sphinx Speaks

WHEN PYE RETURNED TO THE CHERRY ORCHARD, THAT evening, he seemed to have grown in the interval, while his importance was swollen, after the fashion of an inflated rubber toy. With the majesty of the law, he combined the silence of the Sphinx. When Miss Pye met him, with a natural inquiry about the murder, he held her with a fierce blue eye, as he asked, *"What* murder?"

His tone warned her definitely off his domain; but she was debating her own problem and scarcely noticed what he said. All day she had been wondering if it were possible to keep her escapade her own secret. So far as she could judge, no good could come of its advertisement, and might only involve her in dangerous issues.

"Liver and bacon for tea," she said. "Pancakes to follow."

Pye beamed, for she had provided his favorite dishes.

"Busy day?" inquired Miss Pye, as she whisked off a cover.

"That's asking," said Pye.

"Any clues?"

"That's telling."

"Found the murderer yet?"

"Any number of them."

Miss Pye's thoughts were still fixed on those awful moments when she had crept along a maze of nightmare corridors. She continually asked herself whether she had been seen by anyone, or if she had left behind her some clue to her identity.

"You know, Adam," she said, "it has always seemed to me that anyone might get into Jamaica Court and not be noticed in that barracks of a house."

"Wrong," declared her brother.

"Then it wasn't an outside job?"

"No." Pye remembered in time to crush further confidence. "*What* job?"

Miss Pye poured out tea as she nerved herself for confession.

"Adam," she said. "I've something to tell you connected with Jamaica Court, if you will listen to me."

As Pye suddenly stopped chewing and looked at her, she was struck by the penetration of his gaze. The bluff, familiar Adam seemed to be sunk in a new ruthless identity—merciless to judge, swift to sentence.

"Flo," he said, "I'm going to ask you questions, for a change. Did *you* murder Miss Vine?"

"Mercy, Adam, *no.*"

Her scream made him smile grimly.

"I believe you, my girl. Now, another. Do you know *who* murdered her?"

"No. But I——"

"That's enough. Now you listen to me. I don't want to hear one word more on this subject. I've got to keep a clear head and an open mind. I don't want to get it all messed up with crosscurrents and roads that lead nowhere."

"I understand, Adam." Miss Pye changed the subject quickly. "Do you know Betsy refused apple pie for her dinner, today, and when I asked why, she said she didn't like them little black things. Fancy, she'd been chewing the cloves."

"Better men have done that before her," grinned Pye.

With a view to making up his shortage, he went to bed early, and nearly slept the clock round. He was an imposing figure—ruddy and dominant—when he made his appearance at the police court, in his first important case. The conscious-ness that his success was a foretaste of a supreme triumph, lent vigor to his gestures and resonance to his voice.

The court was crowded, although the public interest was, naturally, centered on the crime at Jamaica Court. But even though Miss Vine's anonymous murderer had stolen most of his thunder, Francis Ford was in his element as he looked at his audience. He wore his newest suit—purchased with Miss Vine's money—and his hair shone with a satin sheen.

After he had pleaded "Guilty," he began to address the court, his clear-cut diction being audible in the back benches.

"I wish to make an important statement regarding my relationship with Miss Vine, in order to clear my character of slur and stain, and also to prove that, since I have been her victim, this theft is, indirectly, *her* responsibility. If there is justice on earth, *she* should be standing here, in my place."

He paused with dramatic effect, but was not allowed to continue his performance, for the bench sternly charged him to confine himself to the answers of questions. He availed himself of so much latitude in his replies, and, consequently, had to be stopped so frequently, that the general atmosphere grew heated from friction.

The Colonel gave his evidence in a deadly and lucid man-ner, which marked the degree of his venom. No one in the court, therefore, was surprised when the magistrates made short work of the case and sent it up for trial at the next assizes.

The decision was clearly a severe shock to Francis, who

had counted on an acquittal. He stared at the bench, and then, losing his head, accused its members of injustice and stupidity.

As a result of his outburst he was refused bail. When Charles saw him, afterwards, he was livid with rage.

"It's an outrage," he stormed. "A man of my wealth to be cooped up for a practical joke. I tell you, I can't stand it. You don't know what it's like—confined all day and all night. You must get me out, Charles."

"I'll do my level best," Charles promised. "But you'd better take it quietly. Be civil, and you'll probably get only a short spell in the second division. You can pass the time thinking over investments for your money."

"No, I can only think of those walls, walls, walls," groaned Francis. Then he turned on Pye fiercely. "Instead of chasing butterflies, why don't the police find Miss Vine's murderer? But I know why. You're afraid."

"Afraid? Me?" asked Pye.

"Yes. Too near the bone. *Who*—besides us—stands to gain by her death?"

Pye kept biting on the innuendo all the day. When he went home he saw a familiar red roadster parked in the road before the Cherry Orchard. It underlined a change of circumstance. And he could not ignore the fact that the gloom of the family atmosphere was dispersed by sunshine.

Mrs. Law was radiant as she explained the car.

"No money had passed, so I pretended it was only a joke, and demanded it back again."

"Not afraid of being premature?" asked Pye.

"No, for I rang up Mr. Smart Aleck, this morning, and said I'd close with their offer for the Timberdale Arms. Just bluff on my part, to find out how the land lay. He said that as Miss Vine was prime mover in the scheme for a new Munster Hotel the whole thing had lapsed with her death."

"Isn't it a deliverance?" beamed Miss Pye. "Just like coming out of gas and finding the tooth is out."

Doris laughed loudly as she patted her brother on his back. "I hope you won't be such a rotten sport as to convict the old girl's murderer," she said. "He ought to be decorated as a public benefactor, and I don't care who hears me say so."

Suddenly, to Miss Pye's surprise, her brother dropped his Trappist pose, and began to gossip, over the teacups, about the murder. It is true that he spoke in general terms and gave no information away, so that, to her mind, his action was significant of some underlying purpose.

"The verdict will be 'Murder against person or persons unknown,'" he declared. "Deceased was biffed on the forehead with a weapon which is missing, but was probably, some motoring tool."

"Whose?" asked Mrs. Law.

"Ah, whose?" repeated Pye. "All the young people at the Court, have cars. So we stop there, and go on to the next point—the time of the murder. We fix this for twelve, as I saw her light go out, for one, and she was all dolled up, ready for the night, which was an hour's work. By the way, her maid had put in some good keyhole work over her mistress' secret toilet, for she could give me every detail. My word. Call her a clever woman, when she lets herself in for that. . . . Therefore, on the evidence, Miss Vine was murdered just as she was about to get into bed, by someone inside the house. *Who?*"

Miss Pye felt her knees shake as her brother glared impartially at both the big fair women. But she had received her absolution and intended to give nothing away.

"The servants?" asked Mrs. Law.

"No, for I've taken their statements, and they have all got alibis, as they slept, two together, in the right wing.

252

No housekeeper, and the butler is married to the cook.....
Now for the rest. Miss Vine and the three youngsters slept
in the left wing. I arrested Francis before the murder was
committed. The girl was staying with friends, about ten
miles away. Charles says he was in bed."

"But must it be one of them?" asked Miss Pye.

"No, but it might. Motive was identical, as all benefit
by the will. Now, we'll pass to two other persons, who have
secondary, but equally strong interests in the death of the
deceased. First, Dr. Lawrence. He loses his legacy, but if
he'd had to wait for it, he would probably be sunk. Now,
it's plain he has an affair with the girl, and it would pay
him, hands down, to marry her, now she's rich."

"Yes," nodded Miss Pye, "the marriage is in the cards."

"There is also the secretary," went on Pye. "A cool young
cuss. I believe she means to marry Charles, who is a rich
man now. She also stood to lose her legacy, for, if the crime
had been committed the following night, she would have
been out of Miss Vine's employment. There's a double
motive."

"I'd look no further," said Mrs. Law, who had never
forgiven the unlucky witness of her interview.

"But I am going farther," remarked Pye. "There's this
family. Whoever bumped off Miss Vine did us a good turn.
So you see, I have a fine field of suspects, and the murderer is among the lot. It seems to me simplest to prove
which is innocent, before I tackle the guilt of the lady or
gentleman of the spanner."

"Well, you can count out quite a number," said Mrs. Law.

"I'm not so sure. Take the doctor. He tells the usual tale
of being sent for, and driving out into the country, to find
it was a faked telephone call. Well, his alibi hangs on how
quickly he drove. Same applies to Miss Pomeroy. She had a
car, too, and would make nothing of a few miles. When I

tell you one of the servants heard a car on the drive, about twelve, you will understand that I can place no reliance on the alibis of either the doctor or Miss Pomeroy."

"Well, so've I a car," said Mrs. Law defiantly. "And I was playing nap in my own bar parlor, with three witnesses, and never dreaming some hero was doing my dirty work for me."

Miss Pye, who was watching her brother, saw his lips tighten in a way which always signified that the tap was about to be turned off. Whatever his object in breaking his silence, it was achieved.

"Seems to me," he observed, "that my difficulty lies in the fact that there are too many people with a motive for murdering Miss Vine."

He relaxed in a shout of laughter, as Miss Pye relieved the situation with a characteristic remark.

"Then why don't you look for someone who had no motive?"

CHAPTER XXXI

Inquest

THE INQUEST ON MISS VINE WAS HELD IN A COUNCIL chamber of the Town Hall. A parochial tea was in progress in another part of the building, so that the air held faint odors of tea, hyacinths and currant cake. The Mayoress was entertaining some of the more important parishioners in the Mayor's parlor, which was a few doors down the corridor, and distant bursts of feminine gaiety were sometimes audible.

To the jurymen, who had just viewed an unfamiliar Miss Vine, the ray of spring sunshine which pierced the dust-clogged air, seemed as unreal and stagey as limelight. Few had availed themselves of their privilege of exemption; but the wrinkled parchment face of the corpse conveyed little reality to them, as it held nothing of Miss Vine's identity.

Now that she had gone, they could only remember a rouged, shrill-tongued woman of fashion, dressed in the most extreme and extravagant mode. Even after so short a period, there seemed to have been nothing of her but clothes and noise. The powerful directing will and the busy scheming brain that held together and animated the huddle of draperies and framework, had vanished.

Superintendent Pye was an alert and interested spectator of the proceedings. Although most of the evidence was already known to him, he considered every statement and watched each witness with vigilant care.

When the musician and the restaurantkeeper gave corroborative evidence as to the time when they saw Miss Vine's light go out, on the night of the murder, he nodded at the points which corresponded with his own experience. But underneath the surface currents was the rock of his main interest. Whenever he looked around the court, the reminder floated in his mind.

"He—or she—is here. Which?"

Although much of the evidence was tedious, as it covered the same ground, there were some high spots of drama and suspense. Eames provided a real thrill as she described how she found the body.

"She was lying on the carpet, and she didn't seem to have any face. It looked like bits of mosaic paving, all stuck together with red paint. And then, as I came closer, I saw that she was all plastered up, and the red paint was dried blood."

Pleased with the general sigh of pent-up breath, the maid stepped into the limelight herself.

"And then I dropped the tea, telephoned for the doctor, and went off in a dead faint."

She furnished another tense moment, when she described the mystery of her mistress' evening toilet.

"Mortal eye never saw her like *that,* before. She never let me help her, although it took all of an hour, and she never let me see her, in the morning, until she'd taken off her mask and powdered up a bit. I had to knock and wait outside the door, until she said, 'Come in,'—no matter how long I stood there with the tray. And if it was cold she blew my head off."

Recalled to essentials, Miss Eames stated that Miss Vine had never been to bed on the fatal night.

"She was all ready to go, so she must have been attacked directly after she switched off the light."

A thrill of suppressed horror ran through the court at this suggestion of the poor victim—encased and helpless in the trappings of her vanity—being struck down in the darkness of her own creation.

Although Eames provided the sensational element, there was no doubt that the witness who attracted most attention was Francis Ford, in view of his recent escapade. Although he only threw one glance around him, it was plain that he was conscious of his audience throughout the proceedings and that he was playing up to it.

He wore a suit of deepest mourning and his face was pale. When he gave his evidence his manner was moody and preoccupied, and he confined his replies, whenever possible, to monosyllables. The trouble he gave, in the extraction of his testimony, was a slight gesture of revenge for a former occasion, when his eloquence had been gagged.

In spite of his own restrictions, he managed, however, to give the dead woman one last kick.

"You have stated," said the Coroner, "that you went to the library at eleven o'clock. What was the condition then of the deceased?"

"Drunk," said Francis, acidly.

In marked contrast, Dr. Lawrence made a fluent and resourceful witness. Always a popular figure, on account of his good looks and charm—today, his handsome features were stamped with an air of resolution, and he spoke impressively, in his eagerness to vindicate the character of the dead woman.

He stated that when he viewed the corpse life had been extinct from eight to nine hours, and that although a blow had been inflicted, it was more in the nature of a sharp tap, causing a surface wound. Death had resulted from shock.

He went on to say that he had been in constant attendance on the deceased, who was a woman of advanced age, and, therefore, practically worn out. She was possessed of marvelous mental activity and her faculties were unimpaired, but her body only functioned through the exercise of a powerful will. She was also a woman of frugal habits, and—he would like to stress this point in view of other evidence—markedly temperate.

Pye smiled slightly at this portrait of a Grand Old Lady, painted by her respectful young physician. It fitted so little into his gallery of snapshots of an ancient rouged flirt, with a host of eager courtiers buzzing round her, like flies around a honey pot.

Dr. Lawrence seemed to be pleased with the impression he had managed to create, but his complacency faded before the Coroner's final question.

"You have stated that little force was exerted in striking the fatal blow. In your opinion, could the murder have been committed by a woman?"

It was obvious that the doctor was taken by surprise. He paled slightly and paused before his reply, when his voice was pitched so low as to be almost inaudible.

"Yes."

In spite of the sensation in court, the final honors fell to the young footman who had smoked on duty, for it was he who provided the real punch.

When the inquest was over, Pye returned to the Cherry Orchard, with his face red as a harvest moon from heat and excitement. Miss Pye glanced at him, but decided to ask no questions, to his private disappointment, for *"What* inquest" was already on the tip of his tongue. Presently, when his pipe was drawing well, he himself opened the subject.

"Well, the verdict was just as I said. 'Murder by person or persons unknown.' "

"Not very satisfactory," commented Miss Pye. "I could have said as much, and I'm only one woman to twelve men."

"All they could do on the evidence," explained her brother.

"Is anyone suspected?"

"Yes."

"Who?"

"Charles Ford."

"Oh, not Charles." Miss Pye gave a faint wail. "He couldn't have done it. Not with his wicked, dare-devil grin."

"Not exactly a testimonial to character," grunted Pye. "You see, something rather black against him came out. He had given evidence that he went to bed about eleven. Now there's a footman, whose duty it is to bolt and chain the front door. If any of the family was coming home late he just locked it, so that they could let themselves in with their keys, when they finished the job. That special night he was going to a dancing class with Eames, and he forgot to ask for his instructions before he went, so when he got home, he left the door unbolted, so as to be on the safe side. But he's a conscientious lad, and got worried, so when he woke up, about two-thirty, he thought he'd find out if the young gentlemen were in, so that he could go down and chain up, if it wasn't already done. So he crept along the corridor and peeped into both the bedrooms. They were not only empty, but the beds were untouched."

"My word," gasped Miss Pye. "Of course, Francis was locked up at the station. What did Charles say?"

"Said he was with a lady and he refused to give her name. Oh, he told the tale all right. According to him, it was all daisies and dewdrops, and he said he'd be hanged before he gave the local scandalmongers any chance to chuck mud at the girl."

Miss Pye looked at her brother over her glasses.

"Do you suspect him, Adam?" she asked.

"I keep an open mind. I like Charles."

"So do I. So now, Adam, it's up to you to find out who really murdered Miss Vine?"

"Yes. It's my chance."

As he spoke, Pye caught a fractional glimpse of the gleam. He was aroused by his sister's deep voice.

"Of course, Charles will continue to refuse to give the girl's name. But it's all right. When the woman was here, the other day, I found that hot water had been spilt on a polished table; and when she refused to say who had done it, Betsy, for pure shame, owned up. Mark my words, the girl will speak."

"A conclusion which I have already reached without the invaluable aid of Betsy," remarked Pye. "Of course, the woman in the case, is the secretary. I stopped at the P. O. on my way home and put through a call to London, but she was out. So I sent her a telegram, giving her the main outlines of the situation."

He stopped speaking as Betsy appeared with a message.

"Official, please. A young lady to see the master. She won't give no name."

Without the weakness of a glance at his sister, Pye walked majestically from the room and into his office. A pale, dark girl, of refined appearance, was standing by the fire. He recognized her at once, as the barmaid at the Red Lion.

"Why, it's Miss Belson," he said heartily. "How are you, my dear? What's the trouble?"

The girl twisted her gloves nervously.

"I've come about the murder," she explained. "You know, Mr. Charles Ford and I are old friends, and we have often gone for walks, late at night. There was no other time, for I was in the bar and the old lady used to keep him dancing attendance on her, and I'm not one of those who believe that my character hangs on a watch, or clock, when there's no harm at all, but only a pure friendship."

"Quite right," agreed Pye. "There's never been a young lady at the Red Lion so respected universally as yourself."

"Thank you, Superintendent. You see, it was just because of my good name that Charles wouldn't say he'd been out with me, the night of the murder. Why, when we were sitting together on a gate, we actually saw her light go out. We joked about it, and blew her kisses and wished her nighty-night. I am ready to make a sworn statement, if it is required."

"That does you great credit, Miss Belson," said Pye heartily.

When he returned to the sitting room, he stood, spread-eagled before the fire, in his favorite attitude of victory.

"Thank the Almighty," he said solemnly, "that when He left out a woman's brain, He gave her a heart instead. He knew——"

He broke off at the ringing of the telephone bell in the hall.

"That's probably from Miss Morgan," he said. "Pity I wasted that wire."

His intuition was correct, for he recognized Sally's voice at the other end of the wire.

"Is that Superintendent Pye? Miss Morgan speaking. I want to tell you something important. Charles Ford and I are engaged to be married, and Miss Vine made trouble for us, and discharged me. That night, Charles came into my room, for just a minute, and then he sat down, and we began to talk things over. We got so engrossed, making plans to emigrate, that we couldn't believe our eyes when we saw the time. Naturally, we thought it wiser to suppress the fact that he had been in my room until twenty to three. But

261

since it has come out, I want you to know where Charles really was."

"Thanks," snapped Pye, ringing off.

When he returned from the telephone, his face was grim and his lips compressed to a small rigid line. The first thing that caught his eye was a mauve envelope, addressed in a curly handwriting.

"For you," explained Miss Pye. "Brought by hand."

He tore open the envelope, skimmed the contents of the note, and then crumpled it up in his palm.

"From a local flapper," he explained, "to say that on the date of the murder she passed a passionate night of guilty love with Charles Ford. *She's* been going to the pictures."

As she watched him, Miss Pye saw the veins swell out on her brother's temples. Suddenly he exploded.

"Damnation. Two, at least of these women are lying, and, probably, three. Who can believe one word, now? Between them all, they've wrecked a good alibi."

CHAPTER XXXII

The Tide Turns

MISS VINE'S LAST WILL AND TESTAMENT WAS READ, NOT in the Empire salon, but in the library.

"I couldn't bear it, *there*," cried Iris. "I should remember last time, and I should feel that she was sitting on the yellow sofa, listening, and watching us."

Even under these changed conditions, she found that both her nerves and fortitude were tested by the ordeal. She started at every slight stir behind the ancient stamped-leather hangings, and kept looking nervously around her, as though she feared to see a triangular painted face mocking her from the shadows.

Charles watched her, as he nursed his chin with his hand, for the reading only exacted half his attention. The contents of the will were already familiar to him, and he was prepared for the one change of the addition to Francis' share. Now that he was recovering from the shock of the murder, his spirits were rising. Twice daily he rang up Sally, to exchange confidences over the promise of the future.

It was plain to him that Iris had not rallied to the same extent; she not only looked ill, but she appeared to be suffering from grief or remorse. Her eyes were shadowed, and her conventional red lips made a unnatural flash of color on her pale face.

Although she had avoided Charles for days, when they

met after dinner, in the drawing room, they drew together by a common impulse. The room, as usual, was blazing with light, so that there was no friendly shadow wherein a drifting earthbound soul might linger for a space.

Rather to Charles' surprise, Iris seated herself on the tiny gold brocade sofa, formerly occupied by Anthea, in her pose of a disembodied spirit. She motioned to the vacant place by her side.

"Sit here, Charles, and there'll be no room for *her*."

As he obeyed, she looked at him, and shuddered.

"Isn't it all terrible?" she cried. "I simply can't get it out of my head. I feel we were beasts to her. I know I failed her. What would I be without her? Some nameless workhouse brat."

She overstated the case, since she had been correctly listed on the register of the adoption society; so Charles merely laughed heartlessly.

"Who cares a fig if your name is Iris or Isinglass?" he asked. "Besides, it's no good stirring up mud. It's settled a bit now. But we none of us would care to be a fortnight back."

Iris bit her lip as she remembered that so short a time ago Anthea had been alive and in her most venomous phase.

"We've got to think of the future," went on Charles. "How long are you staying on here?"

"A week or so, until Mrs. Loftus"—she named the new secretary—"has finished up. Of course, I can't stay after she goes."

"She wants Sally back to show her how to deal with a spot of work," said Charles, who was jealous of the capable widow who had supplanted her.

"Oh yes, I forgot." Iris forced a show of interest. "Are you going to marry Miss Morgan?"

"I am."

"Does she get her legacy?"

"She will, unless we like to dispute it. I warn you, litigation is costly, and she'd probably win."

"Oh, *I* make no objection. Let her have the miserable money. I hate it now. Francis might."

"Might show fight? Curse him. But it doesn't matter a hoot. I've enough for us both. That reminds me. I suppose you'll be marrying Lawrence?"

Charles was astonished when Iris' face suddenly puckered up, as though she were going to cry.

"Don't talk of that." Her voice was petulant. "The idea's horrible, when things are like *this*. Everything's spoilt for me. I believe the money is going to be a curse to all of us."

"Not to me," declared Charles with his old impudent grin. "And I'll relieve you of your little lot, if you feel like that."

Iris flashed him a glance of suspicion and fear.

"I believe you would," she declared. "You're like Francis. The money has gone to his head. Oh, Anthea was right. She always said it would. But I never thought he could be quite so vile."

"Now you're springing something new on me," Charles declared. "What d'you mean—exactly?"

"Only, that when I visited Francis, yesterday, he actually asked me to marry him, so as to keep the money together."

As Charles began to laugh, she turned on him passionately.

"Oh, I hate all men. You think of nothing but money, and you're all heartless and cruel. . . . Besides, I—I'm afraid."

She shrank back into a corner of the sofa, and looked at him from under lowered lids.

"I'm *afraid*," she whispered. "Someone—in this house— murdered her."

Charles only laughed the louder.

"It's all right," he said. "I shan't do it twice. In the circumstances, it might create talk."

"What's the joke?" asked a suave voice.

They looked up, to see Dr. Lawrence, wearing a light coat over his evening clothes, and a white muffler wound around his neck. He appeared to be in excellent spirits, although he had assisted, that day at the last rites of the burial of Miss Vine.

"I'm going to the theater," he said. "Traveling company, but quite good, I hear. I had to drop in first, to see you."

He bent over Iris with a tenderly possessive air.

"All right?" he asked. "Don't brood. It won't help her, and it won't help you."

To Charles' surprise, Iris dashed away his hand. Lawrence merely raised his brows and changed the subject.

"What's to become of Jamaica Court?" he asked.

"As part of the estate, it's to be sold," replied Charles, glad to discuss practical details. "Of course, we shan't sell it, for big houses are a drug on the market. But Waters tells me that Francis is full of some scheme of turning it into an hotel."

"That bright youth is suffering from a bad attack of inherited wealth," laughed the doctor. "The poor chap's gone to bits. He caught a fresh cold the night of what he calls—his *faux pas,* which isn't helping him. So far, *he's* getting no good from his money."

"And none of us." Iris sprang from the sofa and rushed towards the door. "This money is a curse, for there's blood on it. And *she* knows, and she's laughing at us all."

Dr. Lawrence made no attempt to follow her, as she banged the door behind her. He merely lit a cigarette and went on talking in his usual voice.

"To resume our broken thread. Where was I? Oh, what

266

about yourself, Charles?... Another match, please.... Are you a member of the firm of Waters, Waters, and many waters?"

"No," replied Charles. "Anthea never sent the check. Of course, now, I'm in a position to sign my own, but I'm holding my hand for a bit. We're going to shut this place up directly, to save for the death duties. And I may prefer to hang out my plate somewhere else. Oldtown stinks a bit now."

"I understand. Thinking of getting married?"

"I'm thinking of buying a dog," grinned Charles. "Whatever there's bad, I'm going to get that much good out of this mess."

Dr. Lawrence thoughtfully blew a ring of smoke.

"Yes, it *is* a mess," he agreed. "The town is stiff with rumors. You're lucky to be able to dig yourself in. We're all of us under suspicion. Amusing, isn't it? Wish friend Pye would hurry up and spot the lady."

Although the doctor had used a common figure of speech, Charles stared at him as he remembered a tense incident of the inquest, and how Lawrence had paused before his admission that the murder could have been committed by a woman.

"You don't think——?"

He broke and glanced involuntarily towards the door.

The change in the doctor's face was startling in its swift transition from tranquillity to storm. It appeared positively dark and swollen by sudden passion, as he glared at Charles.

"You mean—Iris?" he asked thickly.

"I suppose so."

"Then I advise you to keep your thoughts to yourself. Remember, *you* are walking on eggs."

Still in a rage, he snatched up his hat; but when he paused by the door, he had regained his calm.

"I've had a little prison experience," he said meaningly. "So I am familiar with the type of man who is genial with his victim, even when he is killing her."

Charles' jaw dropped when he was alone. Ever since the murder, he had kept within the grounds of the Court. He knew vaguely that Oldtown had gained the distinction of a prominent position in the columns of the press, and that Mrs. Loftus—the secretary—was proving herself resourceful and tactful in dealing with reporters.

But while he had taken the local gossip for granted, this was the first time that he realized the crime was being discussed in every city, town and village where the London papers were delivered. Hosts of unknown readers were finding the mystery a source of interest and speculation.

Charles made a grimace at the reminder that, even at that moment, men in bars and ladies in drawing rooms, might be arguing the possibility of his own innocence or guilt. It gave him a sense of insecurity, even while he was enclosed, as within a fortress, by the solid stone masonry of Jamaica Court.

The gossipmongers could not reach him in the luxurious, brilliantly lighted room; but while he stood staring at the door it might open, to admit the law. Other brains—skilled in criminal investigation—were busy on the solution of the crime. They were on their mettle to prevent it being lain on the shelves, among the files of unsolved murders.

Even now, they might be preparing to spring. Not one was safe, for all human diagnosis was liable to error. In this welter of suspicions and crosscurrents, the innocent might suffer for the guilty.

For the first time, Charles felt desperately afraid, as though the shadows of the gallows was falling athwart the white and golden walls. Unable to endure his own thoughts, he turned to the telephone. Sally, with her unfailing cheer and common sense, was at the other end of the wire. In a few minutes he would hear her voice. But he took off the receiver, only to replace it.

It was not fair to worry her. Keener-brained than himself, she had doubtless already sized up the danger of everyone concerned with Anthea's affairs. If not, it might open her eyes to her own peril.

At the mere thought of Sally standing in the dock, Charles began to sweat. In an effort to escape from himself, he left the Court, and tramped towards the town. Now that the funeral was over, he could join in a game of billiards at one of the public houses, without exciting too much comment.

Just before he reached the shops he recoiled at the sight of a familiar figure. Superintendent Pye—pipe in mouth—was tramping down the street, with his head held high, as though in victory. Outlined against the light of a street lamp, his burly form was magnified by the night mist, so that he appeared as a gigantic, impersonal force.

Charles tried to remember that he had shouted "Old Mince-pie," after him, like all the other boys. Pye was no awful vehicle of vengeance, but merely a good mixer, not overburdened with brains.

He called out to him, with his most impudent grin.

"Hallo, Super. On your way to arrest me?"

Pye looked steadily at the young man before he answered him.

"When I'm ready for you, you'll know it," he said grimly. "I don't deal in suspicion. I always wait until I'm dead sure, and then—I nail my man."

"Pleasant for us, if you guess wrong," laughed Charles.

"I shall be right," was the confident reply.

Pye walked home to the Cherry Orchard, in the majestic abstract which had grown to be his habitual state. He wanted the murder to be his own property, and would have liked to forbid its discussion, by law. Miss Pye's diagnosis of his mental attitude, although slightly exaggerated, was not far from the mark.

"He'd like to bury it, like a dog with a bone, and dig it up, every now and again, just to know it's there."

Although the case bristled with difficulties, which were growing daily more difficult of solution, Pye thrived on his perplexities. At least, four persons had a motive for murder, combined with the opportunity; but it was impossible to prove the actual guilt of any of the suspects, who, therefore, had to be assumed innocent.

For the present, he concentrated on finding some witness who had seen, or heard a motorcar on certain routes, which may have been followed by either Dr. Lawrence or Miss Pomeroy. But, although he cast his net wide, no haul resulted. So he plodded happily on with his inquiries, leaving his problem to incubate within his brain.

The attitude of the London press did not ruffle his serenity, although its pages were spattered with criticisms of the stupidity and conceit of local police, who neglected to enlist the aid of Scotland Yard. He was confident that the Chief Constable, who had entrusted him with the case, would stand by him through all these attacks. It was their own special murder and no concern whatsoever of London Town.

It was Miss Pye who grew conscious of the gradual change in public opinion. At first, everyone expressed excited horror, rather than compassion, over the death of a very unpopular lady, who was a scandal to the neighborhood.

Before long, however, the tradespeople became aware of a loss of valuable custom. Miss Vine never patronized the stores, because she liked the prestige which accrued from her extensive purchases. She would stop her car, with an imperative hoot, before a shop, and, personally, hand the list prepared by her cook, to a courtly manager.

Sometimes, she bought up blocks of tickets for the cinema, and gave them away to favored shop assistants. But, now that this extravagant regime was over, and Jamaica Court about to be shut up, the tide turned in a wave of sympathy toward its dead mistress. Already she was growing to be a legendary figure—a dim, posturing flirt, all paint, jewels, and beautiful clothes.

Until her murderer was brought to justice, Oldtown considered itself to be under a cloud.

CHAPTER XXXIII

Ultimatum

IT WAS A TRADITION IN THE PYE FAMILY THAT ITS MEMbers never quarreled. As a matter of fact, they had their differences, when they preserved their dignity by not speaking to each other, and making any necessary communication through the medium of a third person. Miss Pye, therefore, broke all the rules of the game when she exchanged high words with the privileged younger sister.

In her freedom from worry, Mrs. Law had grown almost blatant with triumph. Like a prosperity campaigner, she could talk of nothing but her own success. She had actually coarsened in appearance, owing to the fact that she had discarded her hat with the advent of the overdue spring.

When she stopped her car, with three signal hoots, outside the gate of the Cherry Orchard, Miss Pye was conscious of inhospitality. Although she remained good-natured and placid, she had reacted to the general tension of the family atmosphere. While Pye wrestled with the problem of finding Miss Vine's murderer, he made her the natural target of his ill-humor, so that she had sunk to the subterfuge of hiding the daily paper and laying the blame upon Betsy.

The sun which had reddened the coarse grain of Mrs. Law's skin, made a glory of her golden hair, which she wore in an incongruous Garbo long bob. As she swaggered up the garden path, she was accompanied by four excited dogs that barked while they leaped at her.

Pye's well-trained Alsatian walked pointedly from the room, to register his disapproval of the intrusion. Mrs. Law nodded to her sister as she lit a fresh cigarette from the stub of the old one.

"Seen today's paper?" she asked.

Forgetful of her own allegiance to a popular and powerful newspaper, Miss Pye tossed her head.

"Yes," she said. "And I seem to remember that it was burnt, publicly, not so long ago."

"Well, what it says is horse sense," commented Mrs. Law. "You know, old dear, public safety must come before sentiment. Now, between you, me, and the bedpost, don't you think Adam has stayed too long in the garden?"

"I don't know what you're driving at," declared Miss Pye.

"Yes, you do. Now, I'm as fond of the old boy as you are, and those darned newspapers get right under my skin. But what *I've* got to put up with is hearing people in my bar passing remarks, and then nearly choking over their ale, when they remember I'm related. It's a bit too thick."

Behind her glasses, Miss Pye's eyes were hard as flints.

"Do you mean," she asked, "that you want Adam to give up his big chance just for you to save your face with a pack of village soakers?"

"No, of course not. But I don't want him to go on making a fool of himself. *He'll* never find Miss V.'s murderer, not if he tries for a hundred years. He's vegetated here too long and his brain is run to seed."

Miss Pye stuffed her fingers in her ears.

"I won't listen to him being insulted in his own house," she cried in a trembling voice. "And from *you*, who couldn't

273

pass your Senior Cambridge. He knows what he's about, but he'll take his own time."

Mrs. Law lit another cigarette and spoke to her Alsatian. "Come here with mother, Sultan pet. We don't want to stay where we're not welcome. No, no biscuits, today, I'm afraid. And never mind about the cards."

It was symptomatic of her demoralization that Miss Pye broke the dignified tradition of the third person, and directly appealed to her sister.

"Don't get mad, Dorrie. I'm—I'm sorry. Do you want to know about the fair commercial? Sit down, and I'll cut the cards."

Mrs. Law bore no malice, so the sisters parted friends. But when she and her tribe of dogs had gone, leaving peace behind them, Miss Pye sat on, mechanically playing patience, as an accompaniment to her thoughts.

Her own common sense chimed with every one of her sister's arguments. Of course, the press was right; if Doris were the victim, she would be first to demand the intervention of Scotland Yard. Besides, she had to admit that, for many years, Adam's mental powers had lain stagnant. His life had been divided up into small interests—routine duties, judging dogs, umpiring matches, growing prize dahlias, playing pyramid or pool.

Yet, when she remembered the extraordinary penetration of his gaze when he had cautioned her not to confuse the issues with her confession, she wondered if he were not playing a very deep game of his own. His temper and gloom might be the result, not of perplexity, but of mental unrest.

"I'm holding back important evidence," she thought. "If he's really barking up the wrong tree, it might be a help to him. But—but supposing, he really *knows*."

She shuddered at the possibility, but her lips remained firm.

"It would make no difference to me, if he killed Miss Vine himself. He knows best, and he's the law. Nothing but happiness has come from her death. Adam may be like Lancashire, and what he thinks today, the world will think tomorrow. It's only common sense to kill a slug in the garden. I'll never judge him, and I'll always be *proud* of him."

Miss Pye mechanically played a game of demon, without noticing the result of the cards she stacked.

"If I tell him what I know," she reflected, "it might complicate things for him, supposing—supposing he did it. And it would raise up a shadow between us. No, silence is best. But—I *wish* I knew what to do."

She felt hopelessly confused and baffled by the clash of her loyalties. But even as her fingers raked distractedly through her mop of ginger-gold hair, the issues had been taken out of her hands, for Pye had received a telephone message from the Chief Constable, bidding him call at his private residence, that morning.

Major Moore lived in a red brick Queen Anne residence, a little way outside the town. When Pye was shown into his study he was writing at his bureau, before the open window, through which flowed the scent of sun-steeped wallflowers.

He was a good-looking man, with thick curly gray hair and pleasant blue eyes. Their expression held friendship and regret as he spoke to Pye.

"Well, Superintendent, where are your investigations leading you?"

"Nowhere," was the blunt reply. "Blindfold me, turn me round three times and say 'Point to the Pole Star.' That's me, sir."

The Chief Constable puckered his brow as he began to draw diagrams on his blotting pad.

"That's not too good," he remarked. "Realize that the press are giving us a blistering?"

"So I'm told."

"Well, there's something to be said for their attitude. There is a small crop of unsolved murders, at present. Besides the Yard gets constant practice in crime. Perhaps, down here, we're apt to grow rusty."

"Meaning—me, sir?"

"Now, Pye, don't get on your hind legs. I'm going to be perfectly frank. When first I heard of Miss Vine's murder, my personal inclination was to call in the Yard at once. But I refrained, for a—a sentimental reason."

"Yes, sir?"

The ferocity of Pye's voice dared the Chief Constable to link him with any mention of sentiment. But there was such a dawn of fear and incredulous dismay in the big man's eyes that the Major was moved to a breach of his usual etiquette.

"I wanted to give you your chance, Pye," he said quietly.

"Thank you, sir," Pye gulped. "I suppose, you mean I've made a mess of it?"

The Chief Constable looked through the window to the snowy blossom of a double cherry tree.

"The fact is, public opinion has grown too strong for us," he said. "Can't you give me something definite to go on? Surely, you must be following up something useful? If there was a real hope of success, I'd hold my hand for a little longer."

"No." Pye's voice was stubborn. "I can promise nothing. All I can say is, I *know* I'll get my man, if I can hang on long enough."

The Chief Constable shook his head.

"Not good enough. I'm sorry. Your old dad gave me a lead over my fences, the first day I went out with the field.

But I can't let the scent grow stone-cold before I call in the Yard. There's been too much delay already."

"I know, sir." Pye swallowed a lump that persisted in rising in his throat, but his voice remained cheerful. "I'll just say this. The Colonel was calling me off his job, too, but I asked for one more chance. That was the night I bagged my man.... Now, I'm going to ask you for the same grace, for I've a hunch I'll strike lucky again."

The Chief Constable nodded, as he touched the bell.

"I wouldn't waste my time looking for a four-leaved clover, if I were you," he said dryly. "I'll give you another day. Good luck to you."

Pye swaggered through the gate and down the lane with his usual confident swing, but, in reality, he walked blindly, seeing nothing. The blow had been so unexpected that he could not realize that it had actually fallen. While he had been battering his head sore against a series of stone walls, he believed his own wrath and frustration to be the measure of his punishment.

It was enough for him to let off steam by snapping at his subordinates and by withdrawing from his domestic circle behind a screen of official dignity. Securely entrenched in his own little kingdom, he had scorned the big guns of the press. But it had never occurred to him that he was being criticized at headquarters.

Confused with his conflict of mingled rage and humiliation, he wanted to walk until he was thoroughly tired, in order to insure against the torment of a sleepless night. Although it was after two o'clock, and his sister was used to keeping his midday meal hot, until his return, he could not endure the thought of meeting her inquiries and sympathy until he was master of himself.

After trudging miles along the budding lanes, past cottage gardens pink and white with appleblossom, he stopped at a wayside inn, famous for its water cress, which grew in a shallow brook, flowing at the bottom of the garden. He ordered bread-and-cheese and ale, at the bar, but, owing to the penalties of fame, he was not allowed to enjoy his refreshment in peace.

Almost immediately, he was hailed by a perfect stranger. "Hullo, Super, how's the murder?"

No one who heard Pye's interchange of broad jokes and the good humor with which he accepted the general chaff, could have guessed at the storm which raged within his heart. The big, confident man shrank inwardly before every criticism, like a pimpernel before rain. Taking the first chance to escape, he plodded up a steep narrow lane, and reached the sanctuary of the hillside.

Miss Pye was not disturbed by her brother's absence from his dinner. But, as though she had received the broken S O S signals of his distress, she suddenly decided to take immediate action.

After she had given instructions to Betsy, she caught the next train up to London.

CHAPTER XXXIV

A Broken Teacup

PYE RETURNED TO THE CHERRY ORCHARD, AFTER HIS interview with the Chief Constable, feeling as though he were winded after a heavy fall from his horse. He had difficulty with his breathing and a weight over his heart.

As he turned in at his gate he looked a vast and important figure of officialdom, with stern eyes and compressed lips. But, inwardly, he felt like a small whipped boy who craved for sympathy, but would repulse it fiercely, were it offered.

He was glad that there was no red roadster parked in the road. At this crisis, his favorite sister, Doris, failed to appeal. She was almost blatant at the turn in her fortunes, and too full of her own affairs to have room for understanding of his trouble.

But he knew that Flo would not fail him. She would say nothing and have an extra good supper awaiting him. Expectant of cheer, he walked heavily into the parlor.

The bright fire and comfortable room welcomed him, as usual, but Flo's chair was empty. To his indignation, his model housekeeper had deserted her post and taken the cheap train up to London.

Betsy aggravated his annoyance by a pert message.

"You're to meet the seven-five train, for certain."

Pye glared down at the girl.

"Are *you* giving me my orders?" he demanded.

"The missus says you are to," amended Betsy.

Pye wrathfully kicked a footstool off the rug, as he told himself that he had done enough tramping for one day, and he would be hanged if he would toil up to the station. Taking off his boots, he sat down in his easy chair before the fire, to get a nap before his supper.

But, in spite of the warmth and comfort, he could not doze. He had an inexplicable longing to see Flo again. Tired, heartsick, and humiliated, he craved the salve of a kindly woman's presence.

Good old Flo filled the bill in every respect. She had no brain, and bored him with her everlasting domestic recitals, but she cooked like a genius, and had an unfailing instinct of a man's requirements.

Stooping painfully, he drew on his boots again, and tramped once more out into the chilly evening. As he did so he had no glimmer that he had just made a momentous decision. The mist of early spring stoppered up the end of every road, with a curtain like the blue bloom on a plum; but the air bit his face and the wind blew shrilly after the comfort of his fireside.

He reached the station when the train was signaled. As he stood staring down the stretch of rails, it seemed to him as though he would never see the heralding puff of smoke blowing around the curve. At that zero minute, horrible little pictures kept flitting through his mind.

He thought of crimes that have been perpetrated in railway carriages, where prosperous-looking women had been the victims. Because he had such an unaccountable craving to see Flo again, he imagined her lying rammed under a seat, with a twisted neck and her loquacious tongue stilled for ever.

At last the lights of the train shone through the deepening dusk, and she glided between the empty fields, like a chain of brilliants, linking the country with the town.

Flo poked her head out of the window—her glasses flashing in the lamplight—in order to see if he were on the platform. At the sight of her ginger-gold hair under her blue beret, and her two chins—one of which rested on a sapphire necklace from Woolworth's—Pye's sentiment was pulped to extinction under the weight of his resentment.

He felt as though he had been pounded all over, and he needed to hibernate in warmth and quiet, instead of being dragged out into the cold to satisfy the whim of fat old Flo. In spite of his joy at seeing her, his greeting was hardly a welcome.

"Well, I'm here. Are you clean off your rocker, Flo? Who's going to run off with an old thing like you?"

Beaming at him, Miss Pye took his arm and leaned heavily on it.

"Corns," she explained placidly. "I've been on my feet all day, in bargain basements, so I knew I could do with a strong man to lean on, on the way home. I've saved you real money, today, my lad."

Insensibly he was soothed by her honey-thick voice.

"We can do with it," he said. "I've some fine news. Seen the Major, this afternoon, and they're calling in Scotland Yard."

"The fool," snapped Miss Pye. "What does the Yard know of Oldtown or local conditions? Why, you had to see Miss Vine, to believe her. . . . When?"

"He's given me two days more."

"Well, that's all right. I expect you've got the real murderer now, mixed up with the rest, inside your head. You've just had a jolt, which will bring him floating up to the top, like cream on milk. You see."

Pye did not know whether to feel irritated by her complacency, or to accept her words as prophetic. So he began to grumble.

"I wish you'd sack your Betsy. That pie-faced idiot gets my goat. She *ordered* me to come to meet you tonight."

Miss Pye sighed gustily.

"My dear Adam," she told him, "I ought to give her her notice the minute my foot is inside the house. She was laughing when I left home, and I said 'When I come back, you'll laugh on the wrong side of your face.' But I can't—because she is an orphan."

"So are you, which makes it level."

"I've got you, old boy. But the deceit of that girl. You know she's a massive breaker. Only yesterday, I said to her, 'Break *another* thing, and you'll pack."

"Has she?" asked Pye.

As a rule he was systematically deaf to his sister's domestic recitals; but, this evening, he actually listened to her story, in some hope of distracting his mind from his worry.

Had he known the importance of this especial story he would have strained his ears to catch each syllable; as it was, he heard Flo's voice absently, through a half-dream, as they began to stumble together down the stony lane.

"It is my custom to go to the china pantry, every morning, to see if there's any fresh damage. I was on my way there, today, when Betsy rushed in front of me, and, in her hurry, let some rubbish fall out of her apron. Something told me to pounce on it, and, lo and behold, I found among it the handle of a cup."

Miss Pye drew a dramatic breath.

"I taxed her—she denied. So I made her come with me, to the rubbish heap, and rake through it. And there, poked under some ashes, I found a broken kitchen cup."

"Um," grunted Pye. "I shouldn't call that much of a cop, myself."

"But that's only half," declared Miss Pye. "I was just going to run for my train, which I'd just time to catch, when the Vicarage phoned for black-currant jelly, for the Vicar's throat. Well, I had to put the Church first—especially as I want the font for Easter—so I let the early train go, and went to the china pantry, instead, to get a pot of jelly. . . . And—*what* d'you think I found?"

As her brother did not attempt to guess, Miss Pye answered her own question.

"I found—my best glass dish in two bits. I rushed at Betsy, like a traction engine, so that she'd no time to think out her tale, but just confessed, straight away."

"The personal punch," nodded Pye. "What did she say?"

"She owned up that she'd smashed it, but she meant to replace it, while I was up in London, so that I wouldn't know, and she'd keep her situation. So she watched me go to the china pantry, and then she dropped down the handle of the cup—*which she'd smashed in advance*—because she felt I might overlook that, seeing it was only an old cracked one. Which I would. . . . But the artfulness of it, knowing I was running for my train, and drawing me off the scent like that. I feel she'll be my master, later on."

"Sack her," growled Pye ungratefully, as his mind swung back to his own trouble at the sight of the dark pile of Jamaica Court, just visible amid the branches of the budding trees.

As they looked, a light shone out, in the left wing.

Miss Pye gave a little scream and clutched her brother's arm.

"Oo," she cried, "it gave me quite a turn. It must have looked just like that, on the night Miss Vine was murdered."

"It did," agreed Pye grimly. "I saw it, coming back from High Gables."

It was bitter to remember his jubilation, and contrast it

with his present depression. He tried to shake it off in concentration on the commonplace.

"You'd think they'd keep that room shut up for a bit, seeing what happened there," he said. "I suppose they've started to root among her things."

"But that's probably not her room," remarked Miss Pye. "I expect it's Miss Pomeroy's. Hers is only a narrow slip cut off the big bedroom and their windows are side by side."

"And how do *you* know, Miss Nosey-Parker?"

"My dear, I live in a small place and I keep my ears open. I could tell exactly where the kitchen sink is in every house in the town including those I've never set foot inside."

"H'm," pondered Pye, "but how is it I've never noticed that light before—say, when the girl was dressing for dinner?"

"Because, in Miss Vine's lifetime, all the curtains were drawn before it got dark. She liked to feel the place was private and all closed in. No one knows the reason for her fancy to keep her own window bare. A signal to one of her lovers, perhaps, or else she was loopy. I expect the servants are slacker now."

Pye made no comment. His brows were puckered in a thoughtful frown when they reached Cherry Orchard. Once again, he sat down and took off his boots, while Miss Pye insisted on putting on his slippers.

"I'm going to the kitchen to prepare supper," she said. "It's something nice and tasty. Suppose you have a good smoke, and don't worry about the old Yard. The cream will be rising from the milk before long."

"Well, I wouldn't call a criminal the cream of society, myself," grunted Pye. "But, as a matter of fact, Flo, I'm getting a new angle on things. If only Miss Vine wasn't so set in her habits, I'd know better where I stand. But they all said she was wound up, like a clock."

Miss Pye looked at her brother in some uncertainty, as though doubtful of her own judgment. Then she sighed gustily, and took the plunge.

"But she broke her rule, the night she was murdered," she said.

Her brother caught her by her broad shoulders and swung her round, to face him. His eyes were a blue blaze, as he shouted, "How d'you know that?"

"Because I saw her, at about a quarter past eleven, and she was dead, then. Murdered."

"My—Gosh. Think again. Are you *sure?*"

"Of course, I'm sure. I heard the town clock strike the quarter. And I know I saw *her,* because I've been trying to forget her face ever since."

Pye began to pace the room in his excitement.

"Why the hell didn't you tell me this before?" he asked. "You have been withholding important information from the police."

"I tried to, Adam," explained Miss Pye. "But you positively forbade me to say another word."

Pye turned and looked at his sister.

"I know I did," he said. "I was a fool. Disloyal, too, for it was my duty to explore every avenue. Only, you told me you'd never murdered her, so I just hung on to that. You see, *I* knew you were speaking the truth, but I couldn't risk things looking black against you, as they sometimes do, against the innocent party."

Miss Pye's eyes grew rather misty behind her glasses.

"I think," she said, "we both felt the same about each other. Miss Vine's death affected us, because of poor Doris, and we were both very hot over her. That's why I couldn't tell them, at the inquest, that I was there, because the Coroner might ask me questions about it, and trip me up to say more than I intended. I had to tell *you,* but you don't know

285

my relief when you took a short cut and finished your inquiry."

Pye reared his sunken chin again.

"That's what it practically came to, Flo," he agreed. "I knew I'd be barking up the wrong tree, if I suspected you, so it was no good wasting valuable time. But now, I want to know *why* you went to the Court, that night."

Miss Pye looked down at the carpet.

"I followed *you*," she confessed.

"Me? Why?"

"Well, you see, Adam, your veins were out."

As Pye stared at her in bewilderment, she touched his forehead and temples.

"Here, and here, Adam. They look like little bunches of berries when you're *very* angry. They were like that when you went to see Miss Vine, so I knew your blood was all swelled up inside, and I was afraid."

"Afraid *I'd* murder the old girl? Well I'm——" Pye gulped. "Whoever heard of a policeman committing murder? We're here to stop it."

"That's what comforted me," said Miss Pye placidly. "I reminded myself that you'd be the last person to be suspected, because you were on the case yourself."

"Well." Again the Superintendent swallowed convulsively. "And what were you going to do about it?"

"Stop you. But if you were too set on it, and you are a masterful man, I was trying to fix up your alibi. In case you were seen going to the Court, I could say I went there, too, and that I'd never left you for a minute."

"You were going to swear this on your Bible oath? And you go to Church, every Sunday?"

"That's where I learned what to do," remarked Miss Pye. "All those old Bible characters were regular twisters, and for ever making bargains with the Lord, and trying to get the better of Him. And, you see, I knew you would not murder Miss Vine, unless you knew it was the right thing to do, in the cause of justice, same as the Judge with his black cap. And I was positive that you wouldn't do it again."

Suddenly the grim lines of Pye's face relaxed and he burst into a shout of laughter.

"Well, I always knew women had no brains, but I did credit them with morals. Never mind, Flo." He slapped her shoulder. "You were matey to me, and that's what counts."

"And weren't you the same, you big stiff?" retorted Miss Pye aggressively. "Shutting me up, because you were afraid it was *me?*"

Pye threw her a sharp glance, as he sat down and began to pull on his boots.

"This makes the third time," he grumbled.

"Yes," said Miss Pye, "when you told me at the station that you had to put your boots on again, to meet me, I knew there'd have to be a third time. Where are you going?"

"For a short hike."

As Pye tramped down his garden path, the sharp air was full of spring scents and the sky enameled with stars. His heart was throbbing like a great engine, from the force of his suppressed excitement.

Miss Pye heard the slam of the gate, and looked at the clock.

"Plenty of time to see about supper," she said, as she turned on the wireless. "Lucky I noticed that the girl always dresses for dinner about the same time. He's got a big brain, like most men, but Dad always said that all science was only applied common sense. Hum. I'll give him three hours."

It was later than three hours, and the supper had been keeping hot in the oven for some time, when she heard her brother's footstep on the path.

He threw open the door of the parlor and beamed at her with his great red face shining like a beacon.

"Well," he said, "Scotland Yard has lost a case by twenty-four hours. I've just come from the Constabulary, where I've just locked up the signed confession of Miss Vine's murderer."

CHAPTER XXXV

Betsy

IN THE OUTSIDE NIGHT, HIGH UP IN THE SKY, THE MIGHTY tangle of Hercules sprawled across the heavens; but, inside the Cherry Orchard, Pye might have been his earthly presentment, as he stood, spread-eagled before the fire. His eyes glowed with triumph as though he had hit his head against the stars.

Miss Pye looked at his massive form, and thought, once again, that he was, indeed, a fine figure of a man. His powerful physique, combined with his confidence, made her understand the force of personality.

She wanted to fall down and worship him for his achievement. Her equivalent was to satisfy his appetite.

"Tripe for supper," she said. "It's keeping hot in the oven. Shall I bring it in?"

"Yes, old girl." In high good humor, Pye slapped her on her broad back. "I'm in for a treat with *your* tripe," he added.

As he spoke, Miss Pye thrust her head right through the crusted star-ridge of the Milky Way, so touched was she by this rare caress. She gave no sign of pleasure, however, as she brought in a steaming plate and placed it before her brother.

"*Who* murdered her?" she asked in a casual voice, as Pye began to eat and drink in mighty mouthfuls and gulps.

Pye shook his head.

"You'll know at the right time," he said. "It's a long tale, and I must tell it my own way. To begin with, I'll own up I went wrong, at the very beginning, through faulty diagnosis. It was this. Because two witnesses have been accustomed to see Miss Vine's light go out, at a certain time, in a certain place, they naturally concluded that it was *her* light they saw go out, at twelve o'clock, on the night she was murdered. And I fell into the same error myself."

"Wasn't it her light?" asked Miss Pye.

Her brother laughed, in high good humor.

"My good girl," he said, "use that speck of brain the Almighty gave you. Just now, when we were going down the station lane, what could we see of Jamaica Court through the trees? Just a dark mass, and you make a rough jab at the left wing. . . . Now, suppose the light I and the other two chaps saw go out, on the night of the murder, was the light in the Pomeroy girl's room?"

"You forget, Adam," his sister reminded him, "that she slept at the Rectory, that night."

"So she did—all but a couple of hours," said Pye. "Tonight, I paid her a surprise visit at the Court. I bluffed her and bluffed hard. She's one of the hothouse kind, so I'd no trouble with her."

"What did you say to her?"

"I said, 'Now, look here, *Mrs. Lawrence,* I have proof that you and your husband were at the Court on the night of Miss Vine's murder. Personally, I believe you both had nothing to do with it. But, if you want me to protect you, you will have to come clean.' "

"*Mrs.* Lawrence?" gasped Miss Pye.

"Yes. As I deduced, they had got married, on the Q.T., because the old girl would have booted them out, if she knew. She was jealous of the doctor."

"That's right," nodded Miss Pye. "It was in the cards. ... Go on."

"It'll soon be announced, now," Pye told his sister. "Well, the girl told me she had a note delivered to her, at the Rectory, late on the night of the murder, and it was from the doctor, to say he'd meet her in her room at the Court, at twelve sharp. The girl's the romantic sort and she loved the secret meetings, so she just ate up the nine miles in her car. When she reached the Court, everything was quiet, and the light was burning up in her window; but she found her room empty, and a note from the doctor to say he'd been called away on an all-night case in the country. So, naturally, she put out the light—*which we all three saw*—and was soon back at the Rectory, and nobody the wiser."

Miss Pye's eyes snapped behind her big glasses.

"And, pray, why didn't she tell that tale at the inquest?" she asked.

"Because she was afraid that it was the doctor who'd done in the old girl. He'd a very strong motive for wishing her dead. When she plucked up her courage to ask him about it, he denied that he'd written either note, or had been there at all, since dinner. But, although he was sure of *her* innocence, he forbade her to say she had been there at all, in case she was suspected."

Pye broke off to laugh.

"Seems as though they were all mighty scared of me," he said proudly.

"They'd need to be, now that you've arrested the murderer," nodded Miss Pye. "Who is he, Adam?"

"He's the chap you said he was."

"I?" Miss Pye looked startled. "No, Adam, I never said so. I'll have the hanging of no innocent man put on me."

"All right, Flo," laughed the Superintendent. "But don't you remember that when I counted up all the folk who'd

291

cause to wish Miss Vine dead you said that perhaps it was someone who had *no* cause. Well, you were right. It was *him*. It was Francis Ford."

His sister shook her fair head.

"But he had a cause," she said. "He was to inherit all that money."

"But that was as good as delivered, about a week before, when she fell into the lake. He needn't have fished her out at all. She was doing his dirty work for him. So you see, he had no real reason to murder her, later on."

"Then—why did he?" demanded Miss Pye.

"Because that young man has been ruled by three strong passions." Pye ticked them off with his big fingers. "*One*. Hatred of old Miss Vine. *Two*. Money. *Three*. You'd never guess this, but it appears he had a violent crush on the girl, which turned to hatred when she just laughed at him, so that he'd have been quite chirpy if both she and the doctor had swung. He didn't care one way, or the other, about Charles; wouldn't have hurt him, or helped him. He hid his passion for the girl from everyone, but when the doctor came on the scene he was mad with jealousy, and worked to do him an injury."

"And who told you all this?" asked Miss Pye.

"Francis Ford himself. I saw him at the jail. He's been in the infirmary, most of the time, with a suppressed chill, and he's not been sleeping, for he's kept going over what he did—although he was proud as Punch about it. So when I laid my hand on his shoulder and bellowed, 'Where were you at *eleven* o'clock on the night Miss Vine was murdered'? he went to bits and confessed."

Miss Pye started at her brother's shout. As she looked at his enormous bulk and his glittering eyes, she understood what he meant by the value of the personal punch.

"Just what I do with Betsy," she nodded. "I never give her time to think up her tale."

Her brother did not notice the interruption.

"I got Francis where I wanted him," he explained, "because I put the last question he expected. But, as a matter of fact, he was spoiling to tell the tale to someone. He was as proud of his cleverness as a peacock with two tails, and he wanted the world to know all about it."

"Young villain," cried Miss Pye. "I hope they'll hang him."

Pye shook his head.

"The fact is," he explained, "the chap is loopy. He's never been normal. Even when he was a kid he used to wash his hands without being told."

"Poor lad. I hope they'll set him free."

"No, but they'll probably send him to Broadmoor, where he'll be nice and comfy and can wash his hands all he likes. I'd no trouble over his confession. He even wanted to spell some of the words for us, and he signed like a bird. It seems, on the night of the murder he got the doctor out of the way by the usual fake telephone call, and then told Charles the secretary wanted to see him in her room. They are sweet, those two, and he guessed they'd stay put, talking. Miss Vine's maid was out, at her dancing class, so he had a clear coast."

The Superintendent refreshed himself with a deep draught of ale.

"And then," he continued, "he sent the old girl to bed at ten o'clock, instead of eleven. He had doped her coffee, so she did not question the time—they've no clocks there—or notice that her window curtains were drawn tight. He let her put on all her contraptions, which would prove she had been in her room, the usual hour over her toilet, and then he paid her a little call, and banged her over the head with

293

a spanner. After that, he switched off her light, and lit up in the girl's room, at eleven o'clock, as per usual. After he'd left the faked note from the doctor he set off to rob the Colonel."

"Then he had found out that the girl was secretly married, and he wrote the note of meeting, which brought her to the Court?" asked Miss Pye.

"Bravo, Flo, the great brain's working, at last. Yes, he made sure that she would be there, at twelve, and then—as a matter of course—put out the light, which was to help his alibi. He'd heard those chaps joke about their time signal, on their way down from the station. And he figured, too, the girl would never squeal, for fear of incriminating herself or the doctor."

There was a pause while Miss Pye digested the facts. Then she pushed her heavy golden hair back from her brow.

"But why did he take all that trouble to murder her?" she asked, "when he could have let her drown in the lake?"

"Ah," explained her brother, "that was where his money complex came in. He didn't want to share equally with the other two, and he guessed Miss Vine would reward him, as she did. And—though this is more difficult to understand, when you're sane yourself—he had planned what he believed was a watertight murder and he wanted to go on with it. He told me he got a mighty kick out of it all."

Pye's face grew suddenly stern as he gave his sister some additional details.

"It was a cold-blooded crime," he said, "for it goes right back to those potty little thefts of Mrs. Antrobus' Dresden china figures. He had to make *certain* of being arrested for burglary, for that was to be his alibi, and he knew that some people could sleep through an earthquake. But he figured that if he did a second robbery, on the same lines as the first, *I'd* be on the lookout for him."

Pye's face relaxed in a grin.

"He got my mark all right. He couldn't take the lid of the vase until the will was altered, and then he was confined to his bed with a chill. But he said he knew I'd hang on. ... By the way, it was not a bad idea to serve a short term for theft. It's a light let-off for a swing."

Miss Pye nodded, but her eyes were abstracted.

"Adam," she said suddenly, "are you sure his confession will stand? It seems that if he's not all there, he might be so proud of his crime as to make it all up."

"Fancy *you* thinking of that, too," said Pye. "Of course, the same idea occurred to me. So I told him I didn't believe a word of his tale, as he'd not the pluck to commit the murder. He rose directly, and furnished the proof."

"Proof?" echoed Miss Pye triumphantly.

"Yes, proof. It's at the Constabulary, under lock and key, at this minute. He told me that, after the crime, there was a little blood on his hand, so he wiped his fingers clean with his handkerchief, and wrapped it round the spanner. On his way to High Gables, he dropped the bundle into the hollow of a certain tree in the grounds. I went there, on my way home, and collected the goods, fingerprints on the metal, and all."

Pye wiped his mouth, rose from the table, stretched himself, and stood before the fire.

"But he told me one lie," he said. "If he'd been nabbed on his trial trip, the whole scheme would have gone West. And he declared that Mrs. Antrobus' puppy saw him in the drawing room, and never barked, although her nephew was just outside. Lies. I know that pup, and he wouldn't let a bishop within a dozen yards of the umbrella stand, without yelping the roof off."

The Superintendent laughed heartily. For he had no knowledge, that—although it was written in the stars that a spinster must be murdered by night—for one brief moment, a mongrel pup was overlord of the gods of Fate.

His sister joined in his laughter. Then, with a mighty effort, she crossed to the rug and solemnly kissed him.

"Adam," she said, "I am proud of my brother."

"Yes." Pye tapped his head. *"This* had to work overtime. ... But the joke is that *you* started me on the right track with your yarn about Betsy. As I listened, it struck me, all of a heap, that Francis was like her. He practically *asked* to be arrested. In a way of speaking, he was showing a cracked cup, to cover up a glass dish."

In high good humor, he patted his sister's shoulder.

"Never mind, Flo," he said, "a fine girl, like you, with your gift for steak-and-kidney pudding, doesn't need brains. And now, I'm off to bed."

When he had gone, Miss Pye crossed to the fire and took off the coals. As she did so, there was a tap at the door, and Betsy entered.

"Why aren't you in bed?" asked her mistress.

"I was waiting to see if you wanted me for anything," replied the girl.

As she spoke, her light blue eyes, which were a compound of rustic sharpness and shyness, were fixed on her mistress' bag.

Miss Pye laughed as she interpreted the look.

"It's all right, Betsy," she said. "You thought I'd forgotten you, didn't you?"

Opening her purse, she presented the girl with half-a-crown.

"Here it is, Betsy," she said. "You've been a careful girl again, I'm glad to say. Another clear month without one breakage."

THE END

≫≫ If you've enjoyed this book and would like to discover more great vintage crime and thriller titles, as well as the most exciting crime and thriller authors writing today, visit: ≫≫

The Murder Room
Where Criminal Minds Meet

themurderroom.com